Days and Nights
of a
French Horn
Player

Days and Nights of a French Horn Player

MURRAY SCHISGAL

Little, Brown and Company—Boston–Toronto

FIRST EDITION

LIBRARY OF CONGRESS CATALOGING IN PUBLICATION DATA
Schisgal, Murray, 1926–
    Days and nights of a French horn player.
    I. Title.
PZ4.S3375Day [PS3569.C5]   813'.54   79–28727
ISBN 0–316–77338–7 pbk.

BP
Designed by Susan Windheim
*Published simultaneously in Canada
by Little, Brown & Company (Canada) Limited*

PRINTED IN THE UNITED STATES OF AMERICA

To Reene

Days and Nights of a French Horn Player

one

My name is Edward Davis. I am forty-four years old. I was born in Brooklyn, New York.

I was an only child.

Once I said to my mother, "Why didn't you have any more children, Ma?"

She said, "What are you driving at, Eddie?"

My father said, "I wasn't cut out for it. But we're glad you're here, nonetheless."

Once I said to the both of them, "Why do you two live together?"

Neither one answered me.

I had offended them.

It didn't matter, though.

I was inside myself, always, and I lived in a place of such rich fantasy that I was constantly surprised when I had to deal with the outside world.

(Bear with me, my friend. Given the choice, I, too, would have had it otherwise.)

Once a teacher said to me, "You are doing very badly in English, Edward."

I couldn't believe her.

I thought I was doing fantastically.

I looked at the composition papers she had returned to me.

3

They were filled with corrections. But I honestly thought she was testing me, probing my character, that she was really saying, "If you have the time, brush up on your spelling and grammar and punctuation, Edward. But don't let it worry you. You are by far the best student I have."

Was she serious about my doing badly? Could she be serious?

I knew that I was the best student she had. I knew that I had a unique way of looking at things, a unique way of expressing myself. I was certain she didn't want me to lose my uniqueness by concentrating on spelling, grammar and punctuation. It was more important that I let my imagination fly and express myself uniquely.

She was testing me, that was it.

She was trying to find out whether I had the courage to stick to my own way of doing things.

She admired me for my uniqueness and was merely playing a game with me.

I remember smiling at her, winking, and walking off.

I also remember her failing me in English two terms in a row.

Reality was always tripping me up.

(Bear with me, my friend.)

But I knew at an early age that style counted for a great deal, so I worked on my walk, left shoulder slightly forward, left hand in left pocket, right arm swinging at side, feet treading lightly, barely leaving the ground.

I had the best walk of anyone I knew.

I worked on my appearance, too. There wasn't much I could do with my face (later on I grew an incredible mustache) or my hair (later on it thinned considerably), but when it came to clothes I had a real flair.

I was the first one in my neighborhood to wear a beret and an ascot.

(Originally it wasn't precisely an ascot. It was an extra-wide polka-dot tie.)

And when I was twelve I started smoking a pipe. I used Sir Walter Raleigh pipe tobacco.

I will say this for my parents: they never prevented me from doing what I was set on doing.

As a matter of fact, both my parents worked and I rarely saw them. We'd meet at the door and say, "Hi, how's it going?" And that would be it until Sunday.

Sunday we all had lunch together, usually spaghetti and meatballs.

We didn't have that much to say to each other.

"Have another meatball, Eddie," my mother would say.

"No, thank you."

"Are you sure you don't want another meatball?"

"Positive."

"I'll have another meatball," my father would say.

And my mother wouldn't answer him.

Nothing really got through to me.

I had my walk, my beret and my daydreams. I could sit on the curbstone, stare down at a puddle of water, and find myself in the Caribbean with a band of pirates.

"One of us has to swim ashore through those shark-infested waters and see if that Island is inhabited," said our Chief.

"I can do it," I said.

"Aren't you afraid, Eddie?"

"No, Sir. I don't know what the word fear means."

"God bless you, Son."

(Bear with me, my friend.)

I went my own way, an enigmatic smile always on my face.

No one knew why I was smiling, why I was so conceited, but I knew.

I was special.

Something was going to happen that would place me among the greats of mankind.

I smiled at buildings, at fire hydrants, at cars, at trees.

I smiled at the policemen and at the sanitation men and at the shop owners and at the postmen.

Everyone knew I was special, but no one would say anything about it.

They were testing me.

That's all right. I was in no hurry.

But one day everyone I smiled at would come up to me and say, "Congratulations, Eddie. You passed the test. Now we can tell you: you're a unique individual; you're really something special."

I bought a pound of apples and went to the movies. I sat in the front row and ate my apples quietly as I stared at the screen.

Wait for me! Wait for me!

And there I was, I was up on the screen with Clark Gable and Claudette Colbert. Passionately I argued with them, pointing out that they had each misjudged the other, that they genuinely loved one another. Can't you see what you're doing, for cryin'-out-loud! You're giving each other needless pain! Now stop it! That's enough! Take each other around and say I love you.

There, doesn't that make more sense than all that childish bickering for over an hour?

They turn to me and say, We love you, Eddie.

I know that. Jesus Christ, you don't have to say it. What kind of a mug do you think I am, anyway?

In my mind I never stopped talking, but with others I had little to say.

I kept it to myself.

I was no doubt considered a quiet kid, shy, introverted, but I thought that all this was to the good, it merely enhanced my image.

I carried about me an aura of mystery, of romance, of infinite possibilities.

I had no friends to speak of.

I walked the streets, with my special walk, beret on head, pipe in mouth, spewing forth clouds of Sir Walter Raleigh.

I talked to myself as if I was my best friend.

Hi, Eddie.

Hi.

How's it going?

Okay.

You wanna go to the park?

Sure. Let's go to the park.

Eddie?

What?

If you found a million dollars, what would you do with it?

I'd give it to my parents.

All of it?

All of it.

There's something I have to tell you, Eddie.

What's that?

They're not your real parents.

You're kidding me.

No. I've been keeping it a secret. Your real parents live in Manhattan.

Where?

On Park Avenue.

You're not...?

No. It's the truth, Eddie. Your real father's name is Nelson; your real mother's name is Amanda.

When can I see them?

When you're twenty-one. They'll pick you up in a limousine.

There was one kid in school who interested me.

He was the ugliest kid I had ever seen. He had a hunchback. He wore thick eyeglasses and had practically no hair on his head. His name was Gerald Hinkey. Out of deference to his personal misfortune, the kids in school called him "Hunchy."

I don't know how many years we were in the same class. Four or five, I would guess. But we never spoke to one another. We never had anything to do with one another.

During my twelfth year, at the beginning of the seventh grade, our relationship changed: whenever my eyes accidentally met Gerald's, his twisted, upturned face would crease in an enigmatic smile.

What was that supposed to mean?

Quickly I turned back to him.

And just as quickly the smile reappeared on his face.

Did he know I was special? Was he trying to tell me something? Was this a test arranged by the authorities or by my real parents, Nelson and Amanda?

One day after school Gerald came up to me. "Hi, Eddie." And he smiled, enigmatically.

"You know?" I asked him.

"Yes."

"Do you have a message for me?"

"Yes. Come this way."

I followed him without saying another word.

Gerald lived in a neat, shingled, one-family house on Alabama Avenue. We climbed a flight of stairs to his bedroom. He locked the door behind us. Then he turned and stared at me, a smile on his face, only now it was a smile that said, I've got you where I want you, Eddie Davis.

I stared back at him and puffed on my pipe.

"Can we talk freely?" I asked.

"Yes."

"What's the message?"

"I'll show it to you," he said.

And he went down on his knees and pulled out from under his bed a strange, bulky, black leather case.

He lifted it onto the bed.

"Is it in there?" I asked.

8

"Yes," he answered, and slowly, deliberately, with great care, he removed from the case what seemed to me several coils of gold that ended in a golden bell.

We stared at each other for a minute. The enigmatic smile was on his face again.

"Is that it?" I asked.

"Yes."

I nodded as if I knew what we were talking about. "Where's the message?"

"Listen," he said. And he put the coils of gold to his mouth and blew into it with all his might.

His cheeks expanded like a pair of small, crimson balloons.

I listened to the music he was playing. At first I tried to decipher it, attentive to the arrangement of the notes and the volume with which they were played. Perhaps the message he had for me was coded. But I soon gave this up and just listened to the music.

He played softly, his hand in the bell, the notes cracking here and there but the melody carrying forward.

His face was twice its normal size now and his eyes were pinched shut behind his thick eyeglasses. His concentration was so great that he looked as if he was making a ca-ca in his pants.

I listened. I closed my eyes, too, and I listened. I was afraid to move. I was afraid to think. I let the music wash over me. I felt terribly sad and at the same time terribly excited.

When Gerald finished playing, he took the coils of gold from his mouth and held them out to me.

"What's a French horn?" my father asked the next Sunday.

"It's like a big, round trumpet. It's a beautiful musical instrument."

"What's a French horn?" he asked again, finding my answer incomprehensible.

My mother said, "He wants to study the French horn, let him study the French horn. Would you be happier if he went to prison?"

9

"Do you know what a French horn is?" He turned to her. "Did you ever see a French horn? Did you ever hear a French horn? What, I ask, is a French horn?"

"You won't spend a nickel on your own son," my mother said. "Do you know he never bought me an engagement ring, Eddie? I was engaged and I never had an engagement ring. I was so ashamed that I used to put a bandage on my finger every time I left the house!"

"All I'm asking is what is a French horn?"

"He has bank accounts, Eddie. All over the city, he has bank accounts. Ask him where he keeps his bank accounts!"

"Why do you have to yell?" my father yelled. "Can't you talk like a human being? We're discussing here what is a French horn. I confess ignorance. I know nothing about music or art appreciation. Now will somebody please tell me, what is a French horn?"

My mother didn't answer him.

I didn't answer him.

My mother finally said, "Have another meatball, Eddie."

I shook my head.

"Are you sure you don't want another meatball?"

"Positive."

"I'll have another meatball," my father said.

We rode the subway to the Bowery. The two of us. My father and I. I don't remember going anywhere with him before, just the two of us. I was very nervous inside and I guess he was, too. (Hindsight makes it possible for me to portray my father in an entirely different light, but I believe my memory of him as he appeared to me then is the wiser choice.) I tried to think of something to say to him; I couldn't. He couldn't say anything either. When we got out of the subway, we walked into the first pawnshop we came to.

"What is a French horn?" my father asked the pawnbroker.

"You don't want a French horn," the pawnbroker said.

"You can say that again," my father said. "It's for my son."

"He doesn't want a French horn," the pawnbroker said. "Buy him a trumpet. It's more practical. He can play at weddings and bar mitzvahs and Polish dances. He can make himself a bundle of dough." He took a trumpet out of the window. "I can give you this one for thirty smackers."

"Wow, it's a beaut. Eddie . . ."

I shook my head.

"Why don't you listen to . . ."

"Tobias."

"Tobias. He knows all about musical instruments. He's an expert on musical instruments."

"I've been selling them for over twenty years," Tobias said. "I sold a Buffet clarinet to Mr. Hoffman of the Philharmonic yesterday."

"Did you hear that, Eddie? Tobias sold a Buffet clarinet to Mr. Hoffman of the Philharmonic yesterday! If he says it's more practical to buy a trumpet, I think the least you can do . . ."

I shook my head.

"How much is the French horn?" My father sounded very tired.

"One hundred smackers, not a smacker more, not a smacker less. You're a fool to buy it."

My father stared down at his shoelaces. "We'll think about it," he muttered, and grabbed my hand and pulled me out of the pawnshop.

He led me into a White Rose bar, sat me at a table, and brought back a small beer for me and a rye and ginger ale for himself.

He finished his drink before he spoke.

"I don't have bank accounts all over the country, Eddie. I give your mother every penny I earn except five or six dollars. I have one bank account, in the Brownsville Bank for Savings. If anything should happen to me, go to Mr. Arthur at the teller's window and say, 'My dad spoke to you about me. I'm four-nine-two-dash-eight-three-six-four.' "

"I'm four-nine-two-dash-eight-three-six-four."

"Again."

"I'm four-nine-two-dash-eight-three-six-four."

"Now say the whole thing."

"My dad spoke to you about me. I'm four-nine-two-dash-eight-three-six-four."

"Who do you say it to?"

"Mr. Arthur."

"What do you say to Mr. Arthur at the Brownsville Bank for Savings?"

"Hello, Mr. Arthur, my dad spoke to you about me before he ... Did you pass away, Dad?"

"Yes, I did."

"How did you pass away?"

"It was unexpected."

"Mr. Arthur, my dad spoke to you about me before he passed away unexpected. I'm four-nine-two-dash-eight-three-six-four."

"Don't forget that number, Eddie. It's your future."

"Do you mind if I smoke, Dad?"

"Smoke? When did you start smoking?"

"Last year. It calms my nerves."

"No, no, go ahead."

I took out my pipe. My father picked the butt of a cigarette from an empty pack and lit it, handing me the flaming match.

"I'm glad you don't smoke cigarettes, Eddie. They're murder."

I looked out the window and watched the derelicts shuffling by on the sidewalk.

"Don't you want the beer?" my father asked.

I shook my head.

"Eddie, I'd buy you the French horn, I would, word of honor, but it's a hundred dollars, a hundred dollars ..." His elbows were on the table, his hands clasped together, tightly, the knuckles white, as if he was arm wrestling with himself. "I don't make that much. You're old enough to know ... Upholsterers are a dime a dozen. It's a dying industry. I have to put away ..." He slapped his hands on the table, leaned toward me, his voice a hoarse whisper. "I have to have something . . ."

And he stared at me, his eyes wet and feverish, his lips still moving but nothing coming out of them.

I said to myself, It's all right, Dad. Forget it. It's all right, Dad. Forget it.

But to him I said nothing. I couldn't go home without the coils of gold. I couldn't.

A few seconds passed, a few minutes, maybe the whole day passed.

The lights went on in the bar.

It was dark outside.

"All right, Eddie." My father stood up. "But don't you ever ask me for anything again, ever! ever! ever!"

Each word grew and grew until it reached the ceiling, burst, and crashed to the floor.

My father walked away.

I rose to my feet, pulled the change from my pocket, and dropped the coins on the table. Then I tilted the beret on my head, tightened the knot of my polka-dot ascot, and followed my father out of the bar.

I waited for Gerald after school. I stood in a doorway across the street. When he came by I hissed at him.

The truth is I was embarrassed to be seen with Gerald Hinkey.

"Did you get it?" he asked me at once.

"Yes. Come this way," I said.

I made him wait for me downstairs. I brought down the bulky case and went to his house. After the door was locked and we were safely in his bedroom, I took the coils of gold out of the case and handed the instrument to him.

He examined it, expertly.

I held my breath.

"The valves have to be oiled," he murmured, "and these dents should be taken out."

What else? I thought. It's no good, right? My father paid a hundred dollars for a piece of junk! Nobody can get music out of that thing, right?

He put the instrument on the bed and went to the phonograph. A record fell into place and I heard a chorus of strings. (It was Mozart's Concerto in E Flat Major.) He put my horn to his mouth and blew into it several times, emitting a hollow wind sound. But as soon as the recorded horn took over the concerto, he joined in and the notes came out in rapid, melodic succession. He played along with the record, and the room filled with the music, reverberated with the music. The walls hugged me, lifted me off the floor, held me gently in their arms, and danced with me. Around and around the room we went, the walls and I, spinning, turning, passing the shaft of sunlight at the window, faster and faster we went, faster and faster and faster, until the whole room was ablaze with light and music and a thousand coils of gold.

When the record was over, I ran to Gerald and kissed him. Inadvertently my fingers gripped the hump on his back and I quickly stepped away from him.

There was a knock on the door. Gerald opened it and his mother came in. I half expected her to be a hunchback but she wasn't. She was very short, though, with impressive breasts, oval eyeglasses and legs like a chicken. She smelled of baby powder and was scrubbed clean, more clean than I thought anyone could be. (Her house was scrubbed clean, too. Later on I was to find out that she worked as a clerk for the Board of Education on Livingston Street. Gerald's father was dead. He had a twin sister who went to a private school.)

"This is my friend, Eddie Davis," Gerald introduced us, his face beaming.

"I'm delighted to meet you, Eddie," she said. "Would you like to stay and have dinner with us?"

I started to shake my head. "I have to . . ."

"We're having pea soup, veal cutlets and mashed sweet potatoes and I bought a cheese cake on Atlantic Avenue."

"Why don't you stay? You can hear some of my records," Gerald said.

"All right. If you want me to."

"Good," Mrs. Hinkey smiled. "I'll phone your mother."

"You don't have to, Mrs. Hinkey."

"Won't she be worried?"

"She's working tonight. So's my father. They like it when I go out to eat."

"Very well. In an hour, Gerald," and she left the room.

I lit my pipe and waited for Gerald to put on another record. But he didn't. He merely stared at me, his eyes blinking behind his eyeglasses.

"You have a nice mother, Gerald," I said for want of something to say.

He smiled, gratefully. And then he put on a record which I learned afterward was Beethoven's Sixth Symphony.

You can imagine my surprise when I met Gerald's twin sister. She was a hunchback. But in all fairness I have to say this right off: she wasn't as ugly as Gerald, although the thing on her back was a little higher and thicker than his. They were about the same height, I would guess no taller than four feet (they didn't grow much above that), and they both had very long hands and feet. But there the similarity ended. Shirley, for that was her name, had a lot of strawberry hair which was meticulously coiffed (like Rita Hayworth in *Gilda*), sea-green eyes (no specs), shiny, well-scrubbed skin, and a pug-nosed, pretty face that was turned perpetually at an angle.

The food at dinner was delicious. I had two veal cutlets and three portions of mashed sweet potatoes and a hefty chunk of cheese cake with honeyed tea. Mrs. Hinkey tried to start a conversation a number of times, but nothing caught on and we ate in complete silence. When we were done she said, "Why don't you children go into the living room and continue the conversation?" which didn't make much sense to me. Obediently we rose from the table and went into the living room.

I sat between the two hunchbacks on the sofa.

I turned to Gerald. He smiled and I smiled.

I turned to Shirley. She smiled and then I smiled.

I let my pipe, crossed my legs, and leaned back on the sofa. I didn't know what was expected of me.

"You two continue the conversation," Gerald said after five minutes of uninterrupted silence. And he left the room.

Shirley and I were alone.

I looked at her out of the corner of my eye. She was staring up at the ceiling, her long hands on her lap, her tennis sneakers several inches off the floor. I thought of saying, My parents are probably home now. Thank you for a lovely evening. But I didn't know how to say it. I sat there, puffing my pipe, still tasting the mashed sweet potatoes in my mouth.

"What kind of pipe tobacco do you smoke?" Shirley asked in a while.

"Sir Walter Raleigh," I said. "Do you like it?"

"Yes, I do," she said. "And I like your beret and ascot, too."

"Thank you very much," I said.

"For a person your age, you look amazingly sophisticated."

"Thank you very much," I said.

"Gerald informs me that you're going to take lessons on the horn."

"I'm gonna be a musician," I said.

"Me, too."

"Do you play an instrument?"

"Piano, violin, flute and timpani. Would you like to hear something?"

"Yes, very much," I said.

She waddled to the piano and sat down on the mahogany bench. After taking a deep breath, she bent over the keyboard so that all I could see was the hump on her back, and she started striking the keys with both hands at once. She was magnificent, really magnificent. She pounded the keys without mercy, relentlessly, huge chords and arpeggios that sounded like exploding cannons of thunder and sky-splitting streaks of lightning.

Then, abruptly, in the middle of what she was playing (Tchaikovsky, of course), she got up from the piano, hobbled quickly across the room, and picked up a violin. If she lost a beat I wasn't aware of it because the violin continued immediately where the piano left off, and there she was, violin snugly under chin, sea-green eyes angled upward, hair flying every which way, humped back swaying as the bow swept fiercely across the taut, vibrating strings.

And now once again, without missing a beat, she put the violin down, and a flute magically appeared above her upturned face; a clear, throaty tone flowed from her in a deluge of sound. Flute down, she was behind the kettledrums, mallets in hand, whacking away, first one, then the other, bouncing the mallets up and down, and building the finale to a glorious crescendo.

I managed to get to my feet. "My parents are probably home now," I said. "Thank you for a lovely evening."

And I moved out of the room with my left shoulder forward, my left hand in my left pocket, and a stream of pipe smoke trailing behind me.

two

I started lessons on the horn at the Porterhouse School of Music which was above a Chinese laundry on Sutter Avenue. One man, Mr. Porter, ran the school and taught all the instruments as well as singing, elocution and gymnastics. He charged sixty-five cents a lesson and worked as a bartender at the Gotham Bowling Alley on weekends and holidays.

He was an ambitious man. You could see it in his eyes and in the tenseness of his neck muscles. He bit his fingernails almost to extinction. There was something definitely off-base about him. For the first few minutes of my lesson he was full of energy, shouting, reprimanding, correcting, exhorting, demanding a high degree of performance and concentration. But for the next twenty-odd minutes, he sat in a chair and stared at the traffic crawling outside the window.

"I think I did that wrong," I would say apologetically after hitting a wrong note.

"I have to diversify," he would murmur under his breath, eyes still pinned to the traffic. "I need greater diversification."

Or I'd say, "My lips are killing me, Mr. Porter. I'm not sure my embouchure is right."

"Do I go heavy in the market?" he would answer, not turning

away from the window, "or do I pull back and retrench in municipal tax-free bonds?"

"Mr. Porter . . ."

"Where goest the economy?"

"I'd like to ask you . . ."

"Where goest the wise investor?"

"How many hours a day should I practice?"

"Synthetics, natural resources, automotive accessories, debentures, commodities, warranties . . ."

Eventually the son of the Chinese laundryman downstairs would come into the room. He'd start doing his acrobatics, somersaults, handstands and what-have-you, while I tried to finish my lesson and Mr. Porter went on murmuring, "Texaco, Boeing, Squibb, Dupont, Westinghouse, Pan American, hocus pocus jimminy crocus . . ."

I had, among no doubt other deficiencies of character, one that was consistent and easy of detection. It was extremely difficult for me to end a relationship. As an example there's Mr. Porter. Although I knew that I was wasting my time with him, it took me over a year to break away and convince my parents that I had to have another music teacher. I wanted Mr. Brooks, Gerald's teacher.

"How much does he charge?" My father wanted to know.

"Two dollars."

"For what?"

"Half an hour."

"He gets two dollars for half an hour?"

"Yes, Dad."

"Does he give you a haircut, also?"

"Mr. Brooks is the best there is. He's a colored man."

My mother dropped a meatball and a tangle of spaghetti on our plates. "Do you wanna take lessons with the nigger?" she asked me.

"Yes, Ma. He's a colored man."

"Then you'll take lessons with the nigger," she said. "And I don't care how much it costs you," she said to my father. "Go to one of your banks and take out the money."

My father swallowed some water. He spoke softly. "Let's talk like human beings," he said. "It's not the two dollars that bothers me. It's the French horn. Eddie, I went to speak to Tobias yesterday. You remember Tobias? He knows more about music than ten professors. He said, 'Don't let your son play the French horn. It's a dying instrument.' Eddie, I'm looking out for your welfare. Transfer to the trumpet or trombone. Tobias said if you . . ."

"I want him to play the French horn," my mother said out of the blue, sitting down at the table.

My father hit his eardrum with a cupped hand, as if he had somehow poured water into it by mistake.

"I like the French horn," my mother went on. "I have always liked the French horn."

"Isn't it a terrific instrument, Ma?"

"Yes. I'll see to it that you take lessons with the nigger."

"He's a colored man, Ma. Dad, do you want another meatball?"

But my father was still too busy trying to get the water out of his ear to answer me.

Mr. Brooks lived with his grandmother (for so I thought her) on the ground floor of a brownstone. He was a fairly tall, slouch-shouldered man, his face a black smudge of gloom with a curved, string-bean nose and a receding hairline. He never sat down but was continually pacing, stopping only to fill a tumbler with wine from a gallon bottle. His grandmother, a fat, gray-haired woman, came in and out of the room; sometimes she sat in a rocking chair and listened to the lesson, at other times she swept the rug or dusted the furniture. Neither Mr. Brooks nor I paid her any attention.

"You're too old," were the first words Mr. Brooks said to me after I played an exercise for him.

"I'm thirteen," I said. "I won't be fourteen until next November."

"You're too old," he repeated, staring at me with angry, bloodshot eyes.

"I'm the same age as Gerald," I said weakly.

"Gerald's been studying music for years." He gulped down his wine thirstily. "His father was a musician. His sister's a genius. Give it up."

"No."

"Study the trumpet."

"No."

"Switch to the drums."

"No."

I seemed to have made him more angry. He had to gulp down another tumbler of wine. "What is it with you? Do you wanna be a second-rate musician for your whole life?" he shouted at me. "Do you wanna go 'round begging for jobs? teaching dumb kids jus' so you can get yourself two bucks for a bottle a cheap wine? We're talking here 'bout bein' a classical musician, Buster! We're talking here 'bout bein' able to play Haydn an' Mozart an' Schubert an' Mendelssohn, in a classical, professional orchestra! How many horn players you think they need, Buster? How many opportunities you think there are? You go on an' tell me that!"

I kept quiet, my eyes never leaving his face.

He paced back and forth, back and forth, long, angry strides that took him across the room and back again every other minute.

His grandmother stood on a chair and changed the light bulbs in an ancient chandelier.

He drank another tumbler. "Okay, Buster; okay. One year. I'm givin' you one year to perform a miracle. If you don't do it, I'm givin' you up."

I got out of bed every morning at five, went into the bathroom, put a mute into the bell of the horn so I wouldn't disturb the neighbors, and practiced until I had to go to school.

After school I listened to records with Gerald, squeezed whatever theory and know-how I could out of him, then went home, had a bite, and practiced in the bathroom until I couldn't stand it anymore.

I prayed to God, asking Him for His assistance and encouragement.

I added to my wardrobe a purple velvet cape which I wore along with my beret and ascot.

I went to concerts with Gerald. Once in a while his sister came with us. We went to Carnegie Hall, Town Hall, the Metropolitan Opera House, to City Center, to the outdoor concerts at Lewisohn Stadium and Central Park. We also went to recitals where we could hear the horn and into people's houses to listen to music.

We started our own orchestra of sixteen kids and rehearsed in Gerald's living room. It was our intention to stick together and all turn professional at the same time. There was one kid in the group I despised. Perry Reese. He played the clarinet. I curse the day I met him and I curse the day he was born. (You'll learn a lot more about him later.)

I collected photographs of famous composers and musicians and tacked them to the walls of my bedroom.

I read everything I could on the lives of the Masters and considered them my personal friends.

Far into the night I had conversations with them and asked their advice.

I had no doubt in my mind that I would perform a miracle and become the best horn player who ever lived.

"Stravinsky is staying at the Geneva Hotel!" Gerald stood under my bathroom window and shouted up at me one Saturday morning.

He didn't have to say any more. I grabbed my velvet cape and ran downstairs.

"*Petrouchka, The Firebird, The Rites of Spring*," I recited as we hurried toward the subway.

"Symphony of Psalms, Symphony in C, Symphony in Three Movements," Gerald hobbled at my side, trying to keep up with his hunchback walk.

"He was born near Leningrad," I said.

"Formerly St. Petersburg," Gerald said. "In 1882. Who did he study with?"

"Rimsky-Korsakov."

"What was the name of the Russian ballet manager he collaborated with?"

"I can't pronounce the name. It's capital D-i-a-g-h-i-l-e-v."

"Sergei," Gerald said, and pronounced Diaghilev for me.

In Manhattan we walked to the Geneva Hotel and waited in front of a stationery store for Mr. Stravinsky to make an appearance.

About noon we got hungry, bought Sabrett hotdogs and Mission orange sodas, and inched our way to the hotel.

It was exciting to watch the people leave and enter the hotel: rich people, storybook people, people in shoes of lizard and alligator, in clothes of brocade and lace, their faces enameled with all the colors in a child's crayon box.

The doorman, in dovetailed uniform, blew his whistle, directed traffic, opened doors, carried suitcases, revolved from curbstone to hotel in a whirl of choreographed activity.

"Scram or I'll break your necks!" he had time to snarl at us.

We moved back to the stationery store, undismayed, eyes fastened to the entrance of the hotel.

It was getting late, but we were determined not to leave until we had seen Mr. Stravinsky.

The sky darkened. A heavy rain fell on the suddenly deserted sidewalks.

"There! There he is!" Gerald hugged me around the waist, trembling from head to foot.

23

"Where? Where?"

"There! There!"

Under an umbrella, in a gray overcoat and gray hat, a spindle-legged man with the shoulders of a football player passed us. I caught a glimpse of his nose.

"Let's go," I said, moving after him.

Gerald scurried at my side. "What will we say to him?"

"Leave it to me. Let's catch him."

We walked faster, but we couldn't walk too fast, what with Gerald hanging onto my arm and holding me back.

Mr. Stravinsky turned and saw us. His expression was one of open-mouthed horror. He, too, walked faster, rounded a corner.

"Come on! Come on!" I urged Gerald. "We're gonna lose him!" We made the corner and there he was. "Run! Run!" I shouted. "We'll never get a chance like this again!"

(Only now do I suspect that being chased by two kids, one a hunchback and the other in beret and purple cape, might not have been a pleasant experience for the Master.)

We broke into a run or something close to it.

Mr. Stravinsky ran. He cut across the gutter, weaving between traffic, his umbrella high over his head.

We went after him.

Cars honked hysterically at us.

Puddles of rain splashed at our ankles. Mr. Stravinsky was now sprinting wildly toward Second Avenue, the umbrella parachuting behind him.

"Run! Run!" We charged after him.

But there was no keeping up with the Master. Gerald slowed down, panting breathlessly, and leaned on a fire hydrant. "I . . . I can't. It's no use. You go, Eddie, go, leave me . . ."

"Did you see his nose?" I shouted at him. "Did you see it?"

"I couldn't. My eyeglasses are wet."

"I saw his nose!" I jumped up and down. "I saw it! It was magnificent! It was the most magnificent nose I ever saw in my life!"

24

"I wish I . . ."

"There! Look there!"

I pointed to a taxi. Seated in the rear was the Master, mopping his brow with a white, silk scarf.

We waved and yelled, "Mr. Stravinsky! Mr. Stravinsky! How's it going, Mr. Stravinsky?"

And the Master did the weirdest thing. As the taxi moved away, he made a face and stuck his tongue out at us.

We entered high school the following fall and immediately applied for the orchestra.

"Two French horns!" Mr. West, the music teacher, was delighted. He led us to a storage room in which there were piles of clothes on the floor and in the lockers. "If you boys can find uniforms that fit you, I want you in the band as well," he said, leaving us alone to scrounge for ourselves.

It took me about an hour to find a uniform that was right for me. I put on the pale blue pants, the brass-buttoned orange tunic with blue lapels, and the conical, imitation beaver bonnet.

I stared at my reflection in a cracked, body-length mirror.

I looked beautiful: very skinny but with the suggestion of a tiger's sinewy strength, near six feet in height, small, intense, brown-speckled eyes, a full, sensual, kissable mouth, acne pimples and prominent nose wiped out by the splendor of the total image.

"Nothing fits me," Gerald whined in despair. "I won't be able to play in the band."

He stood on a mountain of uniforms like some forlorn punchinello, tears streaming down his face.

But I couldn't do anything for him. I didn't have the will to descend from the lofty pinnacle that my new uniform had taken me to.

Giddily I said, "Do not despair, my child. That which I have achieved, thou can achieve. For it is given to no man to suffer without redemption."

And I picked up a silver baton and walked out of the storage room, determined that the world witness my splendor and pay proper homage to me.

Through the corridors of the school and into the street I went, feet barely leaving the ground. I turned and nodded to everyone I passed, muttering a benediction and shaking the baton over their heads.

I knew where I was going. My mother was at work at the A & P and I wanted her to see me in my uniform.

I peeked through the window of the supermarket. There she was, ringing up sales at the cash register, deftly plucking groceries from the counter, and putting them into paper bags. Standing behind her was Mr. Raskin, the manager of the Reo, a neighborhood movie house. He was a stocky, barrel-chested man, hair slicked down on his substantial skull (a la George Raft), wearing a freshly pressed suit, white shirt and pinched tie. He was talking to my mother, grinning widely, showing no teeth. My mother answered him over her shoulder as she worked. I couldn't hear what they were saying.

Mr. Raskin had his hands on my mother's hips and every now and then he would pull her back toward him, bouncing her rear end off the trampoline tautness of his groin.

Mrs. Hinkey cut and sewed a blue-and-orange uniform for Gerald. The day of the first game of the season, I met Gerald in front of his house and we went to the football field. Our naked horns were clasped at our sides and our uniforms gleamed immaculately. We marched somewhat in step, the pipe and the hunchback, going forth to win honor for God, Country and Florence Nightingale High. The game was to start at two in the afternoon and we arrived before noon. No one was there. But we went in, ducking under the turnstile, and we walked onto the field. We had practiced with the band only twice, and neither one of us knew precisely where to make a right or left turn, where to do an about-face or mark time, where and when to hold our horns to our hips, or extend them at arm's reach in a flapping, razzmatazz movement. We decided to practice by ourselves until the others arrived.

Up and down the field we went, the two of us, my friend Gerald and I, our horns bellowing a Sousa in the bright, shimmering sunlight: left turn, right turn, one, two, three, four, horn on hip, one, two, three, four, mark time, mark time, horn to lip, start out, one, two, three, four, one, two, three, four, Night-ing-ale, Night-ing-ale, rah-rah-rah, siss-boom-bah, Victory is ours, one, two, three, four, All must bow to our resolve, one, two, three, four, Take heart, rah-rah-rah, Winners win, siss-boom-bah, start out, arm extended, twirl horn, The Orange and the Blue, one, two, three, four, start out, mark time, horn on hip, here we go, Watch out, The Future's on the march, rah-rah-rah, siss-boom-bah . . .

Glancing over at the bleachers, I noticed that a family of five had entered the stadium and spread a blanket at the periphery of the field. The mother opened a straw basket and gave out pieces of fried chicken to the father and three children. And soon other families came in and sat down on the ground: food was passed, soda and beer cans opened, transistor radios blared, people chatted, moved from one group to another, and there was a noisy, carnival atmosphere about it all.

Several young men were working on the goalposts. I didn't recognize any of them.

We couldn't stop marching, my friend Gerald and I. We were drenched in sweat, bones aching, feet swollen, but the horns and the brass buttons propelled us on. We had an audience and by God they were going to listen to us; they were going to hear the best horn playing and watch the best marching they had ever seen!

Yes, Sir! One, two, three, four, Night-ing-ale, Night-ing-ale, rah-rah-rah, siss-boom-bah, Victory is ours, one, two, three, four, All must bow to our resolve, one, two, three, four . . .

A delegation of men walked onto the field and waved us to a

halt. They were wearing uniforms of short pants and short-sleeved shirts.

"Hey, man, wha' you think you're doin'?" one of them stuck his jaw out and spoke with a Spanish accent.

"Ge' off the field," his companion said, sticking his jaw out and speaking with a Spanish accent.

"Where's the band?" I asked, gasping for breath.

"Wha's he talkin' 'bout?" a third put in, sticking his jaw out and speaking in a Spanish accent.

I turned to the goalposts. They had disappeared.

"We're members of the Florence Nightingale High School band. We're playing Erasmus today," I said, now staring down at Gerald who was squeezing my hand with all his might.

"That's over at Erasmus Field," the first one yelled, pulling his jaw back in and losing his Spanish accent. "We're playin' soccer here today, shmuck!"

And they moved to the sidelines.

"What time is it?" I asked Gerald.

He looked at his wristwatch. "Two o'clock."

I nodded, undaunted.

He nodded, undaunted.

We lifted our coils of gold to our lips and blasted a finale, marching off the field to, if not a tumultuous, at least a respectable round of applause and a couple of *mira miras* thrown in.

I fell in love with the cello player in our high school orchestra. My first love. My first true love. Eleanor Goldsmith. What would my life have been like if I had said to Eleanor Goldsmith at fourteen: I love you; bear with me for a few years; I'll make it up to you.

What would my life have been like?

(You don't know it but right now I'm laughing my head off, seated behind an elegant, patinaed desk in my two-hundred-dollar-a-day suite at the Geneva Hotel!)

I know what it would have been like, my friend, I know.

Anyway, from where I sat in the horn section, I could watch Eleanor Goldsmith without her being aware of it.

Her knees! Her knees! Round and plump and soft as the down on a duck's back! The cello pressed between her knees, cradled between her thighs, embraced by her ballerina arms, bent over and adored by her lovely face! I wanted to cry out, I love you, I will always love you, let me be your cello! Let me rest between your luscious knees, lean over me, hold me, press me to your dimpled chin! Eleanor Goldsmith, I wanted to scream at the top of my lungs, have mercy for God's sake and let me be your rotten cello!

The pangs of youth, my friend, aren't they pathetic? aren't they an embarrassment to us all?

Undoubtedly. Eleanor Goldsmith and I played in the same orchestra for four years, through high school.

I never spoke to her; that is, not until many years later, when it didn't much matter.

It was almost to the day, one year after my first meeting with him, that I went to Mr. Brooks for my weekly lesson. His warning still rang in my head: "Okay, Buster; okay. One year. I'm givin' you one year to perform a miracle. If you don't do it, I'm givin' you up!"

For weeks I had worked hard on the horn, practicing four, five hours a day, skipping school on occasion to put in a few extra hours. Seated in the bathroom beside the tub, exercise book propped on the hamper, mute stuffed into the bell, I huffed and puffed and sweated the valves until I couldn't stand it anymore. I was as ready as I ever would be for Mr. Brooks. Had I performed a miracle? Was I any good? Would he drop me or say, "You did it, Buster. God bless you."

I was frightened when I sat down to do my exercise for him. My throat felt as if it was growing cotton and my hands trembled.

Mr. Brooks paced, back and forth, back and forth, sipped his wine from the gallon bottle. The year had not been kind to him. He had lost weight, his color was that of burnt liver, his clothes hung loosely on his skeletal frame. There seemed little anger left in him.

As I played I waited for his judgment. Now he'll stop me and say . . . Now he'll interrupt me and shout . . . Now he'll grab my shoulder and whisper . . .

Despite all this, I played well, as well as I possibly could, and somehow, inside, I was pleased with myself.

Grandma Brooks sat in a chair near the radiator and quietly peeled potatoes.

I went on to the lesson for the following week. Mr. Brooks didn't stop me once. I was encouraged. It was the best lesson I had.

When it was over I paid and stood by, staring straight into Mr. Brooks' bloodshot eyes.

Tell me. Don't hold anything back. I want the truth.

Mr. Brooks returned my stare, squinting at me. He was clearly puzzled as to why I was remaining after my lesson.

Grandma Brooks held an unpeeled potato in her lap and turned from her grandson to me. She was clearly puzzled, too.

I wanted to say, Did I do it, Mr. Brooks? Did I perform a miracle? Am I any good? The words multiplied in my throat and clotted at the roof of my mouth.

I said nothing.

Mr. Brooks said nothing.

I left the room.

And although I studied with Mr. Brooks for another three years, until I was graduated from high school, I never asked him whether I had performed a miracle or not, and he never told me.

No doubt he had forgotten all about it.

To say what one is feeling. It's the hardest thing in the world to do when one is young and lives inside oneself. But how easy it has become for me now! How incredibly easy! You couldn't possibly recognize in me the skinny kid with the French horn. We are further apart than Arab and Jew, than Greek and Turk, than man and child.

Today there isn't an impulse in my body that doesn't find expression. There isn't a word on my tongue that isn't emitted, disgorged, inflated, improvised on, hurled out like snake's venom into the vulnerable ear of anyone within hearing.

There exists in me no barrier between thought and act, between wish and fulfillment, between desire and gratification.

My volubility has become so unrestrained that, like a modern Dracula, I need fresh ears to bite into. But I've taken a vow, my friend, a strict and sacred vow. I'm determined to call no one, meet no one, initiate no relationship, seek out no diversion, no distraction, until the first of the year, a period of some five months. I can tell you in confidence that I'm preparing myself for several very important auditions and perhaps a concert or two. I mean to give all of my energies and all of my attention to the horn. This is essential if I'm to be as good as I must be. I know this sounds a bit extreme to you, fanatical even, but I'm motivated by my past experiences. Nothing will interfere with my work this time. Nothing, so help me God! Unfortunately, though, I can't practice for more than a few hours at a stretch, especially at the beginning, and during the gaps my craving for fresh ears becomes absolutely unbearable. So here I am, with a monk's cowl on my head, dipping my sharp, glib tongue into the inkwell and allowing it to rant and rave across the empty page in the hope of finding a fresh ear. That I choose to write about the days and nights of the skinny horn player is understandable if not excusable: the story is familiar and of general interest to me. And the wonderful thing about writing the skinny horn player's story is that when I do find a fresh ear to bite into, as I'm sure I will, my friend, my dear friend, my lovely friend, the fleshy, succulent lobe can't talk back to me. I've found the perfect fresh ear! Yummy-yummy-yummy!

Yes, indeed. Yes, indeed. I guess since I already let the proverbial cat out of the bag by telling you I'm staying in a suite of rooms at the Geneva Hotel, that I should fill you in.

At present my assets are close to a million. In banks around the city, in cash (I'm my father's son in this respect, anyway), I have approximately four hundred thousand; the rest is in a town house on East 73rd Street and eleven acres of land in Manchester, Vermont; also various insurance and retirement policies.

Does this surprise you? Really? Well, you shouldn't make the mistake of thinking that the skinny horn player and I are related. As I said, we have very little in common, a few memories, a few scars, the same birthday, that's about it.

I tell you the greatest feeling in the world is to say to yourself, I know, I understand. And to look straight at a situation and to analyze it and to know you're right, you don't have to take anyone's word for anything, you know where it's at.

I know where it's at.

The skinny horn player knew zilch. He was all instinct and naiveté. He rushed from one end of the rat maze to the other, not permitting himself, because of some psychological disability, to stop and look objectively at what he was doing or where he was going. He couldn't own up to the truth about himself.

Frankly, it's merely a convenient fiction for me to write about him in the first person.

three

I sat in Gerald's bedroom, puffing on my pipe, and listening to a record of Weber's Concertino in E Minor which has some beautiful horn chords in it. Gerald sat at his desk, going over my European history homework. Downstairs his mother was preparing a picnic lunch for us. We were going to Highland Park, to play tennis and have lunch on the grass. "Do you know how to play tennis?" Gerald had asked me several days previously. At first I didn't know whether he was joking or not. Tennis wasn't a game frequently mentioned in Brooklyn at that time. His eyes blinked behind his specs and his cocked head stared up at me. He wasn't joking. The fact is I had never played tennis in my life, but I answered him without hesitation, "Of course. What a question." That's how the date came about. The plan was for his sister Shirley to join us with a girl friend at the tennis courts.

"Do you intend to go to college?" Gerald now spoke to the homework paper on his desk, and I spoke to the hump on his back. "I don't know. I haven't given it much thought. Should I"?

"If you want to be a professional musician, you should," he said, whirling around in his chair and handing my homework to me.

He had scratched out a number of sentences, changed a number of dates and names. Characteristically I wasn't displeased. I knew that he knew that I knew all the correct answers, but merely did the homework with my usual disdain for such commonplace chores.

"I want to play the horn," I said. "That's what I want to do for the rest of my life."

"Where?"

I filled my lungs and let it out: "With the Philharmonic. At Carnegie Hall."

"That's tough competition." He took off his glasses to wipe them with a tissue. And as always happened when he took them off, his eyes watered, overflowed. He put his glasses back on. "The more education you have, Eddie, the better it'll be for you. A musician doesn't only play an instrument. He plays musical theory and musical history and personal experience and his own culture, a whole way of looking at things."

(Not bad for a fifteen-year-old hunchback!)

"Are you going to college?" I asked him.

"Yes. Juilliard or Eastman at Rochester. I . . ." He filled his lungs and let it out: "I want to be a conductor. I want . . . to put together sounds . . . never heard before." He lowered his eyes.

"Then you'll be a conductor and I'll be a horn player with the Philharmonic. What are you so serious about? Come on, let's go play tennis." I was up and out of the room before he could raise his eyes.

All right, the truth. I was still ashamed of my friend Gerald. I saw him only on Saturdays. At school I avoided him as much as I could without hurting his feelings. I developed the habit of walking a step or two ahead of him so that if we ran into anyone I knew, I could lengthen the distance between us and pretend we weren't together. I had no excuse for this except a mitigating one. I wasn't morally strong enough to disassociate myself from the prejudices that prevailed. When it came to prejudices of race,

34

color, religion or conditions of previous servitude, I was incorruptible, but when it came to the physical appearance of anyone, I was swept along with the mob, demanding for social equality a facsimile of good looks, sturdy limbs and the projection of impeccable health.

It follows that I was incapable of enjoying Gerald's friendship. I couldn't see under the hump, so to speak. I begrudged him intimacies and withdrew from his touch, posturing a false macho aloofness. Yet I knew full well my indebtedness to him. Perhaps even more important than introducing me to music and instilling in me the desire to be a horn player was his overt acquiescence to my being someone special. He bridged the abyss for me between my inner life and reality. He insisted that I come out of myself, that I read the books he read, saw the paintings he saw, observed the buildings and people and trees and stones that he observed. Impulsively he would point to the sky and say, How beautiful, so that I, too, had to look at the sky and say, How beautiful.

I nurtured the rather feeble hope that he wasn't aware of my . . . prejudice, but I have no way of knowing whether he was or not. We never spoke about it.

My friend Gerald walked a step behind me as we climbed the steep hill of Miller Avenue to reach the park. He carried our tennis rackets, the picnic basket and a blanket. How he was to play tennis I had no idea. Already he was panting, sweat shone on his angled face, the tufts of hair on his bald head were limp and soggy, his eyes were blinded by the magnified rays of the sun; he pulled his knobby, crippled body up the incline, a humped Sisyphus pitting his will against that of the malevolent gods.

Approaching the tennis courts I was met with a sight that literally knocked the wind out of me. Coming from the other direction was Shirley in a white tennis dress of sorts. She was pushing a wheelchair in which sat a girl in a white tennis dress of sorts, her legs ornamented with sparkling aluminum bands. I looked to Gerald for an explanation, but he was in front of me now, moving as quickly as he could to greet his sister and her girl friend.

"Eddie Davis, Bertha Klinger," he introduced me offhandedly, then said, "I'll take over, Sis." He gripped the bar behind the wheelchair and pushed Bertha into the park. I trailed after him with Shirley.

This couldn't be happening to me, I thought. What am I doing playing tennis with two hunchbacks and a girl in a wheelchair?

"You're probably an excellent tennis player," Shirley said. "You have the physique for it."

I nodded and blew a whiff of Sir Walter in her direction.

"This is the second year I'm playing," she continued. "I have a fairly decent forehand but my backhand leaves something to be desired."

I didn't know what she was talking about so I sent out another whiff of tobacco.

"I'll tell you what, Eddie." Her sea-green eyes swung over my face. "Bertha and I will play you and Gerald. If we win, you take me to the movies. But if you win, I'll never bring up the subject again."

"You have a deal, Shirley." I pulled the pipe from my mouth and for no sensible reason started to whistle a chorus of *The Battle Hymn of the Republic*.

Gerald helped Bertha out of her wheelchair. An aluminum cane was appended to her left arm; at the end of her right arm she firmly held a Don Budge tennis racket. "Okay, you guys," she shouted, hobbling on her cane to the far court, "let's hit a few!" And she whacked the ball over the net so hard that I watched it fly past me, too astonished to do anything.

"What's wrong?" Gerald cried over his shoulder as he ran after the ball and returned it with a vicious, crosscourt stroke. Shirley slammed it back to me, almost ripping my head off.

"Hold it! Hold it, everybody!" I yelled, wagging my arms, and when I had their attention, I said, "I haven't played in several

36

years. Let's take it easy at the beginning. Gerald, can I speak to you a minute?" I bent over and whispered into his ear, "Is Bertha up to a strenuous game? I mean, with her condition?"

"Don't worry about Bertha," my friend said, loudly. "She's a high school champion."

"What high school does she go to?" I felt compelled to keep my voice low.

"The same as my sister," Gerald shouted at me. "It's a privately endowed school for exceptional students."

"That's the school I should be going to," I said, softly, and yelled across the net, "Okay, girls, let's play ball!"

We lost the first set, 6 to 0.

There were times when I could have sworn that Bertha was hitting the ball with her cane as well as her racket. She hopped rather than ran, hopped in a perpetually vertical motion, as if she was on a pogo stick, cane and racket slashing at the ball with diabolical accuracy. Shirley wasn't bad either. In fact she was better than Gerald who seemed to bounce his racket off his hump for greater speed and top spin.

Mercifully, during the second set, which we were losing 3 to 1, I got a severe cramp in my leg that brought me to the ground. My kneecap was jammed under my chin and I writhed and moaned in pain.

"What is it, Eddie? Did you break your leg? Is it your leg?" Gerald asked anxiously. The girls leapfrogged over the net and appeared at my side. "He can't breathe," Shirley cried. "He requires mouth-to-mouth resuscitation!" And she leaned toward me, her mouth wide open, like a huge suction cup. "No . . . cramp . . . cramp!" I managed to gasp. "He has a cramp," Bertha said. "Put him in my wheelchair."

They lifted me gently off the ground and sat me in the wheelchair.

Gerald and Shirley ran ahead to spread the blanket for our picnic lunch. Bertha pushed me in the wheelchair to a shady spot near a sycamore tree.

37

"You should take tennis lessons," she whispered to me.

"I will," I said. "As soon as I'm able to walk again."

Shirley Hinkey was my first official date, the result of my losing to her at tennis. I changed my ascot, cornstarched my pimples, darkened the faint hairs sprouting under my nose with my mother's mascara, and went to her house after dinner to pick her up. I planned to take her to the RKO Albee which was on Fulton Street, downtown, so that there would be little chance of my running into any of my classmates.

Gerald opened the door for me. He was wearing a navy blue jacket, white trousers, the collar of his cotton shirt was outside the collar of his jacket, and black-and-white wing-tipped shoes. Was he going with us? I wondered.

"Eddie, how pleased I am to see you," he said, pumping my hand and leading me into the living room. "What brings you here at this unearthly hour?" he asked once we were seated.

I wasn't sure how to answer. "I think Shirley and I have a . . ."

"Oh, yes, yes, you have a formal date with Sis," he said, throwing one abbreviated leg over the other. "Would you care for a cocktail?"

Now I was really confused. "What kind of cocktail?" I asked suspiciously.

"Old-fashioned, martini, whiskey sour, you name it, we've got it at Hinkey's!" He laughed at the ceiling, clapping his hands gleefully.

"No, thank you," I said. "Where's Shirley?"

"Upstairs. Making her toilet."

"Is that so?" A thoughtful pause. "Will it take her long to make it?"

"You know how women are." He winked at me. "It takes them a year to get ready."

"Is that so?" I said a second time.

"They have rites to perform that are beyond the comprehension of any member of the male gender."

Before I could consider saying, Is that so? a third time, Mrs. Hinkey entered, wearing a satiny beige gown, arm-length gloves, and a corsage of gardenias bloomed between her impressive breasts. Was she going with us, too? I wondered. The four of us? To the RKO Albee?

"Eddie, what a pleasant surprise." She glided across the room and sat beside me, holding out her hand for me to kiss.

I looked imploringly at Gerald. He smiled. I looked imploringly at Mrs. Hinkey. She smiled. In the interim some pollen from her gardenias must have crept into my nose because my head suddenly snapped back and I sneezed violently all over her hand.

She stared mournfully at her soiled glove.

"I'm sorry,'" I said, wiping my nose with my jacket sleeve. "I must be coming down with the flu."

She peeled off the glove, tilted and slipped it under her behind. "Don't mention it, Eddie," she said bravely. "Would you like a cocktail?"

"What kind of cocktail?" I asked suspiciously.

"I offered him one already, Mother." Gerald said, and to me, "Ritz crackers and Cracker Barrel cheese, perhaps?"

"Or perhaps slices of banana and Karo syrup?" Mrs. Hinkey put in.

"He can have Poppycock," Gerald said. "Would you care for a cup of Poppycock, Eddie?"

"Or a wedge of rhubarb pie with marshmallow topping and a frosted glass of . . . ?"

It was then that Shirley made her appearance. Seeing her come into the room immediately brought to mind the Celluloid Betty Boop dolls they sold at Coney Island. She was wearing an off-the-shoulder, ruffled, black taffeta dress, white high-heeled shoes that bent sideways under her weight; her hair was done in tight strawberry curls, and hanging from her almost nonexistent neck were countless strings of colored coffee beans. (The Betty Boop

39

image was soon succeeded by one of a Cha-Cha dancer at a Spanish social club for ethnic midgets.)

"Good evening, Edward. Do you forgive me for being tardy?" What was I supposed to say to that!

I jumped to my feet. "Are we all going to the movies tonight?" I asked in my baby voice. "Because if we are, I should tell you, I only have four dollars and fifteen cents."

"Oh, no," Mrs. Hinkey said, rising, and with Gerald at my elbow, ushered me to the door. "Where did you get that notion from?"

"I don't know. I think I'm coming down with the flu," I said, and faked a terrific sneeze into my ascot.

"You will bring my sister home before midnight, won't you?" Gerald opened the door and we all stood on the stoop where the whole world could see us.

I stayed back in the shadows. "Maybe before midnight," I murmured, spotting Mrs. Grosbard at her window.

"I'm certain that Eddie Davis knows how to treat a girl when he takes her out on a date," Shirley shouted to Mrs. Grosbard.

"I'm certain that Eddie Davis knows how to treat Miss Shirley Hinkey when he takes her out on a date," Mrs. Hinkey megaphoned her mouth and shouted to someone living in New Jersey.

"Do you have an umbrella I can borrow, Mrs. Hinkey?"

"Eddie? Eddie, where are you?"

"In here, Mrs. Hinkey. In the corner."

"What do you need an umbrella for?"

"It looks like it might rain and I'm coming down with the flu."

Gerald ducked into the hallway and brought out an umbrella for me. I stepped into the light and snapped the umbrella open, wearing it like a hat. "I'm ready to go, Shirley."

"Eddie, it isn't raining yet," Mrs. Hinkey informed me.

"I know. I just wanna be prepared."

"Good night, Mother. Good night, dear Brother," Shirley embraced and kissed them as if she was never going to see them again.

I didn't wait for her. I ran up the street, wearing the umbrella on my head, hoping I would be mistaken for a rabbi.

I remember the thought I had as we moved toward the bus stop: if I die now, I won't be mad at anyone.

"Let's not go to the movies," Shirley said, clutching my pants' belt to keep up with me. Next to my tall, skinny frame she looked like a little Munchkin and I could have sworn that as we hurried along her feet were off the ground and she was floating beside me.

"Where do you wanna go?"

"To a dance."

"A dance?"

"Yes, I love to dance."

"You wanna go to a dance, just the two of us?" Kill me! Somebody please kill me!

"We can take the bus to Eastern Parkway. They have an Over-Twenty-Eight Club there and we can dance."

"I'm only fifteen," I said.

"So am I. But they'll let us in. With your new mustache you can pass for thirty-six."

"I have four dollars and fifteen cents, including bus fare," I said.

"That'll be sufficient. We'll go Dutch treat and I'll pay for the bus."

"Shirley?"

"Yes?"

"Let go of my belt, please. You're pulling off my pants."

"Oh, I do hope you don't think me lascivious," she said, entwining her fingers in mine.

The Over-Twenty-Eight Club building looked like a mansion to me. It had a columned front porch, a lawn with privets and fruit trees, and large windows glowing with amber light. People left, entered, loitered about on the lawn. I moved up the walk to the entrance with my date, umbrella reopened and pressed to my head.

"If they ask for identification," Shirley said, "ask them where to check the umbrella."

The advice made no more sense to me then than it does now, but I wasn't in a mood to argue.

Of course the Mafia guard at the door stopped me. "Let's see your I.D.," he grumbled, letting Shirley pass by.

"Where do I check my umbrella?"

I admit he was taken aback by that one. "Let's see the I.D.," he repeated, brushing cigar ash from the lapel of his double-breasted gangster suit.

For the life of me (literally) I couldn't come up with another line, so I said, "This umbrella must be checked."

He plucked the De Nobili from his mouth and jabbed it at me. "Hey, kid?"

"Yes, Sir?"

"D'you wan' dat umbrella stuck up your ass?"

"No, Sir. It's not my umbrella."

"Den let's see the I.D."

"He's with me, Rocky." Shirley's head popped in between us.

"Why didn't y'say so, Shirl?" He smiled down at her. "Okay. Dat's four bucks, Valentino."

"He'll give you two and I'll . . ." Shirley started, but the Mafia nixed the deal.

"Butt out, Shirl. Valentino's treatin'."

And treat I did, gladly, sidestepping the hairy ape.

"Y'got mascara underneat' your nose," he whispered as I passed him, and goosed me into the building with a stiff finger.

I gave my last fifteen cents to check the umbrella and we entered the dance hall. At the far end of the room was the band-stand with four or five tuxedoed musicians on it. Dancers filled almost every inch of the place, a dark mass of undulating bodies flecked with bits of tinted light that descended from a revolving global chandelier. Single men circled the dancers, sniffing at the floor. Single women sat rigidly in chairs against the wall, their nylon legs glistening like crossed swords, their faces visored with expressions of contempt.

"Hi, Shirley."

"How's it goin', Shirl?"

"I get the next lindy, Shirl."

Voices flew out at us from the darkness as Shirley pulled me onto the dance floor.

"I take it you've been here before," I said to my Munchkin partner.

"Once or twice. I love to dance. It's my favorite recreation," she said and, wrapping her arms around my buttocks and burying her nose in my navel, she led me in a fox-trot that asked the depth of the ocean and the height of the sky.

"Relax. Just relax. You're too tense." She spoke into my navel as if it was part of the intercom system.

"Shirley, I should have told you, I can't dance."

"I know. You can't play tennis either. Just follow me."

"I have to go to the bathroom," I soon said. "I have an upset stomach."

"After this number you can go."

"My upset stomach is killing me."

"Hold it in until after this number."

"I . . . I can't. I'm sorry," I whined, and hurried off the dance floor.

"Don't take too long," she shouted behind me. "And yell if you need any help!"

I found a copy of a Socialist newspaper on the towel rack and locked myself in a booth for I don't know how long. I was determined to remain in the bathroom until the night watchman came in and kicked me out. Now and then I'd leave the booth, go to one of the sinks, wash, comb my hair, dewax my ears, and pinch to bloody oblivion the pimples budding on my face. This was quite time consuming; so was reading the Socialist newspaper which I tried to commit to memory, but I gave it up when I reached an article on a correspondent's trip to a Soviet poultry farm where the chickens laid eggs the size of softballs. For want of something to do, I cleaned the sinks with my handkerchief, polished to brilliance the mirrors above them, and swept the tiled floor with paper towels.

Still there was no sign of the night watchman. Not having a wristwatch put me at a disadvantage. Whenever anyone entered the bathroom, I was too embarrassed to leave the booth. There were five toilet bowls and at one point I flushed all five in succession, for the hell of it. I noted that they each flushed a different tone. I ran from one booth to the next, experimenting with the flushes, working the stainless steel handles as if they were organ stops. I discovered that I could play the *Halleluja* section of Handel's Oratorio on them, but I had to be quick, getting to a toilet bowl before the flush drained out in the previous one. I sang along with the flushes. "Hal-le-lu-jah! Hal-le-lu-jah!" This was terrific. I was wasting a lot of time and I was having fun. "Hal-le-lu-jah! Hal-le-lu-jah! Ha-ha-ha-ha-hal-le-lu-jah!"

I was really going now, I was really getting into it, dashing from one bowl to the next like a demon, sweating over the flushes, singing louder and louder, and I could have easily continued until the night watchman came, if not for this drunken idiot who staggered in and sat down on my A flat.

That was it. I went back into the dance hall. Everything was as I had left it, the music, the dancers, the revolving light; it was as if I hadn't been gone at all. I looked for Shirley and had no trouble spotting her. She was dancing with a bearded epileptic in the center of the floor, kicking her heels and shimmying in her ruffled dress with exhibitionistic zeal. I sat down in a chair against the wall to wait for her.

The thin, long-faced woman beside me wrinkled her nose. "I smell Lysol disinfectant," she said, fingering her rhinestone collar. "Did someone leave the men's room door open?"

"I don't know, Ma'm. I haven't been in there recently."

"What are you doing?" she asked me.

"Dancing."

"I don't see you dancing."

"I have no one to dance with, Ma'm."

I must have said the magic word because right then and there she turned into a dragon, tongues of fire leaped from her mouth, her eyes started to smolder and smoke. "Oh, you have no one to dance with," she hissed at me. "There aren't enough dancers here for you! There aren't enough dancers in the entire United States of America for you, are there, you little shit!" And she rose high on her scaly tail, scorched my face with her fiery breath, and slithered off to join the other dragons seated against the wall.

Well, that was definitely it. I knew where I wasn't wanted. I got up and went to find Shirley. But where was she? I shouldered my way through the dancers in search of my Munchkin. No, she wasn't dancing now. Could she perchance be having a glass of white wine at the tiny bar in the broom closet? No, she wasn't there either. Could she have gone home without me? Was that possible? I tracked down my Mafia friend. He was seated in the foyer, reading the morning edition of the *Daily News*.

"Hi, Rocky," I said, matter-of-factly. "Did you by any chance see my Shirley?"

He folded the paper to the "Voice of the People" section. "She left," said while chomping on his Italian stinker.

"Left?"

"With Danny the Horse."

"Did she leave a message for me?"

The question warranted no answer.

"Did she leave any money for me?"

Nor that one.

45

I went to the checkroom, redeemed my umbrella, and returned to my Mafia friend. "Would you like to buy an umbrella?" I asked him. "I don't have carfare to get home."

Now he looked at me. But his stare was one of such simple, unaffected directness that there was no misinterpreting his state of mind. Once again my life was in danger. "Thank you very much for your patience," I said, and I lit my pipe, put the open umbrella on my head and walked the ten-odd miles home.

I came down with the flu. Gerald paid me a visit. It was the first time he was in my house and I had to introduce him to my parents. I will say this for them: they behaved with absolute candor. My mother said, "Any friend of Eddie's is welcome, regardless of his disabilities." My father said, "Eddie tells me you play the French horn," and he eyed the hump on Gerald's back as if trying to resolve for himself whether horn playing and spinal deformity were somehow related.

As soon as they were gone, Gerald said, "Shirley sends her condolences. She gave me this billet-doux for you."

I confess I thought he was going to take out a box of candy from his pocket, but it was only a sheet of composition paper folded in the shape of a soldier's hat.

"She asks if you have anything for her," he added cryptically.

"Like what, Gerald?"

"Anything that's personal to you."

I looked around my bedroom which really wasn't a bedroom but a storage area that the landlord had built at the rear of the kitchen. "I don't have anything," I said, dabbing at my running nose with a soggy handkerchief.

"You know what would be nice, Eddie?"

"What?"

"Your beret. She could wear it to school."

I touched my beret to make sure it was still on my head. "I

can't, Gerald, honest. I've had Old Flapjack since the fifth grade. I'm sorry." And after a slight pause, "Is there anything else you think she'd like?"

"One of your pipes," he said without hesitation.

"They've all been in my mouth," I answered weakly.

"That's all right. She won't smoke it. She'll keep it under her pillow to remind her of you." He picked up my favorite Algerian briar. "You rest now. Get better. We miss you, Eddie." And he waddled out of the room, taking along with him my favorite Algerian briar.

I unfolded the soldier's hat and read Shirley's letter:

Dear Edward,

How does one express regret? How does one say I wanted more than anything to turn you green with jealousy and so I left with Danny the Horse, a known gambler and a small potatoes gangster? Edward, I can't forecast the future nor can I presume a knowledge of your feelings for me. Can you presume a knowledge of my feelings for you? How deep is the ocean? How high is the sky? Does that mean anything to you? Regain your health my darling. We have so much to live for. How deep is the ocean? How high is the sky?

Yours eternally,
Shirl the Pearl

I lit a match and burned the letter in an ashtray. Don't ask me why. More than anything, though, I wanted my Algerian briar back.

Shirley Hinkey was the first girl who loved me. Eleanor Goldsmith was the first girl I loved. And so it was that at a comparatively early age I learned a basic principle of human relations: you'll always love the one who doesn't love you, and the one who doesn't love you usually marries young and has two children. That, in any event, was the case with Eleanor Goldsmith. I met her some two dozen years after graduating from high school, in the lobby of the Ethel Barrymore Theatre during intermission.

"Aren't you . . . ?"

"Eddie Davis," I grinned, toeing aside a dead cigarette with my Gucci shoe to catch a glimpse of her knees and to have her catch a glimpse of my Gucci. The years had given her a few pounds, a few creases, but the strings of my heart went zing nonetheless.

"Eddie Davis!" she squealed. "French horn!"

"Ahhh . . . Eleanor Goldsmith! Rotten cello!"

"That's right! How long has it been? Don't tell me. I have a boy and a girl in college, both on academic scholarships, and we live in Mamaroneck, in a positively enchanting house with a swimming pool and an organic vegetable garden. You must meet my husband. He's inside now getting me an orange crush. He's a very, very prestigious corporate attorney. Confidentially I could not have asked for a happier and more fulfilling life, not in my wildest, wildest dreams. But what have you been up to, Eddie? Did I read your name in the newspaper? Was that you? Are you the same Eddie Davis?"

"Well . . ."

"You're famous, that's wonderful!"

"I don't know if I'm famous but . . . I did make a bit of money."

"Did you?"

"Well . . . enough so I don't have to work another day for as long as I live."

She seemed disappointed in me.

"You must meet my husband," she said. "You two would hit it off marvelously. He sells mutual funds on the side."

I delicately lifted my jacket cuff so that we both could see the time on my fifteen-hundred-dollar Cartier Tank wristwatch. "I really have to run. I have an appointment at Sardi's . . ."

"Aren't you staying for the second act?"

"There are no second acts in my business," I said solemnly. "Busy, busy, busy, eighteen, twenty hours a day if I'm lucky. Do you come into town often?"

"On an average of once a week," she said.

I just let it out, no preamble. "I'd like to go to bed with you, Eleanor Goldsmith. I've wanted to go to bed with you since I first saw you at the rehearsal of Schubert's Unfinished Symphony."

That wasn't, as you know, quite accurate. I had never thought of going to bed with Eleanor Goldsmith. I had loved her and had merely wanted to be cradled in her arms. But the intervening years had taught me a trick or two. I knew that a more favorable response could be gotten from an invitation to go to bed than one that revealed an emotional attachment. And I was right.

She didn't blush, her eyes held to mine, and a smile tugged at her lipstick-bright mouth. "It won't be easy," she said.

"Neither was getting rid of Richard Nixon," I said.

"How?" she asked.

"My office number is in the phone book. I do want to see you again, very much. The next move is yours." And I walked off, glancing anxiously at my wristwatch, affirming for Eleanor Goldsmith the penalties incurred by a rich and successful life.

And she did phone, several days later. We made an appointment to have lunch at the Russian Tea Room. But something came up, possibly a trip to L.A., and I completely forgot about it. By the time I did remember, I had lost interest.

Shirley Hinkey loved me. But I didn't love Shirley Hinkey. Not only that. I didn't know what she wanted from me. I couldn't leave the house without bumping into her. "Are you going to the library, Eddie? That's where I'm going. Have you read Kafka? You must read Kafka. Physically you resemble him and he was a neurasthenic, too."

Whenever I dropped in to visit Gerald, she inevitably appeared, wheedled herself into the conversation, and managed to change its direction from the merits of the sonata form to the sexual habits of the African Hottentots.

"A man can only have three thousand twenty-seven ejaculations during his lifetime," she declared once to her astonished audience of two.

"We know that," Gerald mumbled.

"Do you boys masturbate?" She smashed the retort right back at us.

I put a match to my pipe and exhaled a geyser of smoke over her head. If my prayer was answered, I wore an expression that combined the purest elements of ennui with a liberal sprinkling of déjà vu.

Gerald was more furious than I had ever seen him. "That is personal! That is something that isn't spoken of in public! That is a subject that belongs in the bathroom and not in conversation with mixed company!"

"Oh, my God, you've been jerking off!" Shirley exclaimed.

"Where . . . Where . . ." Gerald was struck with a severe stammer. "Where d-d-d-you g-g-g-get that from?" He was on his feet, looking wildly under the furniture, as if he could discover under the furniture where she had gotten it from.

"How often do you jerk off, Jerry?" Shirley spoke with clinical calm to her brother, taking a notebook and pencil out of her schoolbag.

"You, you, you . . . You, you, you . . ." Gerald's head shook in a spasm on his humped back. "You, you, you . . ." I knew he wanted to say something terrible to his sister, but the curse was too heavy to dislodge. He took one last frantic look under the furniture and ran out of the room, slamming the door behind him.

"He jerks off," Shirley said with finality. "Statistically speaking, at his age the jerk-off rate is twice a week, usually on weekends and school holidays," and she jotted the information in her notebook.

"Shirley?"

"Yes, darling?"

"Do you still have my pipe?"

"Is that meant symbolically or realistically?"

"Realistically."

"What pipe are you speaking of?"

"The one Gerald borrowed when I had the flu."

"I think I lost it."

"How could you lose my pipe?"

"Well, I didn't exactly lose it. I traded with a girl friend."

"You traded my pipe? For what?"

"A twelve-inch vibrator!"

Up went her arms and legs and she was howling with laughter.

I admitted nothing to Shirley about my sex habits that afternoon. If I was guilty of anything, it was of assuming an attitude that led her to believe I was statistically above average. But the truth is I experienced no sexual discomfort and/or yearnings until very late in life. For the record, I masturbated for the first time when I was twenty-four, thinking of Eleanor Goldsmith.

51

four

It was during the summer of my sixteenth year that my mother took unto herself a lover.

This I can say with a fair degree of certainty almost thirty years after the event. Of course at the time, given my naiveté and extraordinary preoccupation of self, I had not the slightest inkling (nor of my father's evolving metamorphosis either). At one of our Sunday spaghetti and meatball lunches, Mr. Teddy Raskin appeared in seersucker suit and button-down shirt, his hair brilliantined to a patent-leather gloss over his substantial skull. He made a favorable impression, particularly on my father.

"You say you're the manager of a movie house? That used to be a solid industry, but I heard on the radio that television has made it a thing of the past."

"Not at all," Mr. Raskin responded. "Movies are better than ever. Look, I have some extra passes. Why don't you take your wife and Eddie this week? It's on me."

My father held the passes in his hand and examined them. He was visibly grateful. "Why, that's damn white of you, Mr. Raskin. We haven't been to a movie . . . Would you like that, Eddie? Would you like me to take you to the movies tomorrow night?"

"I can't go," my mother said.

"Why not? Why can't you go? Mr. Raskin was gracious enough to give us these passes. I have the passes in my hand. It would be criminal not to go."

"You can go with Eddie and any woman of your choice," my mother replied without a smile, and to Mr. Raskin, "Have another meatball, Teddy."

"Thank you, I will. Are you working this summer, Eddie?"

I shook my head.

"If you'd like, I can put you on as an usher. You can pick up your expenses."

"Did you hear that? Did you hear what Mr. Raskin said, Eddie?" My father was flabbergasted. "He's offering you a job! As an usher! A regular paying job! Ahhh, what's the salary for that kind of work, Mr. Raskin?"

"He could earn fifteen, twenty dollars a week, depends on how many hours he puts in. And what we'll do, Eddie, is figure out a schedule so you can work part-time when you go back to school."

"Did you hear that? Did you hear it?" My father was too excited to go on eating. "A steady job! After school! I don't know how we can thank you, Mr. Raskin. If there's anything I can do for you, please don't hesitate to ask."

"He can't take the job," my mother said.

"Who can't? Who's she talking about?"

"Me, Dad."

"You can't take the job? Why can't you take the job, Eddie?"

"Why can't I take the job, Ma?"

"You have to continue your studies with the nigger."

"What's that got to do with it?" my father pleaded, grinning incongruously at Mr. Raskin. "He can do both. The kid needs a penny in his pocket. He's sixteen. He can't walk around without a penny in his pocket."

"Then go to one of your banks and take out a penny for him. You can afford it."

"That's not what we're discussing," desperately said to my mother, grinning at Mr. Raskin. "Why can't we talk like human beings? Why? I'm not cut out for these arguments. I'm just not."

"Ma, I think I'd like to try it. It won't interfere with my studies."

"Are you sure? Don't do it to make your father happy. He has money. He's a rich man."

"Who is? Who's she talking about?"

"It's up to you, Eddie," my mother said. "I'm not interfering. Have another meatball, Teddy."

Since I never wore clothes but always uniforms (and do so to this day), I was overjoyed when I reported to work at the Reo and was given a tan tunic with braided epaulets, and a pair of tan trousers with broad, black stripes running down the seams. I was also given a nifty Eveready flashlight that could project a beam of light from the second balcony to the orchestra without losing any of its intensity. I much preferred my usher's uniform to my band uniform, especially as I could wear the usher's uniform wherever and whenever I pleased. But even more wonderful than having the uniform was being allowed to enter the movie house at any time of the day or night. I could just walk in, wave to the cashier, say hello to the ticket taker and slide into a seat and watch the movie. Mr. Raskin went out of his way to be nice, and the other ushers were okay once they got to know me. The only sour note was the captain of the ushers, Perry Reese.

That was quite a jolt to me, finding out that Perry Reese, the clarinetist in our defunct orchestra and a guy I detested instinctively, was the captain of the ushers. Give me a minute to tell you about him. First of all, Perry Reese, in my opinion, was the handsomest student at Florence Nightingale High: medium height, well built, curly, yellow hair, almost perfect features and a smile that could make you dizzy; also, in my opinion, he was intelligent, self-assured and the only person I met during those years who could cause me to feel decidedly uncomfortable. It's hard to explain, but he seemed to see through me, he seemed to say with his piercing blue eyes and dazzling smile, Get off it, Eddie; stop acting, stop pretending; you're more insecure and anxious than the rest of us. He always unnerved me and I stayed away from him. One thing, though. He was a lousy musician; he couldn't play the clarinet to save his life, and in that respect I lorded it over him. Outwardly my conceit remained invincible.

But having him as my supervisor in the movie house created problems. He was on the surface a good friend of mine, but we both knew differently. We were born enemies. Our blood spoke louder than our brains, and no amount of rationalizing could alter what we felt.

His assaults on my conceit were infantile. My first day on the job he asked me to get the keys to the curtain so that the projectionist could start the film. Now anyone who has worked in a movie house for more than a day knows there are no such things as keys to the curtain, but this *was* my first day so I spent an hour or two scrounging around for the mythical keys. I looked backstage, in the offices, in the projection room, here, there, everywhere, all the while urged on by the complicitous ushers who finally gave up and had a good laugh at my expense.

So be it. There's only one first day on any job; after that you get wise and you learn what's what. For several weeks Perry had me cleaning the locker room, sewing buttons on tunics, running to the deli for sandwiches, etcetera, etcetera. But Mr. Raskin got wind of it and called us into his office. He really gave Perry a bawling out and complimented me on my appearance and the work I was doing in the second balcony. It was on this occasion that the cashier came in to tell Mr. Raskin that his wife had phoned and he was to get back to her. I thought nothing of it.

I enjoyed being an usher. It was, you could say, my introduction to show biz. Weekends, when the movie house was jammed with school kids, I'd have to see to it that they didn't get out of hand. Throwing condoms filled with water down into the orchestra and unscrewing seats to take home were among the things I had to be on the lookout for. I had my sticky moments, don't worry. Gangs used to sit up in the second balcony and I had to deal with them.

"Remove your feet from the seat in front of you, please."

"You wanna broken head, kid?"

"No, Sir."

"Den go fuck yourself."

"Yes, Sir. But I have a job to do, you have a job to do; let's do our jobs and respect the rights of his neighbor."

"You're blindin' me wit' dat flashlight, mudder! Go lose yourself or you're a corpse!"

"Yes, Sir. As you wish."

I never pushed it too far because a cardinal rule of ushering is that you don't provoke a fistfight that could lead to personal injury. This has something to do with the insurance rates.

I still practiced the horn every morning, two or three hours, seven days a week, and I tried to keep up with my studies at school. I guess it was to be expected that I'd fall a little behind. In order not to waste time, I got into the habit of wearing my usher's uniform to classes. When the principal, Mr. Butchkis, saw me in the corridor, he took hold of my arm and asked me to join him in the cafeteria. He bought a tuna fish sandwich, a slice of lemon meringue pie and a container of milk for himself and zilch for me. We sat in the teachers' section, away from the animals.

"Edward Davis . . . Edward Davis," he sighed, unwrapping his sandwich and taking a bite out of it. He was an obese man with triple chins and the complexion of someone who had suffered or was about to suffer a major coronary. "What will I do with you . . . What will I do with you?" He wagged his head, bit into his sandwich again.

"Is anything wrong, Mr. Butchkis?"

"Wrong? Wrong? Nooo. Nooooo. Why do you ask if anything is wrong? You're failing four subjects and you're walking around school in an usher's uniform, what could be wrong?"

"Do you mind if I smoke?"

"Smoke? Nooooo. Why should I mind?" The sandwich disappeared and he was cutting into his lemon meringue pie with a plastic fork.

I lit my pipe and waved to Mrs. Alson, my geometry teacher, who was staring at me from another table, grinning from ear to ear. Needless to say, she wasn't a fan of mine.

"Edward, your class will be graduating next June. I don't see how you'll be graduating with them." The pie was gone and he was sipping his milk through a straw.

"You're kidding, Mr. Butchkis."

"Why would I be kidding? What's there to be kidding about?"

"You know."

"What do I know, Edward?"

"My unique abilities, Sir."

"Your unique abilities?"

"School is really a snap for me. Most of the time I'm bored."

"Oh, I didn't know that, Edward."

He hit the bottom of the milk container and made a sucking noise for about two minutes. The sound seemed to relax him. "Edward, you have a sixty-three average. Not only won't you be graduated next June, but there isn't a college in the country that will accept you whenever you are graduated."

"Do you know what disturbs me, Mr. Butchkis?"

"No. What?"

"That you're disturbed."

"Does that disturb you?"

"Yes, it does. It really disturbs me."

"That makes me feel terrible, Edward."

"I'll get into college, Sir. I plan to take the entrance exam, have them waive my high school record, and get a scholarship on the basis of my unique abilities and musical proficiency. As for my work here, I'll catch up, please don't worry about it."

"Worry? Oh, I'm not worried, Edward. I'm not worried at all. I'm not even disturbed. I'm retiring in another eight years." He took a pipe out of his pocket. "What tobacco do you use?"

"Sir Walter Raleigh," I said. "Try some."

"Thank you." He packed the bowl from the tobacco tin.

"You haven't been smoking a pipe for long, have you, Mr. Butchkis?"

"How do you know that?"

"The coke on the inside of the bowl isn't evenly distributed. And the way you're lighting the tobacco. Do you mind if I show you?"

"Mind? Nooooo. Why should I mind?"

I wrapped a napkin around the stem, lit the pipe, and puffed on it until the layer of tobacco at the top of the bowl was burning smoothly. Then I spit on the grainy briar and rubbed it with the napkin; when I could see my face reflected in it, I gave the pipe back to him.

He merely stared at it, with admiration, I think.

"Edward . . . Edward . . ."

"You don't have to say anything, Mr. Butchkis. I know it's not easy for you to single one student out from the entire student body. I really appreciate what's implicit in our meeting here today. Your encouragement means an awful lot to me," and I reached over and grabbed his hand. "Is there anything else, Sir?"

"No, no, except . . . the usher's uniform . . . and the flashlight . . . shining the flashlight in the corridors and during assembly . . . Couldn't you dispense with all that?"

"Would you like me to, Sir?"

It took a beat for it to come out. "Yes, Edward. I think I would."

"Say no more. It's done. But . . . Is it all right if I wear my usher's pants with a shirt and my purple velvet cape?"

"Does that mean you'll be wearing your paisley ascot and your beret again?"

"Yes, Sir. They go together."

Drawn out, "Alllll right. I think that would be alllll right."

"Thank you very much, Sir. And may I say before I leave

that I hope this is the best school year of your career and, parenthetically, there's some tuna fish pasted on one of your chins."

Because of my job at the movie house, I didn't get to see much of my friend Gerald. I saw less of his sister. One evening, though, there was a knock on the door and my father followed Shirley into the living room. I had to introduce her to my parents. I will say this for them: they behaved with absolute candor. My mother covered her eyes and leaned over her lap, rocking in her chair and moaning softly. My father was as fascinated by the hump on Shirley's back as he had been by Gerald's. "Do you play the French horn?" he asked her with great confidence.

"No, I don't, Mr. Davis. I play piano, violin, flute and timpani," she answered him.

My father's face went blank, his paradigm of causality shattered to pieces. He put his arm around my mother's shoulder. It was the only time I had seen him express affection for her. "Come, dear," he said, "let's . . . let's go for a walk." And he helped her to her feet.

"Where does he find them?" my mother moaned, her eyes still covered by her hands.

"I don't know, dear. I honestly don't know."

And they toddled out of the room, arm-in-arm, prematurely aged and withered by an influx of Munchkins coming into their home.

"I like your parents," Shirley said. "They seem very friendly. Can I see where you sleep, Eddie?"

A pause. "Why?"

"I always try to imagine where you sleep, what your room looks like, your bed, your blanket, your slippers . . . I'd like to see how accurate my imagination is. You're not afraid to show me your bedroom, are you?"

She certainly knew how to manipulate a guy, I had to give her credit for that. I showed her my bedroom. She didn't even look at it. She sat on the bed, removed her Betty Boop shoes, fluffed her hair, and crawled under the blanket, clothes and all. "The mattress is somewhat lumpy," she said, her head resting on the pillow, twisted back at an angle so that she was staring up at the ceiling.

On his wedding night, Tom Thumb must have discovered his wife, Lavinia Warren, lying in bed just like that.

"Shirley, will you get out of here? If my parents walk in . . . you'll give them a heart attack!"

"Lock the door, Eddie. Do I have to tell you everything?"

I locked the door. "You better tell me everything because I don't know what you're doing in bed. This is crazy."

"I told my mother I was sleeping over at Bertha's," she said, smiling mischievously. "Come, lie down next to me." She flipped over the blanket.

"Shirley . . ."

"If you don't do exactly what I say, I'm going to scream," she said, shutting off her smile.

"You're gonna scream? Whatta you gonna scream?"

"Oh, I don't know. Whatever comes to mind. Something like . . ." She sat up in bed and screamed, *"Eddie Davis is pulling off my bloomers!"*

I jumped into bed before the word "bloomers" was out of her mouth and covered myself with the blanket. "All right! All right! You don't have to scream. I'm in bed. There's no reason to . . . Shirley, will you tell me what we're doing in bed at seven o'clock in the evening?"

"This is better, isn't it?" She snuggled against me, her head wedged in my armpit. "Since you're working, I rarely see you anymore. We have to consummate our friendship, my darling. Now where is your pretzel? What did you do with your pretzel?"

Without knowing what she was about, I suddenly felt an excruciating pain between my legs. It was as if my penis was slowly being pulled out at its roots by an iron claw.

I was so surprised and/or intimidated that I peed in Shirley's hand.

"Ohh, are you fast. Ohh, Eddie, you're so fast, how can I keep up with you?"

"I'm all wet," I said.

"I know you're all wet. I'm all wet. What a come that was. It's unbelievable. It's mind-boggling."

"I have to change my underwear," I said.

"No, don't change it. Let it dry by itself."

"If you think that's advisable."

"Eddie?"

"What?"

"Can I have it?"

"Can you have what?"

"Your underwear."

"You want my underwear?"

"I'd like to put it under a microscope."

"You'd like to put my underwear under a microscope?"

"For my science class."

"If I give you my underwear, will you go home?"

"Yes."

"Here's my underwear."

You see, I had no interest in sex. I know how naive this sounds and I admit I'm uncomfortable telling you about it. Nowadays a sixteen-year-old kid is already into the kinky. My impulses were normal, however, and eventually I went the way of my peers, with a vengeance, I might add. It just took me longer, that's all.

Unfortunately the usher's uniform attracted girls like flies to a cube of sugar and there was no avoiding them, especially in the second balcony.

"Sit down and rest your tootsies, Eddie," one of the girls was sure to say to me, dropping the empty seat beside her.

Or another would approach me as I stood my post at the exit door and say, "Let me hold your flashlight, Eddie." I knew what that meant. They start holding your flashlight and they end up holding your ding-a-ling-a-ling. "Please return to your seat, Miss. You're prohibited by the Fire Department from loitering at an exit door."

I didn't give an inch and eventually they got the message and respected me for my integrity and professionalism.

But one Friday night when I was on the tapes, Perry came at me and said, "Meet me in front after work. I have two live ones," and he was off before I could say, No, thank you. I have to practice in the morning; I don't have time for girls.

I certainly had no intention of going with him and I rehearsed what I was going to say when we met after work; naturally, I said nothing, and I was introduced to my first blind date.

"Buffy the K, Eddie Davis," Perry said, and walked away, taking his own date under the arm and heading up the street.

Buffy the K nodded and I nodded and we followed our friends like a couple of stray alley cats. We watched their every move for a clue as to how to behave, but the more Perry and his date talked and laughed and carried on, the more tongue-tied and awkward we both felt. Buffy the K wasn't a bad-looking girl. She had a decent figure with plump, bouncing boobies. There was something the matter with her skin, though. It was a bit more serious than acne. There were clusters of pimples around her mouth and on her forehead, and she kept popping them open with her handkerchief.

We walked some fifteen-odd blocks without a word passing between us. It's true. We trailed Perry and his date into Sweeny's, an ice-cream parlor on Saratoga Avenue. Right off Buffy the K started talking to her girl friend and I started talking to Perry. Neither one of us stopped talking until we had finished our sundaes and shakes and egg-creams and we were out on the street again, walking behind Perry and his date. Then we stopped talking.

"Do you go to the Reo often?" I finally tore the words out of my gut.

She was popping away at her pimples, her handkerchief hanging over her mouth so I could barely hear her. "So-so," she said. "Do you like to . . . ?"

"Yes, very much," I answered. "I see every . . ."

"What was that?"

"Well, I don't see every . . . Where do you . . . ?"

"Thomas Jefferson. You . . . ?"

"Florence Nightingale."

"Do you know . . . ?"

"Is she . . . ?"

"That's right," she said.

"No, but I know her friends," I answered. "Do you know . . . ?"

"What does he look like?" she asked.

"He's hard to describe."

"Does he . . . ?"

"That's him," I said. "You know him." A long, long pause, then: "Boy, it's a hot night tonight, isn't it?"

"It's a hot night for October," she said, popping a whopper on her chin.

"I have to agree with that statement. During the summer we don't have nights as hot as this hot night we're having in October."

"I like hot nights," she mumbled.

"I do, too. Hot nights are my favorite nights."

"Mine also."

"Boy what a hot night this is!"

Buffy the K's girlfriend lived in a tenement next to the one Buffy the K lived in. Perry gave me the go-ahead sign before taking his date inside. I followed Buffy the K into her tenement. We climbed the stairs and stood at her door, stood there for maybe ten minutes without saying anything. I peeled paint from the wall with my fingernail, and Buffy the K searched through her pocketbook for a key. Where she had successfully popped her pimples open, there were tiny dots and rivulets of blood; her face looked as if it had been tattooed by a palsied aborigine. I was scrounging for the words to say good night when she said, "I can't see you anymore, Eddie. I'm engaged to be married."

I thought about that for a minute. "You should have told me," I said.

"This was kind of a last fling for me. If my fiancé knew what I was doing tonight, he'd kill the both of us."

I thought about that for a minute. "You should have told me," I said, and on further reflection asked, "Where is your fiancé tonight?"

"He's in jail," she said.

I thought about that for a minute. "You should have told me," I said. "What is your fiancé doing in jail tonight?"

"B and E," she said.

"B and E?"

"Breaking and entering."

And I thought about that for two minutes. "Boy, it sure is a hot night for October," I said.

"He gets out tomorrow. Eddie, when I kiss you good night, it's no more fooling around for Buffy the K," she said, and held out her arms like a sleepwalker.

Instinctively I looked behind me, but there was no one there, and when I turned to her, I was in her arms, her legs were wrapped around me, and she was sitting on my hips.

"What are you . . ." I began, but her mouth was on mine and her tongue was halfway down my throat, licking my tonsils.

I tell you, it was unbearable, absolutely unbearable. I jumped up and down, trying to shake her off; she held on like a rodeo cowboy, her fingers and heels digging into my spine. I couldn't breathe, I swear. I was suffocating to death. I pulled my head back as far as I could and I shook it furiously from side to side. That didn't do any good, so I started smashing her against the wall, desperately fighting for my life.

"Shhh, you'll wake my parents," she said.

I gulped in air and pushed my elbows into her boobs to keep

her away. "Why . . . Why are you hurting me?" I yelled at her. "Is it because I didn't talk to you most of the night?"

"No, Eddie. I like you."

Her mouth stretched out toward me, but I held her off. Stalling for time, I asked, "Why . . . Why do they call you Buffy the K? What's the K for?"

"K is for kissing," she said. "That's my specialty."

It was about a week later that I noticed a red swelling in the middle of my lower lip. I rubbed it hard with soap and water and tried to forget it was there. But it throbbed and festered and when I examined it the next morning, it was decidedly larger and in the process of developing a white cap. I wet a strip of toilet paper and covered it as though it were a razor nick. That didn't work too well. From a distance it appeared as if I had a roll of toilet paper in my mouth. I peeled it off and put on a bunion Band-Aid — we didn't have anything else in the house. Throughout the day I peeked under the Band-Aid. Oh, boy. Ohhh, boy. There was something there, all right, and it was a beaut. It could be a cold sore; it could be an infection; it could be . . . the Syph! What an idiot I was! That was it! I went out and got myself the Syph! Buffy the K gave me the dreaded, infectious and easily communicable Syph!

It came to me, just like that. Everything added up. She had chancres all over her face, her boyfriend was in jail on a B and E, and her specialty was kissing! It was the old Humphrey Bogart/ Claire Trevor story in the movie *Dead End.* It was the same exact story! What more proof did I need? There it was, a classically documented case history!

In a panic I went to the dictionary and read:

syph·i·lis\sif-(e)-lis\, *n* (Mod. L. *Syphillis sive Morbus Galli- cus*, title of a poem, 1530, by Giroloan Frascastore; so named after the hero Syphilus, a shepherd . . .)

A shepherd! How do you like that? It was a shepherd! The whole dreaded, infectious and easily communicable Syph started with a lousy shepherd fooling around with his lousy sheep!

... an infectious venereal disease caused by a spirochete and usually transmitted by genital or oral intercourse...

Oral intercourse! That was me! I had had oral intercourse with Buffy the K in her hallway on Georgia Avenue! Oh, my God, what do I do now? How could I ... I read further:

... if untreated, it usually passes through three stages, the first (primary syphilis) characterized by a hard chancre on the genitals or other point of inoculation...

That was it! That was me! Mouth-to-mouth inoculation! I ripped off the bunion Band-Aid and examined the sore. That was a chancre, all right, there was no mistaking it. That was a chancre's chancre!

... the second (secondary syphilis) by variable lesions of the skin and mucous membrane...

Back to the bathroom mirror. There they were, staring me right in the face, variable lesions of the skin and, by God, there was a small sore beginning to sprout inside my left nostril, mucous membranes. I was in the second stage already!

... and the third (tertiary syphilis) by the infection and disablement of bones, muscles, nerve tissues...

I had to lie down. I felt the disablement taking place in my bones, muscles and nerve tissues. I couldn't move. I couldn't even light my pipe. My first truly sexual encounter (I refused to count peeing in Shirley's hand as being my first truly sexual encounter) and I was paying a price for it, and what a price! How long would it be before I couldn't move at all? How long before the bones and muscles and nerve tissues started down the road to complete deterioration and atrophy? I would be a basket case. I would go blind and deaf. And for what? For a few slobby wet kisses that I didn't even want? Was that fair? Or . . . was this supposed to be another test for me? Was I to be the first famous French horn player who had been crippled by syphilis? The Friedrich Nietzsche of French horn players? Was that it?

I reached for my horn and cradled it in my arms. I hadn't practiced for days and I was afraid that I'd never play again. My beautiful horn. My coils of gold. I curled around it and ached to kiss its cool, perfect loveliness. But I wasn't going to betray it. I wasn't going to give it my spirochete germs; no, Sir. I put it back in its case and kissed the case, which I then wiped with a cloth soaked in rubbing alcohol.

I took a hot, steaming bath and scrubbed myself thoroughly. Please, God, if Thou hast any mercy, if Thou hast any compassion for one of Thy most humble devotees who has not been in communication with Thee of late, please don't let this happen. God, if Thou gettest riddest of the Syph for me, I will do whatsoever Thou wishest, and I will offer unto Thee this fragile life, so helpest me God.

When I got out of the bathtub, I looked in the mirror. There it was, only bigger and redder, a veritable white-capped volcano ready to discharge its pus and goo at any minute. I went to the window and stared up at the sky. God! God! Didn't Thou hearest me before? I was talking to You! Why are Thou angriest with me? Other kids my age are getting laid all over the place! I'm innocent! She kissed me, You saw that, didn't you? weren't You watching? I didn't even kiss her back! God, I ask You to reconsider my importunities. If Thou takest away from me this spirochete sore by tomorrow morning at eight o'clock, I will keepeth my parteth of the bargaineth and become a religious fanatic. Okay? Okay? Whatta You sayeth?

In the morning at eight o'clock, the swelling was still there, as bright and vivid as a snow-capped rosebud. I was too sick to go to school so I made some excuse and waited in bed until my parents went off to work. Purposefully I didn't use any of the towels and I sterilized under scorching water the dishes and utensils I came in contact with. If my parents got the Syph because of me, I'd never forgive myself, nor would they. I could imagine the scene: they were sitting in the living room, listening to the radio, covered from head to toe with spirochete sores. My father would say to my mother, "Don't get upset. Let's discuss this like human beings. Did you or did you not have sexual intercourse with a total stranger?" My mother would say, "If I had sexual intercourse, it would have to be with a total stranger!"

I paced through the rooms (a habit I picked up from Mr. Brooks), talked to God seriously for an hour or two, haggling with Him for a deal, then I rushed out to the public library on Arlington Avenue. There was no one there except the librarian.

"Hi," I said, as if I didn't have a worry in the world. "Get any good books in lately?"

She stared at the bunion Band-Aid on my mouth.

"What's new in medical research?" I asked her. "I'm fascinated by the genre of medical research. I've been thinking of becoming a medical researchist."

"What do you want? I'm tired," she said.

"You're always tired," I said. "You probably have chronic fatigue and hereditary anemia. Incidentally, just for conversation's sake, where do you keep your medical research archive?"

Her finger directed me to the reference section. I took down all the medical encyclopedias and dictionaries, sat on the floor behind a bookcase, and started turning pages. I read:

Very soon after the appearance of the chancre the nearest lymph nodes become enlarged and indurated. The mucous patch, *condyloma latus*, or moist papule, occurs on most areas, usually where two skin surfaces are in contact. All these lesions harbor many of the spirochete. The gumma is a rounded nodule, varying in size from the dimensions of a pea to those of a small apple. Its favorite seats are over flat bones, the membranes of the brain, the liver, spleen, and testis . . .

Oh, boy. Ohhh, boy. I was getting sicker and sicker. I struggled to my feet, head reeling, and staggered to the bathroom. In a booth I removed my shirt and dropped my pants, poked and probed and pinched every inch of my body for anything resembling peas and small apples. Perhaps I didn't have the Syph. There wasn't a pea or small apple on my entire body! Perhaps I had a cold sore on my lip and that was it. I could have scrubbed so hard with the soap and water that I had brought on the rash myself. In front of the mirror I gently peeled off the bunion Band-Aid. And would you believe it? The chancre was arrested! It was retrogressing and regenerating! It had shrunk considerably and felt softer under my fingertips!

Thank Thee, God. I do humbly thank Thee and henceforth promise Thee a life of purity and chastity and if I ever kiss another girl again, may Thy wrath descend upon me and may my testes fall off and may my whole body be rampant with peas and small apples.

I went to work, singing and dancing inside myself like a drunken Cossack. But as soon as I walked into the locker room, the first words out of Perry Reese's mouth were, "So you got yourself the Syph, huh?" That stopped me. That killed the drunken Cossack. The other ushers gathered around me and stared at my spirochete with more than casual interest.

"It's the Syph, no doubt about it." One of them shook his head unhappily, and a second asked, "Who gave it to you, Eddie? You can save the rest of us from a life of misery if you told us her name."

"He was out with Buffy the K last week," Perry said.

"Buffy the K!" an astonished chorus rattled the lockers.

"How could you let him go out with Buffy the K?" a third shouted angrily at Perry.

"I tried to warn him," Perry said, "but he was like an animal. Buffy's girl friend told me. He smashed Buffy against the wall until her face was a bloody mess!"

"Is that true?" two or three voices, simultaneously.

I nodded. It sounded right to me.

"You're not to use the bathroom, Eddie. Under no circumstances are you to use the bathroom or sit on the toilet bowl," a voice barked at me as they all moved out of the locker room.

Work was out of the question now. A quick glance in the mirror and I was back where I started. I had to talk to someone. I had to ask someone for advice, but who was there? Who could I ... Mr. Raskin! He'd keep it a secret. And maybe he'd send me to his doctor. Maybe he'd tell me I was being silly and that there was nothing to worry about. In my street clothes I made my way to his office door. I hesitated long enough to hear that he was quarreling with a woman. Their voices were muffled, indistinct.

"I didn't make any promises," Mr. Raskin was saying. "What you thought, I'm not responsible for."

The woman's voice: "Did you suppose this was gonna go on forever? How was this gonna go on forever?"

Mr. Raskin's voice: "I don't want us to break up. But if you have in mind for anything to change, for me to get a divorce or anything like that ..."

The woman's voice: "Now you say it. You didn't say it a year ago, did you? You said ..."

Mr. Raskin's voice: "I'm not proud of myself for what I said or for what I did. You're a very attractive woman. The past year was . . . I don't regret it. But everything has to come to an end, Sylvia."

Sylvia was my mother's name. It could have been my mother or it could have been another woman named Sylvia. I didn't wait to find out. I had my own problems.

From my medical readings and research I knew that I had to take a Wassermann test. I don't remember who told me to go to the Board of Health on Flatbush Avenue, but the following day I was there. And believe it or not there was a line, a line that began at the entrance of the isolated stucco building and wound itself around the block and down the next block! I was stupefied. Did all these people have the Syph? And if so, why were they allowed to congregate in one solid bunch? Wasn't this a health hazard created by the Board of Health? Could modern science say with absolute certainty that the disease could not be transmitted by inhalation? I pulled my purple cape over my head and wore it like a burnoose, wrapping my face in folds of velvet.

I stood in line behind a paunchy postman who was carrying his mailbag and had his peaked cap resting on his eyebrows.

"Is this where you get a Wassermann test?" I asked him, pushing aside the folds of my cape to speak to him.

He looked toward the Brooklyn Bridge as if appraising its value.

An emaciated, whiskered old man guided by a Seeing-Eye dog came up to me. "Is this for the Wassermann?" he asked.

"I don't know, Sir," I said, and tried the postman again. "Excuse me, there's a blind man here who wants to know if this is the line for the Wassermann test."

The postman wouldn't even turn to answer me.

"I'll go and ask somebody else," I said to the blind man. "Save my place."

I asked two or three people before I got an answer from a pregnant woman who was breast-feeding her baby. I went back to my place and patted the dog and told the blind man he was in the right line. By now there were others standing behind him. A gum-chewing girl in a dirty T-shirt and sunglasses said, "Get in the rear, kid. You wait like the resta us is doin'."

"Yeah," said the boyfriend in a matching dirty T-shirt and sunglasses, "get in the rear, whatta you t'ink you're doin', sneakin' in on us?"

"I wasn't sneaking in," I said. "I was here before. You can ask the blind man. He saw me."

"Back dere! Back dere!" they yelled, and I had no choice but to give up my place and stand at the end of the line.

I'm not exaggerating when I tell you that it took me about three hours to get into the building and be seated in the reception room. There were a dozen of us sardined on a wooden bench. My arms were pinned to my sides by a very pretty woman with a scar on her cheek and hair in pink curlers on my right and the blind old man with his Seeing-Eye dog on my left.

"Where's your chancre?" the pretty woman with the scar on her cheek and hair in pink curlers spoke to me *sotto voce*.

"Pardon me?"

"I asked where your chancre was."

I whispered through the folds of my burnoose. "My lower lip, in the middle, under my nose."

"Can I see it?"

"Pardon me?"

"I asked if I could see it."

Our heads were pressed close together and I thought no one could hear us, but the blind man said, "I got myself the clap. I been drippin' like a leaky faucet the whole week."

The pretty woman with the scar on her cheek and hair in pink curlers pretended he wasn't there. "I wanna compare it with mine," she said to me.

"I'd rather not," I answered her, thinking of "Bartleby the Scrivener."

"Would you like to see mine?" she then asked me.

Suspiciously, "Where is it?"

"Way in here," she said, opening her mouth wide, and jabbing her finger at its gummy interior. I shut my eyes. "Don't you wanna see?"

"I'd rather not," I said.

"I show you mine," the blind man said.

"How'd you get yours?" she soon asked me.

"A girl," I said.

"That's not unusual," she said. "Was it a straight lay?"

"Not exactly."

"Was it sixty-nine?" she wanted to know next.

"Not exactly. It was more like a number eleven."

"What's that?"

"Oral intercourse," I said.

"Was it any good?"

"Suffocating. I found it suffocating."

"Mine was as good as a crap in the mornin'," the blind man said.

"How did you get yours?" I asked her.

"It's hard to tell," she answered. "What are you doin' after they take your blood?"

"They're gonna take my blood?"

"That's what you're here for, ain't it?"

"I didn't know they were gonna take my blood."

"They take everybody's blood. How 'bout a drink after?"

"After they take my blood?"

"I go wit' you," the blind man said.

"You have somethin else t'do?" she asked me.

"After they take my blood?"

"Yeah, whatta you gonna do after?"

"I don't know. I think I'll go home and rest," I said.

"Don't you wanna have any fun?"

"I go wit' you," the blind man said.

The nurse motioned her to the desk.

"Let's wait a few days," I begged off.

"Okay. I'll meet you across the street, on Wednesday at one

73

o'clock," she said. "Don't stand me up." And that was the last I saw of her.

The nurse, Miss Dooley, the nameplate on her desk so announced, scanned the card I had filled out for her.

"Is the information on this card correct, Mr. Nightingale?"

"Yes, Ma'm."

She looked up at me with a spinster's face that was faintly rouged and didn't seem to have any lips at all.

"Your name is Flavius Nightingale?"

"Yes, Ma'm. I was named after Florence Nightingale, known universally as the lady with the lamp."

"And you live at the Geneva Hotel?"

"Yes, Ma'm. On the sixteenth floor."

"You should know that the results of the test are mailed to you within ten days. If the information on this card is incorrect, you will not receive the results and the Wassermann will have been taken for naught."

"In other words, Ma'm, you wish my name and address for the next ten days."

Silently she counted up to three, then, "Yessss," squeezed out of her lipless face.

"I misunderstood the imputations of the questionnaire, Ma'm. My apologies." I took the card from her, crossed out the name and address, and wrote down my correct name and address. "This will be my name and address for the next ten days," I said to her.

"May we have the name of the party whom you believe responsible?"

"Responsible for what, Nurse Dooley?"

"Responsible for your being here."

I really didn't want to squeal on Buffy the K, but I wasn't going to lie anymore and make an enemy of Nurse Dooley. "Buffy the K," I said very quietly.

"What do you spell K?" she asked.

"K," I said.

"K like in K-a-y?" she asked.

"No, K like in kissing," I said.

Silently she counted up to four, then, "In! In there!" she snarled, motioning me into a room, and there were her lips, all right, thin and livid, like those on the blind man's dog.

I skipped a class every school day to be at home when the mail was delivered. You can well imagine my anxiety so I won't go into it, except to say that the next ten days were the longest ten days of my life. The letter finally arrived and I climbed the ladder to the attic to read it. Crouched on my knees under the cobwebbed skylight, I slowly opened the envelope and held the letter in my trembling hands, upside down and reverse side up. That's how I read it. I couldn't have done it otherwise. It took me quite a while to make out a crayon check mark beside the printed word EVITAGEN. Quickly I turned the letter face up and upside up and read it. NEGATIVE. The results were negative! I had beaten the Big S! I clasped my hands and stared through the skylight. Thou hast been more than generous to me, God. I am Thy servant and I am prepared to execute Thy every command. But as Thou knowest, God, I have been finding of late an excessive amount of loose hairs on my comb and pillow. God, we have worked terrifically together in the past. If Thou canst stop the hair from falling from my head, there is nothing, absolutely nothing, I would not doeth for Thee, so helpest me God.

five

It became apparent during the Christmas holidays that if I was to be graduated in June, I would have to quit my job at the movie house and really concentrate on my school work. It was a heartbreaking decision, but that's how the cookie crumbled. I left the Reo, rolled up my sleeves, and gave my undivided attention to, as they say, the curriculum.

Once again I needed the tutorial assistance of my friend Gerald. After school I was in his bedroom, pacing, puffing my pipe, staring out the window as he threw questions at me, reviewed dates and facts, and forced me to memorize whole passages. He was a stern taskmaster. My failings were more of an affront to him than they were to me. I didn't know at the time what he was going through. It would have helped to explain his sudden bursts of temper, his tireless, monotonous insistence that I do better, that I work harder, that I stop pampering and deluding myself.

By March he was into the habit of lecturing me. Specs off, eyes brimming over with tears, his angled, balding head twisted back on his hump, the words spilled out of his mouth, ran down his chest and legs, and threatened to flood the room. Music, he said, there's music. We can create, Eddie, the two of us; we can make out of nothing something, something beautiful, something

76

that will echo in the heavens for all eternity. I'm not being romantic, he said. I'm not being metaphorical. On the contrary, I speak the plain, simple truth. We're made of finer stuff than nature, Eddie. Mankind is. Human beings are. The worst of us is infinitely superior to nature, infinitely more moral, infinitely more compassionate. I hate nature, Eddie. Hate it to the core of my innermost being. I love man. I love what man is capable of doing. I love what man has done. His creations are infinitely superior to those of nature. Yes, yes, he said. And don't tell me about the Grand Canyon and the sun rising on the horizon. The price is too high, much too high. Tell me about earthquakes and epidemics and drought and death. If mankind in its madness slaughters millions, that's peanuts compared to the mindless devastations of nature. And don't forget, Eddie, mankind can change, mankind can exercise a moral imperative. What can we hope for from nature? A dying sun that turns to ashes the beauty we create. Eddie, listen to me . . .

"All right, all right, I heard you! Jesus Christ, I have a test Friday. We can talk about this later!"

Listen to me, Eddie. Listen to me . . . His face always looked burning hot, and tears frequently streamed down his cheeks, as if there were too many of them now to contain under the veined lids of his eyes. And he talked, lectured, on and on, endlessly, repetitively. Listen to me, Eddie. Listen to me . . .

The only time during those months that he smiled was when I asked him about Shirley. I hadn't seen her in I don't know how long. Then he smiled and his hot, flushed face seemed momentarily relieved.

"She's engaged. She met a boy, a very talented composer who teaches at Curtis."

"That's terrific. Now how the hell do you conjugate . . ."

Listen to me, Eddie. Listen. If there's a tomorrow, if mankind persists, survives, and evolves a way of living in this world, the tomorrow-people will say when talking about us, the today-people, they'll say, how did they do it? How did they manage to get through a single day knowing all they knew, knowing that time is a noose that tightens by the hour? Eddie, they'll have to say, They were a noble people, a glorious noble people whose courage was so great, whose aspirations were so high, that they spat in the face of nature and defied to live for no other reason than to create beauty.

Listen to me, Eddie. Listen . . .

What I didn't know then, what I didn't even suspect then, was that my friend Gerald was dying.

I got through high school by the skin of my skin. I wrote Mr. Butchkis, the principal, a letter saying that I would be unable to attend the Commencement exercises because of a previous obligation and would he be kind enough to mail my diploma to me. (If you haven't already guessed, I'll tell you: I was ashamed of my parents, too.) Mr. Butchkis wrote back saying that if I wanted my diploma I could pick it up at the clerk's office and that he no longer smoked a pipe.

My mother gave me a Bulova wristwatch and my father gave me a twenty-five-dollar government bond that was worth eighteen dollars and seventy-five cents. I cashed in the bond and bought a marine's dress jacket with gold master sergeant's stripes on the sleeve. I wore it everywhere, beret still on head, but now a narrow aviator's scarf wound flamboyantly around my neck, replacing the ascot.

I had somehow convinced myself that the school I wanted to go to was the Grand Army Plaza Conservatory of Music which required no more than a high school diploma. Students were given private instrument instruction and attended classes in musical theory, composition, conducting, etcetera, etcetera. After four years you received a certificate that stated you had been a student for four years. I connived a partial scholarship, but would still need about eight hundred to make up the difference. In reality the scholarship was a gimmick.

"I don't understand why you don't go to Brooklyn College," my father went into it one Sunday at the end of June. "They have music there and there's no tuition; it wouldn't cost you a penny. I spoke to Tobias, you remember Tobias, Eddie, don't you? He runs the music department where you bought the French horn. His son goes to Brooklyn College and he's a musician, a trumpet player, and Tobias says that there isn't a better school for music in the whole country."

"Another father would say, 'Here's the money, Eddie, and here's another hundred for expenses,'" my mother said, forking a meatball into quarters. "But not your father. Oh, no, not him. He's just looking how to save a penny, that's all that counts with him."

"Do you think money solves everything? Do you think all you have to do is pay money and everything comes up roses?" my father asked, not expecting an answer.

"Yes," my mother answered.

"Well, that's not how it works. I want Eddie to have a chance in life. I want him to ..."

My mother let go, throwing the fork across the room where it bounced off the wall and shook itself to death on the floor. "And me?" she shouted. "Do I have a chance in life? What do I have? Tell me!" She glared at him, smothering his eyes with her own as if she meant to drown him in her misery.

In the past my father would have answered her, he would have said, Let's talk like human beings, or something like that, but he didn't say anything to her now; he brushed bread crumbs together on the table with the palm of his hand and then dropped them fastidiously into an ashtray.

Their marriage was cracking at the seams.

Anger and Bitterness filled every room in the house; it became harder and harder to find a place to sit without having them crawl all over you; it became harder and harder to breathe, too.

(I can say today, Yes, my mother's affair with Mr. Raskin was over and she was in the hell of a loveless marriage again. And I can say today, Yes, my father was wrestling with his own demon and asking himself who he was and why he was experiencing so much pain and emptiness.)

"I'll get a job this summer," I said. "I'm old enough."

"Your father will pay," my mother said.

"I can help, Eddie. I can give you something ..."

"I'll pay, Dad. It's all right." I wanted to say, Why don't we separate? I'm finished with high school. Why don't we move and get our own apartments?

But I said nothing. And we sat there, bent over our plates of cold spaghetti and meatballs, talking inwardly words that should have been said to each other.

Well, what can you do, my friend. That's life. You won't find one in a million who can't tell you what a rough time he's had of it. My suite of rooms at the Geneva Hotel is on the sixteenth floor, by request. (I smile as I write this.) It costs two hundred a day, not including food and tips. (That's on paper. Did you think I'd forget to hustle for myself a monthly rate and a businessman's discount? Did you, really?) Right now I'm wearing a pair of silk pajamas, three hundred, give or take a buck. I'm not wearing slippers. I enjoy walking barefoot on the cream-colored Aubusson rug. Napping like an angora in the armchair are my coils of gold, an incomparable Kruspe, worth two thousand, easy. Vetault suitcases, Meladandri suits, Turnbull & Asser shirts, Gucci shoes, Sulka underwear, Lapidus ties, Cartier wristwatch, Tiffany bill clasp, Mark Cross wallet ... Oh, dear. Oh, dear. The times they have achanged. Money to burn now. Money to flush down the drain. Money to open doors and legs and lipless faces.

I could have done wonders for the skinny horn player, if I had been around in those days. I could have given him an allowance every week, let's say, conservatively, a hundred and fifty. I could have bought him things, a car to knock about in, a soundproof apartment, a better horn, better teachers, introductions to people in the know, people who could push him along, wise him up, tell him where it's at. I could have . . . I could have. If I had been around in those days.

Tomorrow is Labor Day. I've been here approximately a month, and during that time I haven't violated my strict and sacred vow to keep to myself once. There must be some trait in me that's responsive to the monastic life. I go about my chores with buttoned lips and a buttoned fly. I am ennobled by my resolve. It gives me strength.

The longest conversation I've had since I checked into the Geneva was with the hall porter, Mr. Alfred, a rather tall, dignified gentleman who wears spotlessly clean white cotton gloves.

"Do you have to vacuum the carpet in front of my door every morning, Mr. Alfred?"

"That's what they pay me for, Mr. Davis."

"And if I paid you, would you forget to vacuum the carpet?"

"I'd lose my job, Mr. Davis. But how much would that be in terms of dollars and cents?"

"Five dollars a week."

"For not vacuuming your carpet?"

"Five dollars a week."

"I have a manual vacuum that doesn't make any noise at all. Would that be satisfactory?"

"Are you sure it doesn't make any noise, Mr. Alfred?"

"Yes, Sir. I can guarantee it."

"Okay. Your money will be at the desk every Friday, with Mr. Burton."

That was it. It's been a little creepy, I admit, but it would be too easy for me to get caught up in one thing or another, at the expense of my work. I am not the skinny horn player. Yesterday I threw away a pair of matching English Dunhill pipes and poured a quart of Stolichnaya vodka down the drain. I am now practicing the horn on an average of five hours at a stretch.

I doubt that I could have achieved as much as I have in this short a period, if I didn't have your delectable ear to nibble on, my dear friend. And for that I do sincerely thank you.

Evenings I go out. I walk the streets for exercise, window-shop for entertainment. Usually I slip into a restaurant about seven with a newspaper or magazine, and I have dinner. It seems everyone is out of town. So far I haven't bumped into a single soul I know. Sunglasses, straw hat, and the beginnings of a speckled gray beard serve adequately as both uniform and disguise. Diligently I avoid the restaurants where I used to hang out.

No one knows I'm staying in New York. I said I was going off to Greece until the first of the year, cutting myself loose for a while, pressures of business, etcetera, etcetera. I don't believe this inconvenienced too many people.

I did get a job that summer. It was as a waiter in The Chocolatte Shoppe on Pitkin Avenue. I wore a maroon vest and a maroon bow tie. I put in about ten hours a day and slept and practiced the horn with what was left over. Early one morning Mrs. Hinkey phoned, whispered in a broken voice that Gerald was in the hospital, would I visit him? What's wrong, Mrs. Hinkey? We had no idea, Eddie; it was years ago when he had, when he was struck with, when he . . . I'm going over now to see him, Mrs. Hinkey. I'll cheer him up.

I never did find out what was wrong with him.

Was he at Kings County Hospital? The Lutheran hospital on Jamaica Avenue? I don't remember. There were four beds in the room and Gerald's bed was behind a screen. His head was twisted on the pillow. The white sheet reached his chin. I sat in a chair beside the bed and waited for him to take notice of me. His eyes were open, but they had no shine to them which was odd because he wasn't wearing his specs; they were absolutely dry, tearless, desiccated. I didn't want to be there. I couldn't stand being in a hospital and watching someone, anyone, die.

Listen to me, Eddie. Listen to me, my friend Gerald said, rolling his desiccated eyes and staring at me. You're special, he said. You're a unique individual. I don't know how good a horn player you can be. I don't know how far you can go. But stay with it. Be the best you can, even if the best you can isn't as good as somebody else. Don't let them beat you, Eddie. Don't let them discourage you. Music isn't a rat race. Music is loving to play music. Music is loving to listen to music. You're a musician, Eddie. You're as much of a musician as anybody who ever lived because you need music to live, because without music you can't talk about what you feel, because without music you don't know what you feel. Eddie, the ape men who painted deer and bison on the walls of their caves were no less the artist than the Sorbonne graduate who knows by heart every school of painting, every theory of painting since the beginning of time. Art is democratic, Eddie. Art says to everyman: what you create counts regardless of race, religion, background or ancestry. Listen to me, Eddie. Listen to me. All I want is to live. I don't want to die. If I could live, I wouldn't care if I wasn't a musician. Maybe that's hard for you to understand. Maybe you can't understand it because you don't feel the coldness in your chest and you don't say to yourself, This is weird, this is a dream I'm having, a hump on your back is one thing, but what's going on here? what are we doing this number for? Listen to me, Eddie. Listen to me. I love you. I value your friendship more than anything. All I want to do is to live.

I said nothing. I couldn't talk to him, to my friend Gerald. I put my hand on his arm and said, "You'll get better. Take care of yourself. I'll come by and see you tomorrow." And I left. I left without saying anything I felt. I didn't know what I felt.

Mrs. Hinkey flew to Phoenix with Gerald in the hope that a change of climate would be beneficial to him. It wasn't. He died in July, and she flew back with his coffin while I was working at The Chocolatte Shoppe. Gerald's body was in the Dumont Funeral Home on Glenmore Avenue. Mrs. Hinkey and Shirley, both in layers of black, were seated by the coffin when I walked in. Standing behind Shirley was a short, heavy version of the young Cary Grant. I assumed, correctly, that he was her boy-friend. He didn't have a hump on his back. I nodded to them, touched the varnished wood of the coffin, conscious of their stares which said, Say something, Eddie.

But I said nothing and retreated to the shadows.

"Let's go for a drink, Buster," a muffled voice said, and I turned to see Mr. Brooks, my former horn teacher, leaning against the wall, his hands in his pockets. A baggy suit hung over his skeletal frame; he wore a ridiculously small felt hat, and his skin looked muddy, not black, a gray, ashen color that seemed to have been rubbed on, like a paste.

As soon as we were out on the sidewalk, he lit a cigarette and I lit my pipe. We walked to a nearby bar. Inside, Mr. Brooks asked me what I was drinking and I said, "The same as you, Mr. Brooks," and that was a mistake for two reasons: one, I didn't drink, and two, he ordered beers and shot glasses of rye. He sipped a little of his beer and dropped the shot glass, with the rye in it, straight into the beer glass. (A boilermaker.) I did likewise and drank along with him. Not for a minute did I believe that the terrible tasting stuff I swallowed was meant to be enjoyed. But somehow I had convinced myself that I was drinking for Gerald's sake, that I had to shock my senses in order to respond to his death.

I told Mr. Brooks that I had been accepted at the Grand Army Plaza Conservatory, and he waved for two more beers and two more ryes. I hurried to keep up with him.

"How's your grandmother?" I asked him.

"She's not my grandmother," he answered, drinking.

"What did you say?"

"I said she's not my grandmother. She's my wife."

You're kidding me was on the tip of my tongue, but I let it stay there.

"How old do you think I am?" he asked me.

"I don't know. Thirty-five?"

"Fifty-four," he said. "I'm fifty-four an' my wife is sixty-seven an' we have been married for 'bout thirty years, living together in mutual respect an' harmony." He laughed, slapping his thighs, then drank deeply, gargling the stuff before letting it slide down to his stomach.

"I never thanked you for all you did for me, Mr. Brooks. I feel that I learned more with you . . ."

"Crap! That's a load a crap!" he barked at me, and the old anger was back in his face. "Not taking the horn away from you, Buster, was the worst crime I committed," he said. "Not taking the horn away from every one a my students was a crime for which I do not forgive myself. I rue the day I ever did see the horn. I rue the day I ever did see my first music teacher who said to me, 'You can have a brilliant career for yourself, Buster. You are a born, natural musician, the best I have seen in all my years.'" He laughed again, banging his fists on the bar, howling and screeching until the other people in the place turned and glared at us.

I stopped trying to keep up with him and he stopped ordering drinks for me. I was starting to feel woozy. "I'm gonna be a musician, Mr. Brooks. I'm gonna be the best I can even if the best I can isn't as good as somebody else," I repeated almost verbatim what Gerald had said to me in the hospital.

"You do that, Buster. You do that," he laughed, wagging his head. "You be the best. You knock 'em on their asses. You . . ." The laugh evaporated and he pushed his gray, skeletal face close to mine. "The horn is the devil," he hissed at me. "The horn'll kill you. It killed Gerald. That's why that boy is layin' stiff an' cold in his coffin. Don't be a fool, Buster. Throw it away. Bury it in the backyard an' put a tombstone on it. Get yourself a job, get yourself a new suit a clothes an' a little girlie an' forget you ever did see the horn!"

There were two couples seated at a Formica table behind us and three or four men at the bar. One of the men at the table — he had a tattoo of an eagle with a banner flowing from its hooked beak — put a coin in the jukebox. A thumping, jarring vibration of pop music shook the room as the jukebox rocked from side to side, its lights blinking garishly.

Mr. Brooks stared down at his hands for a minute, then got to his feet, and moved to the jukebox. He bent over and pulled the plug from its socket and returned, a bit unsteadily, to his stool at the bar. "Forget you ever seen the horn, Buster," he said, holding a beer in one hand and a shot glass in the other and taking turns sipping from each of them. "Forget you ever had anything t'do wit' it. The devil lives inside the horn. I seen him. I looked in an' I seen him sitting in there with his tail caught between his teeth. For years I been trying t'grab that son of a bitch!"

"Leave the jukebox alone," the bartender said in a whining voice, picking up the empty glasses.

Mr. Brooks didn't miss a beat as he went on, "But the devil, he always gets away from me, he always hides in the valves an' tubes so I can't lay my hands on him. He stays in there, Buster. Sometimes he peeks out of the mouthpiece, sometimes he goes into the bell an' leers out at me wit' his devil's face, teasing me t'smash the horn with him inside it, smash the fuckin' horn once an' for all an' . . . But I can't do it, Buster. I think a Haydn an' Mozart an' Schumann an' just can't . . ."

The jukebox was suddenly blaring again. Mr. Brooks sucked in his breath and stared down at his hands, sniffing through his string-bean nose. "Go on home, Buster. You go on home. There's gonna be trouble."

"What kind of trouble?"

He didn't answer me. His skin was the color of slate now and tiny bubbles broke and splattered at the corners of his mouth. The men at the Formica table were giggling with their girlfriends.

"You sure . . . ?"

"Go on home," he said wearily.

I knew there was going to be a fight, but I didn't want any part of it. As I moved to the door I could feel Mr. Brooks staggering toward the jukebox plug and I could hear one of the men warn him to leave it alone. The minute I was on the sidewalk, the jukebox went dead, there was the sound of scuffling, shouting, something smashed, and Mr. Brooks tumbled out of the bar, arms and legs flying, laughing wildly, maniacally, until his head smashed against the curbstone.

I ran to him. "Mr. Brooks . . ." There was a bad gash on his temple and the blood pouring from it was a phosphorescent blue in the light of the streetlamp. I helped him to his feet. Once erect he tore the ridiculously small hat from his head and puked into it. He handed the hat to me and held a handkerchief to the gash on his temple.

"Are you all right, Mr. Brooks?"

"I nearly went an' did it, Buster. I nearly went an' got the devil by the throat. He was sitting in that there jukebox," he said, quite pleased with himself, and with one arm on my shoulder, he led me away from the bar, softly singing a Puccini aria in a remarkably sweet voice.

His grandmother, rather his wife, was waiting on the stoop of the brownstone, her eyes welcoming us. Mr. Brooks passed her without a word. I gave her his hat and she thanked me, then followed her husband, who was still singing Puccini, into the house.

I had a hangover when I went to Gerald's funeral the next day. In a chauffeured limousine I rode to the cemetery with Mrs. Hinkey, Shirley and her boyfriend — his name was Nathaniel Eliot. The sky was overcast and when we were on the expressway a steady drizzle started pecking at the asphalt. I watched the windshield wipers scrape across the window. Luckily I was seated in front with the chauffeur so I didn't have to look at Shirley or her mother. Every now and then one of them would collapse into choking sobs and Eliot would have to commiserate with her. In a while Mrs. Hinkey said, "Eddie," and I had to look back at her.

"Yes, Mrs. Hinkey?"

"I want you to say something at the services. You were Gerald's best friend, his only friend, his dearest . . ." Her veiled face dropped to her knees and she was sobbing again.

"I . . . I'm sorry, Mrs. Hinkey. I . . . I couldn't. I . . . I can't," I stammered, and blessedly my body broke, and I sobbed more loudly and more wretchedly than both Mrs. Hinkey and Shirley put together.

I heard Shirley say, "He can't, Mother. Don't ask him or me or anyone who loved . . ." and she sobbed, and I heard Mrs. Hinkey say as she continued sobbing, "It's all right, Eddie. I understand. We don't have to say anything for Gerald. He knows, he knows . . ."

And what neither one of them knew was that I was crying because I had a hangover, my head was splitting, and I didn't know how I felt after Gerald's death.

The drizzle ended. A patch of sunlight was on Gerald's coffin. Standing around the grave I saw Mr. Butchkis and Mr. West, the music teacher at Nightingale. Mr. Brooks wasn't there. I didn't know any of the others. All told there were about a dozen mourners. I inhaled the crisp, morning air and my head cleared a little. It was like being in the country. I couldn't stop myself from enjoying the open space and the meticulously trimmed greenery. Whatever services were being performed I was hardly aware of them. I read the names on the tombstones, stared at the diggers squatting behind a mound of newly turned-over soil, and watched the cars arriving and departing with their grief-stricken passengers. Before I knew it, Shirley's arm was linked to mine, and we were moving toward the limousine.

"Nathaniel and I are getting married," she said, in full control of herself now. "We're going to live in Philadelphia. Mother will be staying with us."

"Congratulations." I tried to smile and felt stupid. I wondered why a good-looking guy like Nathaniel Eliot wanted to marry a hunchback.

The chauffeur opened the door for us, but before stepping into the limousine, Shirley stood on her toes, her sea-green eyes shining bright in her angled face, and she hugged and kissed me with all her might.

By the time I got home I was drunk again, more drunk than I had been the previous evening. I didn't answer my father who asked me from the living room how the funeral went. I stumbled into my bedroom and pulled my horn out of its case. I knew exactly what I wanted to do. I took the horn with me to the attic, unlatched the skylight, and climbed on to the tar-papered roof. There I found an old crate box. I sat on it, raised the coils of gold to my lips, and played two movements of Mozart's Concerto in E Flat Major. I played to the clouds and to the bruised orange sun. I played cleanly, roundly, pure warm tones that spread like a canopy over the entire neighborhood.

Gerald was dead. Through the music it came to me. I would never see him again, never have his hunched, misshapen body trailing a few steps behind me, his proud, twisted face trying to catch up to me. Gerald was dead. Through the music it came to me. Who was there to take the place of my friend Gerald? Who was there to say that I was special, that I was more than I appeared to be, that I was capable of creating something of beauty? No one. There was no one. I had lost my friend. I had lost my mentor and my disciple. Gerald was dead. Through the music I grieved and came to know my own feelings.

SIX

Friendless and fortuneless, the skinny horn player entered the Grand Army Plaza Conservatory of Music that fall. In his marine sergeant's jacket, aviator's scarf and delicate Erroll Flynn mustache (the beret had been discharged, accused falsely of aiding and abetting the migration of his hair), he registered, paid his fee, and attended classes with a regularity and resolve that elicited the following response from the dean, Mr. Gilcrist, some twenty years later:

"Davis? Did we have a student here named Davis?"

Yes, my secretary informed him; he studied French horn and would like to start a scholarship fund in memory of Gerald Hinkey.

"How much money would that be?" Mr. Gilcrist asked.

I couldn't restrain myself and shouted into the phone box: "Mr. Gilcrist, it's me, Eddie Davis, the skinny kid in the marine jacket, do you remember me?"

"Is that you?"

"It's me. How have you been, Mr. Gilcrist?"

"Lousy. I've been growing gallstones as big as rocks," he whined, and, "How much money are you sending us . . . did you say your name is Freddy Davis?"

That bit of nostalgia cost me a cool five thousand tax-deductible dollars.

The Conservatory was housed in what was formerly an industrialist's residence, a three-storied limestone building catercornered at the junction of two streets, close to Prospect Park. Steps led up to a pair of massive doors and into a large foyer and sitting room. Mr. Gilcrist's office was at the rear of the foyer and a wide banistered staircase ascended to the classrooms on the second and third floors. Ensemble and orchestra rehearsals were in the basement.

There were at the Conservatory about two hundred and fifty students, most of them interested in jazz and popular music, and most of them veterans of the Second World War who were taking advantage of their educational benefits. As a precaution, I removed the sergeant's stripes from my marine jacket. There was no sense in asking for trouble. Frankly, the veterans put me off. They were a slovenly bunch, always hanging out in the sitting room, gabbing, horsing around, pitching pennies, sleeping on the sofas, etcetera, etcetera. A good many came only to keep their attendance records in order, this to receive their monthly allowance checks. From time to time one of them would go berserk and do himself or someone else an injury. I remember seeing an ex-boatswain's mate who was studying piano smash his fist through a classroom window and shout, "I hate these fuckin' sharps an' flats! I hate 'em worse than the kamikazes!" And an ex-paratrooper who was studying saxophone put his saxophone between his legs and flew from the second floor to the first, landing on top of a viola player and breaking his collarbone.

Ah, but there was a select and dignified minority of which I counted myself a member. This group consisted of the classical students, the acolytes of the Masters. We were a small, valiant band trapped in a jungle inhabited by bebop savages who worshipped at the stomping feet of Dizzy Gillespie, Lester Young and Charlie Parker. For some bizarre reason, the jazz students thought that we, the classical students, were all gay, and this led to some embarrassing encounters. For instance, there was an ex-marine corporal who fell in love with me.

His name was Peter Scharf and he was much shorter than I was but pot-bellied, with washed-out, shifty eyes in a ruddy, pock-marked face. He wore, without fail, a sheepskin coat, spiked boots and a huge, turquoise pinky ring. The rumor was that he had participated in planting the flag at Iwo Jima. I don't know whether he was first attracted to me by my marine jacket or by my shoulder-forward-left-hand-in-left-pocket walk, but, unannounced, he appeared one night at The Chocolatte Shoppe.

Innocently, "Aren't you . . . ?"

"Peter Scharf, drums," he said, a funny pumpkin-grin splitting his face.

"Eddie Davis, French horn."

"I know. I heard you. You blow a mean horn, Eddie."

"Thank you very much. Can I get you anything?"

"Whatta you have?" he grinned.

"Sundaes, malteds, hamburgers . . ."

"The treat's on me, Eddie."

"I'm not allowed to have anything when I'm working," I said, looking over at the tables that needed my attention.

"How about after work?"

"That's very kind of you, but I ate already. Besides, I don't get off until midnight."

"That's okay. I'll walk you home."

And would you believe it? He waited for me, drinking four cups of Sanka coffee and smoking four White Owl cigars! The luncheonette was empty when I was done, except for Mr. Kamlot who was counting his loot at the cash register.

"Good night, Mr. Kamlot," I said, leaving with Peter Scharf.

"You made me lose my place," Mr. Kamlot said, and started counting all over again.

Out on the sidewalk, we walked toward my house. I thought,

Gee, I made a friend tonight, how do you like that? Maybe he wants me to play in his band or go to the movies with him.

It was chilly, a stiff autumn wind came off the side streets, and I buttoned my marine jacket.

"Why don't you take my coat?" Peter Scharf offered me his sheepskin.

"It's not necessary. Thank you very much. So . . ." I had nothing else to say to him.

"How old are you, Eddie?"

"I'll be eighteen, the second of November."

"I'd like to throw you a birthday party," he said.

I couldn't believe I was hearing right. Here was a guy, a total stranger, and he wanted to throw me a birthday party!

"Gee, that's real swell of you but . . ."

"We'll invite the gang from school and I'll ask them all to bring presents," he said, brushing aside my objections before I could figure out what my objections were, and then he went on to tell me about his experiences during the Second World War (he had been at Okinawa, not Iwo Jima), about his boyhood in Little Rock, Arkansas, and the problems he was having with his best friend, Jackie St. Claire.

Unfortunately I didn't learn how to say no until very late in life. Now I say it for the mere fun of it. Now I say it out of habit, gratuitously, with the knowledge that one derives strength from the word no.

The next morning Peter Scharf was at my front door.

"Hi," the pumpkin-grin was on his face, a quarter moon of wet hair hung over his eye.

"Hi. What are you . . . ?"

"I'll carry your horn for you, Eddie." He took the bulky case out of my hand and we headed for the subway.

"I didn't know you lived in my neighborhood," I said.

"I don't."

"Where do you live?"

"Near school, on Montague Street."

Food for thought. He lived near the school, we were going to the school, the school was at least forty minutes away by subway. "It was nice of you to come by. Thank you very much."

"I like being with you, Eddie."

"I like being with you, Peter. But about my birthday party . . ."

"It'll be the best party a guy ever had, you can depend on that."

"I rather you didn't . . ."

"What can I get you for your birthday?"

"You don't have to . . ."

"Okay. It'll be a surprise."

My horn playing was going well. My teacher, Mr. Noonan, a dapper little man with a bobbing Adam's apple and sharp face, was encouraging. He never touched on my deepest fear: did I have what it takes to be a professional musician. And I was grateful to him for that. (Of course I never asked him.) We proceeded on the assumption that after four years at the Conservatory I would be capable of earning a living as a horn player. He kept himself at a distance, neat as a proverbial pin in his vested suits and butterfly bow ties. I knew nothing about him away from school, and I don't recall him ever asking me anything personal. Looking back I'd have to say that we were both jerking each other off, but he was getting paid for it.

Because there were so many dumbbells at the Conservatory, I was an outstanding student. My work in all the classes was somewhere at the top. With the exception of Peter Scharf, there was no one at the school I spoke to socially. I hurried from class to class with great impatience, jotting down cryptic notes to myself and evolving a style that was meant to say, I'm eccentric, do not disturb, I am potentially violent. I bought and wore a pair of tortoise-rimmed specs with tinted windowpanes and reverted to my nasty deceit of using mascara on my mustache. I scrounged record shops for old records of horn music, listened to QXR

94

religiously, and tried to catch a concert or recital once a week. Every other Saturday I'd be in the lobby of Carnegie Hall to collect all the brochures and flyers of coming events. Then I'd sit on the steps outside, with my horn pressed between my knees, and I'd pretend I was there on business.

"We'd like you to join our quintet." I was invited by a fellow student who wore tortoise-rimmed specs and used mascara on his mustache. He introduced himself, Mario Dinato. He was as tall and as thin as I was, but made points by having a less prominent nose and an abundance of wavy black hair. "The horn player we had moved to another state," he explained. "We're having a re-hearsal this evening at my home, can you come?"

"I have to work, I have to . . . There's really a lot I have to . . . I don't know . . . Yes."

He wrote down the address and told me to be there at seven-thirty. I was excited, nervous, flattered, anxious, etcetera, etcetera. I went straight to an empty room in the basement and worked on the horn for hours, stopping only to phone Mr. Kamlot and tell him I couldn't be in that evening. About five I left the school and walked to a discount salvage store in the area and bought an Australian trooper's hat with chin strap and side brim tacked to the crown. I thought it went marvelously with my marine jacket, aviator's scarf, tortoise-rimmed specs and mascaraed mustache. In a cafeteria I tried to swallow a vegetable cream-cheese sandwich and a cup of hot chocolate.

The bus dropped me off near Mario's. I passed his house two or three times before it dawned on me that he lived in a dress shop; that is, he lived with his parents in the rooms at the back of a dress shop that his parents owned. I entered the shop. A bell tinkled over my head. There were dress racks everywhere, ar-ranged in a kind of maze with barely enough space to walk between them. Mario came out from behind a beaded curtain, chewing on a lamb-chop bone.

"You're early," he said. "It's seven o'clock."

"Oh. I . . . I thought I'd practice before the rest . . ." I started toward him, but I evidently made a wrong turn as I squeezed between the dress racks because I found myself facing a blank wall. I turned to him, saw his head above a tangerine negligee. "If you want I can come back . . ."

"No, that's all right. Give me a hand and we'll get these racks out of the way."

"How do I get to you?"

"Walk between the prints and solids, then veer over at the chambray skirts."

It wasn't as easy as it sounded. But after several false starts I did manage to get to him and we moved the dress racks to the sides. Mario passed five folding chairs and five metal music stands out to me from behind the beaded curtain and we set them up in the middle of the room; it was still a pretty tight squeeze. The dresses on their hangers encircled the chairs like a crowd of headless spectators.

"Here's the music we've been rehearsing," he said, dropping a bundle of sheet music into my arms. "You practice. I have to finish dinner," and he retreated behind the beaded curtain.

I picked out the horn parts and looked them over. I was familiar with most of them, but there were pieces by Danzi, Villa-Lobos and Alvin Etler that I hadn't seen before. I took out the old *Trompe de chasse* and began working on the Danzi, softly, not wanting Mario to hear me until I was ready. And then it happened. I don't know if it was from sheer nervousness or the vegetable cream cheese and hot chocolate, but my stomach started to act up on me. I had to go to the bathroom worse than I could ever remember. I ran to the beaded curtain, holding my legs together, and hissed, "Mario? Mario? Can I see you for a minute?"

The curtain parted and there was a small, pudgy woman with bare arms glaring at me. "Why don't you let Mario eat? The music is gonna make him crazy. They gonna take him away t'the lunatic house wit' the music."

"I have to . . ."

"What's the commotion?" A scarecrow of a man in shirt-sleeves and wide suspenders appeared at her side. "Why don't you let Mario finish his dinner, mister? Where's the fire?"

"I have to ... if I can go to the bathroom ..."

"You come here t'go to the bathroom?" the man asked.

"Mario! Mario!" the woman yelled. "Why your friends come here t'go to the bathroom? Whatta you doin' t'my place?"

"It's the door on your left," Mario said, taking his parents under the arms and pulling them behind the beaded curtain.

Well, I was sick, I was wretchedly sick. I could hear the others arrive and start to warm up, but there was nothing I could do about it. Every time I got off the bowl my stomach began to rumble and I had to sit down again. I sat through Malcolm Arnold's *Sea Shanties*, Marcel Poot's Concertino for Wind Quintet, Leonid Balai's *Divertimento*, and an arrangement of some of Bach's Brandenburg. And still there was no end in sight.

"Hey!" Mario's mother pressed her mouth to the crack in the bathroom door.

"Yes?"

"How long you gonna be in there?"

"I don't know, Mrs. Dinato."

"My husband, he has t'go," she whispered. I could actually see her lips moving in the crack of the door.

"I'll be done soon, Mrs. Dinato."

"You be a good boy an' come out," she said. "My husband, he's an old man, okay?" The lips disappeared.

"Mrs. Dinato?"

The lips returned.

"Wha'?"

"There's no toilet paper in here."

"Whatta you do, eat the toilet paper?"

"Someone used it up."

"Nobody use' it up. You use' it up. You kids don't know the value of anything anymore." The lips disappeared.

"Mrs. Dinato?"

97

No answer.

"Hey!" There were the lips again.

"Yes?"

"Open the door."

Squatting, with my pants bundled at my ankles, I waddled to the door and opened it slightly for her. A *Daily Mirror* flew in and skidded across the floor.

"Use all you wan'," she said. "It'sa yesterday's paper," and the lips disappeared.

I wasn't all together when I pushed my way past the dress racks and met Julius Heller, the bassoonist, Alice Bageris, the oboist, and Gloria Hotchner, the flutist. I had seen them around the school, so a brief nod sufficed. Mario called for a piece by Strauss and as soon as I blew the first note, my stomach rumbled, growled, dug into my bowels. I put my horn on the chair and moved quickly to the bathroom. But as luck would have it, Mr. Dinato was already in there.

I pressed my lips to the crack in the door. "Mr. Dinato?"

"Wha'?"

"How long will you be in there?"

"Go 'way, mister."

"If you just gave me an idea . . ."

"Go 'way from the door, mister, or I call the cops!"

"Five minutes? Ten minutes?"

I heard him shuffling about and then the door slammed shut, almost clipping my lips off.

In a sea of dresses my four musician friends were still at the Strauss, seemingly indifferent to my erratic behavior. I leaned over Mario, "Keep playing. It sounds terrific. I'll be back in a minute." I smiled at Gloria Hotchner and hurried out of the shop, my legs held tightly together to keep it all in.

As was to be expected at that late hour, every lousy store in the neighborhood was closed, and I couldn't find a bar. I ran up and down the street, my body jerking in epileptic spasms. A woman was seated in a window of a tenement, spitting sunflower shells on the sidewalk.

In desperation, "Miss, I'll give you a dollar if I can use your bathroom!"

She looked behind her and screamed. "Tony! Hey, Tony, come here, quick! There's a maniac startin' up wit' me!"

I didn't wait to meet Tony.

I ran to an intersection, hopped into a taxi, and gave the driver my address. "You get an extra dollar if I get there in five minutes," I said, tossing and squirming on the rear seat.

"Don't dirty the floor an' I'll give you an extra dollar," the cabbie said, and all I could say was, "Hurry up, for God's sake, it's an emergency!"

I made the stairs in two jumps and headed in a beeline for the bathroom. I didn't answer my father who was watching television in the living room and asked me how it was going. Door locked, pants down, ahhh, bliss, ahhh, ecstasy. Pants up, dab of mascara on mustache, door open and out of the house I ran, with my father asking me if I'd like a dish of compote he had cooked that evening.

I rode a bus back to the dress shop. It was dark, deserted. I knocked, anyway. I had to get my horn and explain to Mario that I had been ill. No answer. I knocked again, louder. And would you believe it? As I stood there knocking on the dress-shop door, my stomach began to rumble and I had to go to the bathroom worse than I had to go to the bathroom earlier, which was worse than I had to go to the bathroom at any time I could remember.

I really knocked now, rattling the doorknob and kicking at the door. Oh, boy. Ohhh, boy. It was starting. It was beginning. Ohhh, boy.

Someone pulled a feeble bulb to light, and the door cracked open. Mrs. and Mr. Dinato, both in oversized flannel bathrobes, looking like reservation Indians, stared up at me.

"Where . . . Where's Mario? I have to . . . see Mario," I breathed the words out slowly so as not to disturb anything that was going on inside me.

Mr. Dinato: "You crazy, mister? Why you drag us outta bed?"

Mrs. Dinato: "Mario, he's sleeping. Why you bother him? Does he owe you money?"

Mr. Dinato: "Go home, mister. Go, go, forget you know Mario." He flapped his hand as if he was shooing away a pigeon.

I couldn't waste another minute, believe me. Before Mr. Dinato could slam the door in my face, I pushed myself into the shop and rushed toward the bathroom. But those damn dress racks were in the middle of the room again, and I tripped over one, banged into a couple more, and finally sprawled to the floor hanging onto the prints and solids. I was buried in dresses, drowning in dresses, and I couldn't get on my feet without slipping and bringing down another rack or two. I could hear the Dinatos yelling and Mrs. Dinato picked up a broom and took a few whacks at my backside. Lucky for me she was cockeyed and I was able to scramble out of reach. Mario came in, wearing nothing but his jockey shorts; he yawned sleepily and scratched his testicles. I got to my feet at last and, dragging dresses and belts and skirt and blouses after me, I made it into the bathroom. Door locked, pants down, ahhh, bliss, ahhh, ecstasy.

Not even the hysterical screams outside the door could dispel my feelings of absolute oneness with the universe.

Mario's parents wouldn't take any money for the damage I had done. All they asked was that we rehearse elsewhere, which we did. We met three afternoons a week at the school and after a while I settled in and was quite comfortable with the other members of the quintet. I didn't particularly like any of them except, naturally, Gloria Hotchner, the flutist. But I still enjoyed playing with them. You have to be a member of a musical group to know what that's about. Everything personal gets wiped away. To be part of: music had the power to give me that, too.

Ah, but there was Gloria Hotchner, my dark, darling Gloria Hotchner. Auburn hair tumbling in a frothy cascade on her broad shoulders; deep, lively brown eyes and a full laughing face; she had a body like a farm girl's, bones and curves hidden beneath layers of baby fat and smelling of fresh milk and creamy butter.

Dear, sweet, vivacious Gloria Hotchner, I wanted to cry out, let me be your flute! Once, just once, raise me to your ripe mouth and blow into me, fill me with your warm, scented breath, close the orifices of my body as you do those of your instrument, play on my skin with your fingertips until my veins burst with the joy of you. Gloria, Gloria, Gloria Hotchner, I beg you, I implore you, have mercy for God's sake and let me be your crummy flute!

Of course the skinny horn player pretended she didn't exist. Whenever she spoke to him, he looked elsewhere, and busied himself with one thing or another. She liked him, that was apparent; she went more than halfway to let him know how she felt. But it was a thankless effort. She stared at him in the present, accepted him in the present, but he stared back at her from somewhere in the distant future and found her wanting. I think: what would I do if Gloria Hotchner walked into my suite of rooms at the Geneva this minute, now, as she was then? Laughing, lively, seventeen-year-old Gloria Hotchner? What would I do?

Well, for one, I'd unbutton my lips and grin like a cat. And for two, I'd take a holiday from my strict and sacred vow to keep to myself and I'd take full advantage of the occasion.

Come in, come in, my dear Gloria Hotchner.

Is it . . . ?

Eddie Davis! Grand Army Conservatory! My, my, you look wonderful, Gloria Hotchner, Absolutely wonderful!

Thank you, Eddie. You . . . You look older.

Oh, I put on a year or two, nothing worth mentioning. Say, I have an idea. Why don't you have dinner with me? You have time, don't you? Wonderful! Wonderful! Let me order, please.

Hello, room service? Mr. Davis here. We'd like a dozen Blue Point oysters and some of your house pâté, a couple of steamed lobsters . . . Do you like steamed lobsters, Gloria Hotchner? Wonderful! Wonderful! Steamed lobsters, room service, a dish of fruit and cheese, make that Gorgonzola, Roquefort, Bel Paese, peaches, plums, cherries if they're in season, a pot of espresso, and send up a bottle of Dom Perignon and a bottle of Remy Martin. Thank you. So . . . Gloria Hotchner. Sit down. Sit down. Don't be bashful.

What happened to your hair, Eddie?

My hair?

It's thinner.

Oh, that's nothing. I pulled out a couple to even them out.

You're getting a paunch, Eddie.

A paunch? Nooo. Why do you say that? I'm wearing a pillow under my shirt, for laughs, don't you get it? Ha! Ha! Ha! Ha!

Do you still play the horn?

Play the horn? Of course. Of course. Why, right this minute I'm preparing myself for several important auditions and a concert is in the works. You didn't think I'd give up, did you?

You're the only one I know from the Conservatory who didn't give up.

What can I say?

You're special. You always were special.

One has to do what one has to do. Ah, here's dinner, that was quick. You may light the candles and recite the benediction, waiter. I'm joking! I'm joking! Doesn't anyone have a sense of humor anymore? Thank you, waiter. Look under your pillow tonight; your tip will be there. Ha! Ha! Ha! Ha!

So . . . Isn't this nice, Gloria Hotchner? Isn't this cozy? Gobble-gobble-gobble. Gobble-gobble-gobble. Well, all done with dinner. More champagne? brandy?

I don't drink, Eddie. You know that.

Just a little brandy.

A little. It makes me dizzy.

Good. Did you enjoy the meal?

It was the best I ever ate. But I should go . . .

Gloria, why? why? Haven't we waited a lifetime for this? Stay. Live with me. I'll pay your expenses.

My parents are expecting me.

Phone them. Tell them you're staying with a girlfriend for the weekend.

I don't have a change of clothes.

I'll buy you a change of clothes and a Cartier wristwatch so you'll know when the weekend is over. More brandy?

Please. I never thought this would happen, Eddie. You're . . . different. You're so . . . self-assured, domineering, sophisticated, worldly, suave, cultured, verbal, witty, imposing, knowledgeable, virile . . .

It's true. Everything you say is quite true.

I'm getting drunk, I swear.

Good.

Eddie, inside I'm glad all this is happening, but . . .

Be quiet, my darling. You don't have to talk. Let's lie down on my Beautyrest mattress for a while. I'm getting sleepy. Yawn. Yawn. Isn't it nice to be in bed, just the two of us?

It's what I always dreamed.

Don't move, my darling. Just lie there, like that. How young you are, how incredibly soft you are, how nice it is to touch your breasts . . . Let me take off your clothes, sweetheart.

Eddie . . .

Shhh. Shhh, my darling. First your dress, then your little shoe-sies, sniff, sniff, they don't even smell, now your panties . . . Ohhh, Gloria Hotchner, how could you hide all this? Your body is beautiful, positively beautiful.

I'm heavy. I have no waistline . . .

No, no, my darling. Your body is beautiful. You must love your body as I love it. Let me kiss you . . . Let my tongue touch yours . . . Let me put my mouth on your nipple, first one, then the other, we don't want to show favoritism, do we? Ahhh, your breasts are delicious. Yummy-yummy-yummy. Ahhh, Gloria Hotchner, how long, how long we waited. We could have done this years ago, nights of it, days of it, with my mouth on your breasts, when I needed . . . so much . . .

Aren't you going to take off your clothes, Eddie?

No, no, my darling. I want to delight in you. I want to give you pleasure. I don't care about myself. I want to do this for you, for you, my sweetheart. I want to bring you to orgasm, multi-tudinous orgasms, one after the other. I want to get you wet inside and watch your body tremble and shiver and thrash with orgasm, multitudinous orgasms, one after the other, rippling through every pore of you until you can't stand it anymore. For you, darling. Oh, let me touch you down there, let me rub your cushy-wooshy little bird's nest, let me feel inside of you, the wetness, ahhh, you feel terrific, sweetheart, you're opening up and I can smell your luscious wetness, let me . . . Gobble-gobble-gobble. Gobble-gobble-gobble-gobble-gobble-gobble.

seven

Don't think Peter Scharf dropped from my life. No such luck. If I didn't fall over him at the door of my house in the morning or at The Chocolatte Shoppe in the evening, I was sure to do so at school, where he waited outside my classrooms to grab hold of me.

"I've decided to cater the affair," he said as he walked me to my next class.

"What affair?"

"Your birthday party, stupid! It's in two weeks. I have to send invitations for Sunday the third."

"Peter, I don't . . ."

"Listen, you deserve a birthday party. I've been watching you. You've been working your ass off. By the way, your parents can't come."

"My parents?"

"I spoke to them on the phone."

"Why can't they come?"

"Your father has to wallpaper your bedroom to surprise you."

"Who told you that?"

"Your mother."

"Peter, why don't we forget . . ."

"I'm inviting Mr. Gilcrist."

"The dean?"

"Right. And Mr. Noonan, Mr. Fosdick, Mrs. Hermann, your friends, Mario Dinato, Julie Heller . . ."

"Why do all those people have to come to my birthday party?"

"Do you want there to be just you and me? A quiet Chinese dinner and drinks after?"

"Yes, I'd prefer that."

"I would, too. I'll pick you up on the third."

That Sunday my mother prepared a birthday breakfast for me: chicken fricassee, eggs, a pot of coffee and two packages of Twinkies. My father couldn't join us because he was wallpapering my bedroom. I practiced for an hour or so, ran off to the luncheonette to work the noon shift, returned, showered, shaved, mascaraed, and read a bit until Peter arrived. Under his sheepskin and over his spiked boots, he wore a rust-colored suit, pleated shirt and shoestring tie with a brass buffalo-head clasp. His hair was shellacked in place, quarter-mooned over one eye, and he emitted a pungent odor of bay rum and White Owl cigars. In his stubby hands he carried a bouquet of chrysanthemums which, to my mother's disappointment, he gave to me.

"You must be very proud of Eddie," he said, sitting down and taking a Ritz cracker from the dish on the coffee table.

My parents didn't know how to react to the compliment. They slyly peeked over his shoulder to see if he was concealing a hump under his sheepskin.

"Music is a tough business," my father said, "especially the French horn. It's a dying instrument."

"I sacrificed everything for Eddie to study the French horn," my mother said.

"The thing about Eddie, Mrs. Davis, is that he works, he's a worker, and there aren't many kids his age who are workers."

"He works, all right," my father said, "but can he make a living playing the French horn?"

"That I don't know, Mr. Davis."

The answer depressed both my father and me.

"What instrument do you play, Mr. Scharf?" my mother asked.

"The drums. I played the drums with the marines in Okinawa; that was after I received the Bronze Star."

"So you're a war hero," my father inquired with interest.

"I don't like to boast," Peter said, glancing at his turquoise pinky ring, "but I believe in this country, Mr. Davis. I believe in its mountains and its fields and in its huddled masses yearning to be free. Anyone would have done what I did, caught in the same situation." He raised his pale, shifty eyes, taking a small package from his sheepskin. "Eddie, this is for you. Happy birthday from your one and only," he said.

"You didn't have to . . ." I unwrapped the package and dangled a Bronze Star in the air.

"You're giving Eddie your Bronze Star?" My father was dumbfounded. "You can't give Eddie your Bronze Star. Is he giving you his Bronze Star, Eddie?"

"Peter, you don't have to . . ."

"Keep it, Eddie. You deserve it for the work you've been doing at The Chocolatte Shoppe," he said without flinching.

I thought then, for the first time, that there was something definitely off-base about Peter Scharf, but I attributed this quality to the fact that he came from Little Rock, Arkansas, and not to the more relevant fact that he was a genuine whacko.

"Why don't you pin the Bronze Star on your marine jacket?" my father suggested.

"They'll be taking Eddie to Korea now that he's eighteen," my mother said. "We don't want him to go, but if our country needs him . . ."

"There's a lot that can be said against this country," my father added, "but I'd still rather live here than in Australia."

"I'm not going to Korea," I said, pinning the Bronze Star on my marine jacket.

"What do you mean you're not going?" My father's voice went up a couple of notches.

"You have to go, Eddie," my mother said. "Whether you like it or not, you're an American."

"I'm not going," I repeated. "I can't afford to be away from my horn for any extended period of time."

"You'll play the horn in the army," my father said. "I heard it's the only place left where they still use French horn players."

"My family has been in all our wars." My mother was getting very angry.

"If not for Eddie, I would have been in the last one, too," my father said to Peter.

It was nice having my parents agree with each other, but they were in an area where I was impregnable.

"No, I'm not going."

My father: "We have neighbors, Eddie. Some of them lost their sons in Korea."

My mother: "What do we say to them?"

My father: "How do we explain your presence?"

My mother: "I have a job in the A & P. If they ever heard you didn't wanna go to Korea, I could get canned."

My father: "You're going too far, son."

My mother: "He's going to Korea whether he likes it or not."

"No, I'm not."

"Yes, you are."

"I'm not."

"You are."

"Wait a second," Peter broke through with a toothy grin. "Maybe they'll reject Eddie for reasons of mental or physical health."

"There's nothing physically wrong with Eddie," my father said.

"How about mental?"

My father looked at me sideways.

"I'm not saying there has to be anything mentally wrong with Eddie, Mr. Davis, but if the army thought there was . . ."

"That's possible," my father said.

"Some guys are too sensitive for army life. I think your son is one of them. Would you like to be rejected for a mental reason, Eddie?"

"Yes. Very much."

"Leave it to me. I know just who we can see about it. Now if you'll excuse us," Peter said, getting up from the sofa, "we have reservations for dinner at Po Ping's Oriental Gardens."

Po Ping's Oriental Gardens was in Chinatown. After we had dinner, what it was I don't remember, we went to a bar in Brooklyn Heights called Christy's. It was there that I was supposed to meet someone who would tell me how to avoid being drafted for a mental reason. The place was crowded, noisy and, not surprisingly, filled entirely with men of every age and ilk. We sat at the bar, in the corner, and Peter ordered Gallianos for us. I declined his White Owl and lit my pipe instead. I half listened to him tell me he wasn't sure he wanted to be a professional drummer, that he had thoughts of returning to the service, that it was rough being an out-of-towner in New York, etcetera, etcetera. He interrupted himself to wag his arm and shout, "Jackie! Jackie St. Claire!" to a strikingly good-looking, red-haired young man whose posture was so rigid I suspected he wore a back brace.

"I thought you weren't coming here anymore," Jackie St. Claire said, lifting Peter's Galliano and downing it; he then lifted my Galliano and downed it as well. "We'll have three more," he said to the bartender, pushing himself between the two of us. "So you've won a Bronze Star from Peter," he said to me. "Shame. Shame. Shame."

"Jackie, this is . . ." Peter began.

"I know what this is," Jackie answered, peering at me from atop his elongated neck. "The question is, what is this doing here and what are you doing with this?"

"He goes to the Conservatory with me."

"That piece of information leaves me panting for breath. The repartee at this end of the bar is fastly becoming vomitous." He swallowed some of his drink, patted his crown of red hair, and glanced quickly around the room for a friendly face.

"It's Eddie's eighteenth birthday," Peter persisted. "I took him out for dinner. In Chinatown."

"That must have been enthralling. Did you have consommé with wontons or bat shit?"

Peter winced, rubbed his pinky ring on his coat sleeve. "He's worried about being drafted into the army. I know you avoided the draft, Jackie, and I thought if you gave him a few tips . . ."

"Tips I do not give. Lessons I do give." He swung his head around to me. "Are you interested in taking lessons on draft evasion? Three lessons for twenty-five dollars. I guarantee you will not be inducted. Yes or no, and take that foul-smelling protuberance from your mouth, please. It reminds me of someone I loathe."

I knocked the pipe clean and put it in my pocket. "What kind of lessons are they?" I asked in my squeaky Little-Bo-Peep voice, and stared past him at Peter who said, "You can trust Jackie. If he guarantees he'll get you out, he'll get you out."

"You can pay me when you receive your second lesson which will be given one week from today. Your first lesson will be given tonight, now, at my *pied-à-terre*. And you," he swung his head back to Peter, "if you wish to accompany us and observe in silence, you're required to pick up a bottle of Galliano as your admission fee," and with that he moved off, pushed his way through the mob of men to the exit, saying, "Do you mind? Am I disturbing you?" as he advertently banged into every pair of shins that blocked his path.

He lived in a room without kitchen or furniture, a couple of buildings from Christy's. One wall was covered completely with a beveled mirror, the other walls and ceiling were painted black, and there were giant-sized pillows on the bleached wooden floor. When we entered, Jackie lit countless candles stuck in countless Chianti bottles; if there was any electricity in the room, he didn't bother to turn it on. He poured Galliano into paper cups and motioned for Peter and me to sit down on the pillows. Then, staring at his reflection in the mirror, he raised himself on his toes, his body as straight as a steel shaft, and sliding his hands over his rib cage, a la Isadora Duncan, spoke to his mirrored double in a deep, resonant voice.

"I am an actor," he said. "I am a student of acting. I take from my craft those ingredients that are necessary for my survival. No one should have his education disrupted to go off to wage war in Korea. What is Korea? Where is Korea? Does anyone presume to know?" He darted across the room, whirled about, and spoke from the shadows. "It is possible, very possible, when one is adequately equipped, to evade the onslaught of military service. However . . ." And now he threw his arms out and in a single leap was back at the mirror, lowering himself on his haunches to a pillow. "However, that requires skill, discipline and the ability to admit to oneself what one has perhaps concealed from oneself. I . . . I am a homosexual." He bowed his head reverentially. "I can be, if I so choose, a variety of types that exemplify the homosexual persona. But for the purpose of draft evasion, I, you, we are compelled to choose from our repertoire of prototypes the most extreme and flamboyant. We cannot confuse the military hard hats with nuance, and thereby fail to be rejected on the grounds of aberrative, antisocial, sexual perversity."

"If you play queer," Peter murmured, "they're gonna reject you."

"But your performance must be without flaw," Jackie cautioned me. "Your manner must be impeccable; your delivery and enunciation must be on a par with the inimitable Garbo and the incomparable Bankhead. Can you do it, Edward?"

"I'm not an actor. Isn't there anything else . . . ?"

"What? What else could there be?" Jackie poured himself another Galliano. "I am giving you the enormous benefits of my own experience, the cabala of my own success. Does the notion of performing the part of a homosexual frighten you? Are you perhaps prejudiced against the practice of homosexuality?"

"No, no. Everybody can do what he wants to do so long as he doesn't hurt schoolchildren."

"That's what he believes in," Peter said.

"My dear boy, I have nothing more to offer you. Three lessons in faggot behavior to free you of your military service or a fraternal pat on the *tuchis* and a fond *au revoir*, which shall it be?"

"I don't have time to go to the army. I have to practice . . ."

"Stand up. Stand beside me. And let's get started. I promise that you will not be asked to do anything that violates your conscience. Unlike other instructors in the vicinity, I will not call upon you to swallow a hot sausage while whistling 'How Much Is That Doggie In The Window.' Our mutual friend, Peter Scharf, can attest to the propriety of my instruction."

"I'm not queer," Peter said.

"Ha!" Jackie huffed, throwing back his red-crowned head, and he clasped my hand and led me back and forth in front of the mirrored wall. "Remember, Edward, what I'm asking of you is a performance. I'm going to give you acting lessons; I'm going to ask you not merely to imitate what I do, but to draw from the resources inside yourself and to use those to convince the army psychiatrists that having you in the service will be detrimental toward winning the war. Use the faggot in you, Edward. We all have a faggot in us. Some of us have a big faggot in us and some of us have a teensy-weensy faggot in us. Now look at your reflection, walk, walk, swing your buttocks, roll them, that's it, do what I'm doing, do what strikes you as appropriate, excellent, excellent, you have a natural faggot's walk, ten cents a dance, don't go walking down lover's lane with anyone else but me, excellent, excellent, now say as you walk, and lisp it, lisp it, don't be subtle, exaggerate, 'Sally sells shells on the seashore since Sammy sucks shoes in the shoe store.'"

We did this exercise for quite a while before sitting down on the pillows again. Peter filled our cups with Galliano and said, "I'm enjoying this. For my money you two are doing the best acting jobs I ever saw."

"Tell the psychiatrist you're a transvestite, Edward, that you frequently prance about in your mother's clothes, and that for you there is no sensation comparable to that of being waltzed around the dance floor by a Nazi storm trooper."

"I'm not . . ."

"Lisp, lisp when you speak. Get into the habit."

Lisping, "I'm ssssorry, Jackie. I'm not wearing my mother'ssss clothessss. They don't fit me!"

"You sssshould wear them," Peter lisped. "You'll look fantas-ssstic!"

"What I will insist is that you wear silk stockings."

"Why do I . . . ?"

"During the interview I want you to pull up your trousers and allow the psychiatrist to peek at your silk stockings. I think I have . . ." He dug under the pillow. "Here you are, Edward. Put them on." He tossed a pair of silk stockings at me.

"I . . . I can't, Jackie. I can't go through with this. I'll never convince anybody I'm a homosexual."

"Yes, you will," Peter said.

"You're resisting me." Jackie's head rose on his giraffelike neck, his red hair bristling. "He is resisting me," he snapped at Peter, "and I will not tolerate any resistance!"

"Eddie, what are you doing? Jackie's breaking his hump trying to keep you out of the army and you're resisting him."

"You can go!" Jackie shrieked at me. "But if you're killed in Korea, you have no one to blame but yourself!"

I put on the silk stockings and shut up for the rest of the evening. When I left with Peter, Jackie gave me a card on which the following was written: Grade for first lesson — B. Comments — Needs improvement.

Of course I didn't go back to Jackie St. Claire. I sent him a money order for ten dollars and a letter thanking him for his help. I found out from Perry Reese (he was going to Long Island University and I bumped into him now and then) that it was possible to avoid the draft by joining the National Guard and attending weekly training sessions. And that's what I did. The first time they saw me in my army fatigues, my parents were dewy-eyed, and I took that as a sign of approval. I must say, things were getting pretty bad at home. I don't know precisely when it started, but one day I realized that my parents hadn't spoken to each other in months; whenever they were forced to communicate, I conveyed the message.

"Tell your father he owes money to the telephone company."

"Dad, you owe money to the telephone company."

"Why do I owe money to the telephone company?"

"Ma, why does Dad owe money to the telephone company?"

"He used the telephone last month and I'm not paying when he uses the telephone."

"Dad, you used the telephone last month and Ma isn't paying when you use the telephone."

"I used the telephone once. That's five cents. Here's five cents. One, two, three, four, five. Give it to your mother, Eddie."

"Ma, here's five cents. One, two, three, four, five. Dad asked me to give it to you for using the telephone last month."

"It's unacceptable."

"Dad, Ma says . . ."

And on and on it went until I heard myself say, "Why do you two live together?"

Neither one answered me.

I had offended them.

So I said, "Why don't you get a divorce?"

They couldn't have been more astonished. It was as if I had said, Why don't we all make a ca-ca on the floor?

"Divorce? Did you say divorce?" my father asked.

"Don't you ever mention that word in this house again," my mother said. "Do you hear me, Eddie?"

"Tell your mother I couldn't agree with her more," my father said.

"Ma, Dad says he couldn't agree with you more."

"Tell your father there has never been a divorce in my family."

"Dad, Ma says . . ." And then I heard the voice inside me say, "Why don't we separate? Why don't we each live in our own apartment?" I listened to the voice and admired it for its maturity and good sense.

But my mother reacted quite differently. "If you ever leave this house, Eddie, if you ever move out, I'll kill myself, do you hear me? This is no idle threat. The day you leave this house is the day I end my life and don't you ever forget it!"

Which was, in view of what occurred several weeks later, a peculiar thing for my mother to say. I came home from school, I believe it was in March, and my father was waiting for me on the stoop.

"She's gone, Eddie."

"Who's gone?"

"Your mother."

My heart started pounding. "I didn't move, Dad. I didn't get my own apartment. Why . . . ?"

"She moved, Eddie. To North Hollywood, Florida. Come on, I'm taking you to dinner. It's on me."

We walked to a local diner and sat in a booth. My father ordered the blue-plate special and I passed.

"What is she doing in North Hollywood, Florida?"

"I'm not sure. She phoned me at work this morning. She said she had the rare opportunity to get into the motel business."

"The motel business? How did she get into that?"

"I don't know. Your mother's a strange woman. I could tell you stories about her that would turn your stomach. Would you like to hear them?"

"Not now, thank you."

"She's, you know." He twirled his finger around his ear. "I've known it for years. She said she'd phone you tonight. But I don't want you to worry. We'll do fine, the two of us. We'll have a little peace and quiet."

My mother did phone me that evening.

"Eddie, this is your mother calling you from sunny Florida, the land of the orange and the grapefruit," her voice cackled in the receiver.

"How are you, Ma?"

"I've never been happier. I'm . . ."

I didn't get all of it. "What did you say, Ma?"

"I said I'm happy! I'm happy!" she screamed at the other end. "It's a relief to be out of that horrible depressing house!"

"When are you coming back?"

"Never! I'll kill myself first!"

"Ma, we miss you."

"That's how it should be. Eddie, I have eight studio rooms and a volleyball court."

"Where?"

"My motel. I'll tell you about it when you visit. When can you come down? I'll make reservations for you."

As it turned out, my father was also happier than he had ever been. He came in from work bursting with enthusiasm. Jacket still on, whistling cheerfully, he'd start rearranging the furniture, put a new curtain up somewhere, beat a carpet or two, and then prepare a beef-and-potato stew which he'd watch simmer with loving care. There were hot rolls for breakfast, plastic containers of tuna and egg salads in the refrigerator, and my bed sheets were washed and changed twice a week.

If I had thoughts of leaving home, they disappeared when my mother left home.

She phoned infrequently.

"Ma, I don't understand. Do you know you haven't called me in over a month?"

"Is it over a month?"

"It's five weeks and four days to be exact. For Christ sake, I was getting worried about you."

"Do me a favor and don't worry about me, Eddie. I'm old enough."

"I really don't understand, Ma. You have one son and you can't pick up the lousy phone!"

"I've been busy . . ."

"How busy can you be? You don't have a minute to pick up the lousy phone?"

"Business is booming, Eddie. I have all the rooms rented until the middle of May."

"The least you can do is give me your phone number. You could be dead and I'd be the last one to know it."

"The number changes. They keep changing it. I'll call you every week from now on, I promise. When are you coming down?"

"The first week in July."

"You'll have the Brazilian room. It has bamboo shades and a twenty-four-hour electric coffee maker."

The only real sour note in all of this was Peter Scharf. Somehow he and my father became friends and it was the rule rather than the exception to arrive home and find him at the dinner table. By now I was onto Peter, but I didn't know how to get rid of him. My father was indignant whenever I suggested he not allow Peter into the house.

"He's a war hero, Eddie. You don't kick a war hero out of your house."

"He's a whacko, Dad. A real whacko."

"A winner of the Bronze Star? A man who fought at Okinawa so that you and I could enjoy the benefits of democracy?"

"Dad, I just don't want him hanging around. I don't like him."

"Don't like him? How can you say that when he loves you?"

"He loves me?"

"He told me so himself."

"I don't care if he loves me or not. I still don't like him."

"You should, Eddie. Love is hard to find, especially between men. When you've lived as long as I have, you'll appreciate what I'm saying."

There was no convincing him without bringing up the homosexual thing, and I wasn't up to doing that, not with my father. He was more naive, at that period of his life, than I was.

The friendship between my father and Peter flourished. They began to spend whatever free time they had in each other's company. You have to put this in its right context. My father never had a friend; he never had an interest beyond his job, his family (me) and what was to be seen on evening television. The departure of my mother and the appearance of Peter Scharf altered his habits radically. He had lost a wife, but he had gained a friend, and anyone with two eyes in his head could see that he felt he had gotten the better of the deal.

You wouldn't believe the improvements they made in the apartment. The stairway was carpeted, the bathroom was painted and tiled (black, no less), lineoleum laid in the bedrooms and a wall-to-wall rug in the living room. They were constantly at work on some project or other. By the end of the day they were sure to be in the kitchen, preparing dinner from a cookbook, my father in an apron of my mother's and Peter in a truncated chef's hat; they'd chat and laugh like a pair of schoolgirls as they sliced peppers and mushrooms and bits of fish and meat, stirred batter, simmered onions and garlic, twisted braids of dough, then set the table with an embroidered cloth and pewter candlesticks purchased at a charity thrift shop.

Once a week they went off to bowl with a team called The Alley Cats. On Tuesday nights two men from the brewery on Liberty Avenue came over and they all put on turtleneck sweaters with "Mellowlarks" printed across them, and they harmonized, on key for the most part, such old favorites as "For Me and My Gal," "Don't Sit Under The Apple Tree With Anyone Else But Me" and "Till The End Of Time."

My father was ebullient. His life was full, gratifying and without discord. In July when I was getting ready to visit my mother, he said, "Guess what, Eddie?"

"What?"

"I've asked Peter to stay with me while you're gone."

"Peter?"

"Peter Scharf. He can use your bedroom."

"My bedroom?"

"We're planning to spend a weekend hiking in the mountains."

"Hiking in the mountains? With Peter?" I had to say something. "Dad, there's something I have to tell you."

"What's that?"

Deep breath, "Peter Scharf is queer."

"Aren't we all, son?"

"Dad, didn't you hear what I said?"

"What's that?"

"Peter Scharf is a homosexual."

"What does that mean?"

"He prefers men to women."

"Is that bad?"

"For sex."

"A corporal in the marines? Don't be silly."

"Dad, not all homosexuals are effeminate, just as not all blacks are necessarily black."

"What does that mean?"

"You don't have to be yellow to be Chinese either."

"You've been working too hard, Eddie. Why don't you stay with your mother for the summer? You can use the rest."

119

"Dad, if I left you a couple of books on the subject, would you read them?"

"Books?"

"They'll explain what happens when you go hiking in the mountains with someone like Peter Scharf."

"I'll be very happy to read books on hiking. I'm sure Peter would like to read them, too."

"In any case, carry a knife with you."

"What?"

"When you go hiking with Peter, always have a knife ready."

"We're only going to the Palisades, Eddie. There are no wild animals up there."

"That's what you think. Dad, did you ever have a homosexual experience?"

"Only with your mother."

"Goodbye, Dad. I'll phone."

"Goodbye, son. If I'm not at home, I'll be up in the mountains with Peter."

eight

Fall is coming on like winter this year. I went down to Central Park yesterday, Sunday, and I sat on a bench and watched the bicyclists swoop along the trafficless roads. My beard is filling in nicely. I wore my belted Burberry, my Polo gabardine slacks, Calvin Klein plaid shirt, Jaeger shawl-collar cardigan, buckled Gucci shoes and a tweed, Eddie Bauer slouch hat. I looked scrumptious. There was plenty of loose fluff around. If not for my vow to avoid such entanglements, I could have scored easily.

I felt proud of myself.

I felt like an athlete in training.

I felt that everyone was staring at me, that everyone knew I had the inner strength and willpower to turn my back on all that was extraneous in order to concentrate on my music.

I felt that at any minute someone would come up to me and say, You're special; you're a unique individual; congratulations.

A splash of sunlight fell over my shoulders like a glittering, iridescent cape.

It seemed as if half the city were out. There was a Hispanic parade on Fifth Avenue. Kids were flying kites in Sheep Meadow. Public relations men from the Mayor's office were giving away

Big Apple posters and buttons. Save Our Town! We're Number One! New York Is Beautiful! Once I was part of this, the park, the people, the sense of the city, but I'm not anymore. Nothing is familiar to me. Nothing says anything to me. The thrill is gone. It's a bit depressing.

On a bench I closed my eyes and raised my face to the sun. And suddenly I heard a horn playing. I thought I was hallucinating. I looked around and I saw, seated on the ground with his back against a tree, a young horn player wearing a purple beret on his head! He was skinnier than even the skinny horn player, his almost albino face as sharp and pointed as a brand-new hatchet; long, stringy, colorless hair hung down from beneath his purple beret to his spindly shoulders.

I couldn't help laughing, aloud. He stopped playing and stared, with a hurt expression, at me.

"I'm sorry," I said. "Please, go on."

He nodded and continued playing, Beethoven's Sonata in F Major.

To play the horn in the park, out in the open, that was something that had never occurred to me. How gutsy he was, sitting there against the tree, his coils of gold hurling shafts of sound up into the sky. I envied him. Greatly.

But he wasn't that good a horn player. I doubted if he had had any formal training, and yet everything about him suggested that he was a music student. His technique was deplorable. He rarely hit a note that wasn't slightly higher or lower than it should have been. The odds were heavily against his making it.

As if reading my mind, he jumped to his feet, looking very grim and disconsolate. He tucked the golden horn under his arm.

"Do you need anything?" I asked him without thinking. "Can I help you?"

He shook his head, his cheeks flushed crimson, and he moved off quickly.

I grabbed a taxi to the Geneva, put out the Do Not Disturb

sign, took the phone out of its cradle, and I played the horn all afternoon. I played until I couldn't stand it anymore.

It was during the first week in July that I went to Florida to visit my mother. I stepped off the train in Miami, suitcase and horn in hand, and I rode the bus to North Hollywood. From the depot I walked along something of a highway, then turned down a sandy, shell-graveled road that led to the ocean. There were about a dozen motels on either side of the road, it was called Balboa Drive, and I searched among the competing marquees and signposts for Sylvia's Sunshine Villa.

It was unbearably hot. I could see the ocean in the distance, but it offered no breeze or spray of relief. Fortunately, I had on (with my marine jacket) my Australian trooper's hat and it kept the sun from my face. The area was deserted. I saw no one. A dozen empty motels, garishly painted in pinks and blues, a few scrawny palms, not much else, a kind of ghetto resort area for underprivileged tourists. I read signs: Oceanside Paradise, Benny's Valhalla, The Beach Ball Country Club, and stared up at crudely built billboards of flamingos, dolphins, pineapples and tropical sunsets. I thought of knocking on a door when I heard a voice singing "The Donkey Seranade" from Rudolph Friml's movie version of *The Firefly*.

I tracked the voice to my mother. She was hanging bed sheets on a volleyball net between two stuccoed pink buildings. She really looked great in a starched cotton dress, hemmed above the knees, and a floppy straw hat. I couldn't understand why I had always been ashamed of her. She was unquestionably an attractive woman, with chestnut hair cut in a bob, chestnut eyes in a small, oval face and a remarkably youthful body. She sang loudly, joyfully, "There's a song in the air, but the fair Senorita doesn't seem to care, for the song in the air..."

I put my things down and took a couple of steps toward her. Squinting, I stared at her youthful body. It was not, on closer inspection, so youthful. In fact my mother was pregnant.

"So I'll sing to the mule, if you're sure you won't think that I am just a fool . . ."

I called to her. "Ma? Ma?"

"Amigo mia, does she not have a dainty way . . ."

"Ma, it's me, Eddie!"

She seemed astounded at my being there; her brow furrowed and she stopped singing, but continued hanging the bed sheets.

"You're not Eddie," she said, dismissing me without a second glance.

"What do you mean I'm not Eddie?"

"You're not Eddie," she repeated, flapping a bed sheet and draping it over the net.

"For cryin'-out-loud, Ma, I spoke to you last week. You told me how to get here. How would I know how to get here if you didn't tell me and if I wasn't Eddie?"

That got to her, somewhat. "What's your father's name?" she asked me.

"Phillip."

"Where were you born?"

"Brooklyn. I'm . . ."

"Don't tell me how old you are. It's nobody's business. Do you have a birthmark on your right leg?"

"No."

"On your left leg?"

"No."

"Can you speak any foreign languages?"

"No."

"Eddie, it's you!"

"That's what I've been trying to tell you."

"What a shock this is. What a shock. I left behind a sweet little boy and I find standing in front of me a grown-up man who's bald-headed!"

And she started to sob, burying her face in a pillowcase. I put my arm around her and kissed her gingerly on the cheek.

"I'm fine, Ma. I'm in good health. And you look wonderful, really wonderful. Is this your place?"

She blew her nose in the pillowcase and pointed to her signpost which was too low to be seen from the road. "It's not the season now, Eddie, so we're slow, but until a few weeks ago, we were booked to capacity. Do you like it?"

"Very much. Ma, can we sit down and talk? There's something I have to ask you." My glance slid down to her swollen stomach.

"Later. You have to meet Angel."

"Who's Angel?"

"He's my boyfriend and my business partner," she said, brushing the lint from her dress and moving away from the volleyball net. "You'll take to him, Eddie. You two have a lot in common. He plays the maracas."

Behind one of the buildings, the recreational facilities of my mother's motel were wisely kept out of sight: a couple of rusty swings, a deflated, rubber wading pool and several metal tables and chairs planted crookedly in the sand.

Seated in one of the chairs was a bare-chested Cuban, reading the morning newspaper with the intense concentration of a Biblical scholar. He had a pencil-line mustache, tiny eyes and ears and thick, wiry hair that sat on his head like a pad of Brillo.

"Angel! He's here! He's here! Eddie's here!" my mother shouted excitedly, pumping her fists in the air. When this didn't arouse him to any discernible movement, she said to me, with reverence, "Eddie, this is Angel Medina, a man who gave me more pleasure in five minutes than your father gave me in nineteen years."

Evidently pleased by this remark, Angel now turned his head and slowly ran his tiny eyes over me. He fastidiously folded and placed the newspaper on the table, rose from the chair to his full height, which narrowly escaped falling into the midget class. Slowly, fastidiously, he put on a silk orange robe, knotted the belt around a slight paunch of waist.

"You are the son of this woman?" he asked with a pronounced accent.

I didn't know what else to do but nod.

"You have come from the bowels of this woman?"

I thought of correcting him, but I noticed that my mother was nodding fervently, so I deferred to her judgment and nodded again.

"Then I say to everyone living in North Hollywood, Miami Beach and Havana, Cuba, that the son of this magnificent woman is welcome to my home, and if anyone in those vicinities dares do him harm, I will personally see to it that his memory is revenged!" And with that he stretched on his toes, grabbed my head between his tiny hands, and brought me down to his level, kissing me passionately on the mouth.

"Sylvia, my darling woman, my jewel of all jewels," he then said, "go bring out the wine and the cigars and the kosher salami. We will celebrate your son's return!"

My mother rushed off as if she had been shot out of a cannon. Angel sat down, crossed his legs, and motioned me into a chair.

"How does she look to you, Eddie?"

"Wonderful. Really wonderful."

"She is happy. Always she sings and always she works and always we make hot love on the beach in the moonlight."

"That's . . . terrific. Where did you two meet?"

"Oh, many years ago when I work at the A & P in Brooklyn. I swore to myself that one day I would make plenty of *dineros* and I would go back and take your momma away with me and make her into a happy woman. She was not a happy woman with your father, Eddie."

"I know."

"Your father, he has no balls."

"I know."

"I have balls, Eddie. I have big balls."

"I know." Thoughtful pause. "That's what I want to talk to you about, Mr. Medina."

"Poppa. You call me Poppa. I will be like your own father. And don't say to me what you are thinking. I am the one who put the goose in your momma's oven."

"That's exactly what I was thinking."

"What should I do, my son? She can be a difficult woman. I want to marry her. I do not want her to have any basteed from me. But she refuses."

"My father would give her a divorce."

"The same is so for my Anita."

"You're married?"

"Oh, for many, many years. I have kids from all ages. I would like you to speak to your mother, my son. Convince her that for the sake of the unborn child, we must get our divorces and be married legally. It will also be good for the business."

"I'll try, Mr. Medina."

"Poppa. You call me Poppa."

Gulp. "Yes, Poppa."

"Try. We will both try. She has to listen to us. It would be a shameful thing, my son, if we have a little basteed in the family."

I drank two glasses of wine and swallowed a slice of salami before bringing up the subject to my mother.

"Ma, it seems that everybody would be happy except for this one small thing that's making everybody unhappy."

"What thing?"

"You know, Ma."

"The basteed! Our son is talking to you about the basteed!" Poppa emptied his wine glass over his shoulder and refilled it from a second bottle. There was no denying his anger. His mustache started to wiggle under his nose.

"Angel, I asked you not to mention it to Eddie. He doesn't have to know I'm pregnant."

Poppa was on his feet, his orange robe catching fire in the rays of the sun. "You can be a foolish woman, woman. Eddie is our oldest son and it is his future, too, we are talking about. What name will you give the basteed? It will not be Medina. There is no Medina who is a basteed! There will never be a Medina who is a basteed!"

That sent my mother into another fit of sobbing. With her hands covering her face, she ran into the motel, leaving the door open behind her. From where we sat we could hear her crying.

"My son?"

"Yes, Poppa?"

"Talk to her. Convince her that marriage is the only honorable way."

"Poppa, maybe you should . . ."

One look at him and I knew that Poppa shouldn't. I went into the motel and found my mother sprawled on the bed, still crying. I sat down on the edge of the mattress.

"Ma?"

She sat up, rubbed her eyes, and tucked her legs under her rump.

"Ma, I think it's terrific. I mean, you really have a new life for yourself and . . . it's terrific. But I think Poppa is right. I really think you ought to marry him."

"I don't want to hurt your father's feelings, Eddie."

"You won't hurt his feelings, Ma. He'd be happy as anything to give you a divorce, I guarantee it."

"Are you sure?"

"Sure I'm sure. Right now he's hiking in the mountains. He's having the time of his life."

"Anyway, I don't wanna hurt Anita's feelings. And there are the kids."

"How many kids?"

"Six. I don't wanna hurt anybody's feelings."

"Ma, you have to let them decide for themselves. Give them the courtesy of saying no if they're against your marrying Angel."

"You think they'd all approve?"

"From what I can judge, yes, definitely."

"I'll tell you what, Eddie. If they all approve of the marriage and if business picks up in September, I'll marry Angel in October, but only if he never mentions the subject to me again."

"Now you're being sensible."

"Go out and tell him, Eddie. I'll wait here for his reply."

Poppa was reading his newspaper, legs crossed, a dirigible of a cigar in his tiny hand.

"Poppa?"

Eyes on newspaper, "Yes, my son?"

"My mother says that if everyone who is involved in this affair approves of your marriage to her, and if business picks up in September and you never mention the subject to her again, she'll marry you in October."

Eyes on newspaper, "Tell the woman I will agree to her conditions but she must come with me for one week in December to visit the shrine of the Lady of Guadalupe in Mexico City."

I returned to the motel. My mother was at the bureau mirror, putting on makeup. "What did he say, Eddie?"

"He'll agree to everything except he insists that you go with him in December to visit the shrine of the Lady of Guadalupe in Mexico City."

"He wants me to visit a lady?"

"The Lady of Guadalupe in Mexico City."

"What does he want me to visit her for?"

"I believe she's the Virgin Mary."

"He wants me to visit the Virgin Mary?"

"That's what he said, Ma."

"Eddie, I can't do that."

"Why not?"

"It's against the Jewish religion."

"I don't think it's against the Jewish religion just to visit some-one."

"Still . . ."

"He doesn't want you to convert to his religion, does he?"

"No, but I feel peculiar, regardless. We are Jewish, you know."

"I know. But when you get down to it, we're not really Jew-ish."

"My father was . . . a little."

"What should I tell him?"

"Tell him all right. But tell him I'm not getting down on my knees or doing anything like that. I'll stay in the hotel room when he visits what's-her-name."

"Poppa?"

He put the newspaper aside.

"My mother says she agrees so long as you don't ask her to participate in any observances that are contrary to her religious beliefs."

His dark, round face cracked in a smile. "Have a Havana, my son."

"Thank you very much."

"From this day you are of my family, too; you are of my blood and of my heritage. I remember what it was like to be a young man when always there is a broom between the legs. It is easy to do stupid things and bring shame and dishonor to those who are closest to you. Do not do so, my son. Do not. Am I making myself clear to you?"

"Yes, Poppa."

"Remember. Remember what I tell you." He lifted himself from the chair, bellowed his chest as he knotted the belt around his orange robe. "Now I must do what is required of me. Drink wine, my son. Eat of the kosher salami. Celebrate the marriage of your momma Sylvia to a man who has a destiny in the fields of real estate, used automobiles and Bendix washing machines."

He swaggered off, rolling his body with a kind of guileless arrogance. At the motel door he turned, grinned brightly at me, patted the pad of Brillo nesting on his head, and quietly closed the door behind him.

The next day I rode the bus to Miami Beach. It was, as you can expect, nothing resembling what it is today. There were a good many fewer luxury hotels and the hub of the shopping district was at Lincoln Road, downtown. Quite by accident I spotted a Busboy Wanted sign in a cafeteria window on Washington Avenue. I walked in and was interviewed by the owner, Mr. Wallach, a stout, middle-aged man with a square jaw and rimless specs; he smelled like a dentist. (Later on I learned he was a dentist.) He had me fill out a reference card, a request for a work permit and a tax-witholding form before leading me into the kitchen. There I met the day-shift captain of the busboys, a sandy-haired young man with a light, pasty complexion; a set of badly fitting false teeth rattled loosely in his mouth and he spoke, when he did speak, with the broad, nasal inflection of a Bostonian.

His name was George Brenner and he assigned me a hook on the wall for my street clothes. I was then given a white uniform of pants, jacket and apron, a large, rectangular, synthetic sponge, and instructed on how to wipe a table and stack dishes in an aluminum cart. Within the hour I was at work, earning forty dollars for a six-day week, from seven to four, with breakfast and lunch thrown in.

The first week I traveled by bus from the motel to the cafeteria. My mother and Poppa were very proud and supportive. When I told them that it was impractical for me to bus to work every day, they were even more proud and supportive, and they packed my suitcase for me. I moved into a room above the South Seas Saloon on Collins Avenue, with George Brenner and an asthmatic baker named Harry Klein. I have to confess that I neglected my horn that summer, practicing less than an hour a day, generally between five and six, when George was having his swim and Harry Klein was twisting bagels at the Rodney Plaza Hotel. I was into a whole new thing.

You see, George Brenner was a gambler, his specialty was the greyhounds, and every night I'd go off with him to the Flagler racetrack and bet the dogs. As I already mentioned, George wasn't a particularly talkative young man — he could have been inhibited by his clattering false teeth — and it took me a long time to get to know anything about him.

"Don' trus' me, Eddie. I'm a gambler. Y'don' trus' a gambler. They rob y'blind."

We were walking home from the racetrack, nearly fifteen dollars of winnings in our pockets.

"What did you come to Miami for?" I asked him.

"I go wit' the dogs. Where the dogs go, tha's where Georgie Brenner goes."

I was curious to learn how he had lost his teeth. "Did you know Mr. Wallach is a dentist, a real dentist?"

"Tha's how I got me job busin'," he said, flattening his vowels behind his wobbly dentures.

"What do you mean?"

"Me mout' got itse'f infected or somethin'. I was spittin' out all me fuckin' teet', like they was fish bones. I wake up one mornin' an' there's the rest a me fuckin' teet' layin' nex' t'me. Wallach, he put these here plates in me mouth' an' he gimme the job busin' in the caf' t'pay him back."

"They must hurt. They look . . ."

"They're killin' me! These fuckin' teet' are killin' me!" He shook his head in agony, jammed his thumb into his mouth to rearrange the plates. "They're in here temp'rary, t'ough," he continued in a minute. "These here teet' belong to some ol' geezer who didn't pick 'em up. Wallach says soon as I get me anudder bundle, he's gonna gimme a new set that he's makin' special for me. He's not a bad egg."

"What's the most you won on the dogs, George?"

"Oh, I made a bundle, Eddie; a bundle. I once had near six t'ousand clams. I bough' meself a car, I bough' meself a lot a suits, a bough' meself a leat'er coat . . . I had meself some fun wit' those winnin's, Eddie. An' I'm gonna do it ag'in but maybe a hundred times better. But y'listen t'me. Don' y'trus' me, wha'ever I say. I'm a gambler. It's like dope wit' me. Don' y'ever trus' a gambler."

After the track we'd drop into a luncheonette and have a cup of chili or a hamburger before going to bed. The girl working at the counter was named Vicky. I knew she was named Vicky because pinned to her blouse was a chip of wood on which it was spelled out with strips of uncooked spaghetti. To be blunt about it, she was an incredibly fat girl. But she had a pretty, dollish face, the kind of face that God frequently gives to incredibly fat girls to compensate for their incredible fatness. She used pancake makeup and eyeshadow to excess and invariably wore a pair of plastic heart-shaped barrettes in her billowy brown hair.

She had many admirers, Vicky did, particularly among the local cabbies and members of the food-handlers' union. They sat on the counter stools like crows on a telephone wire, waiting for some signal from her before fluttering their wings and flying recklessly around the room to provoke a smile on her pretty, painted face.

"How'd it go tonight?" she'd ask as soon as we walked in, setting teaspoons and paper napkins in front of us.

George would mumble, his nose already buried in the next evening's scratch sheet, underlining time, distance and past performance with the gnawed stump of a pencil.

I'd tighten up and I couldn't say anything other than, "A bowl of chili and an extra pack of saltines, please." Inwardly I knew that Vicky liked me and that if I could put together a string of words, she'd go out with me. But I didn't know what I'd do with her if she did go out with me, and I didn't know if I liked her, anyway. So far as I was concerned, the only thing she had going for her was that she was a girl, and that I knew her by her first name.

We'd go to bed about midnight and sometime during the night Harry Klein, the baker, would come in, light a cigarette, and convulse immediately into an asthmatic cough.

George would take his teeth off the night table and slip them into his mouth. "Jesus Chris', Harry, we tryin' t'sleep. Y'can be sharin' a room wit' anybody wit' your sickness. Jesus Chris', Harry!"

"Water, water," Harry Klein gasped, and I would have to get out of bed and pour it for him.

After a swallow he'd sneak another drag, cough briefly, then break the cigarette, and tuck the cover under his arms. I could see his face in the flickering neon of the South Seas Saloon. He couldn't have been much over fifty, but his vacant eyes were those of an old man, and I suspected that there was more than asthma wrong with him.

"I've been a baker since I was a boy of fourteen," he would murmur to himself, staring at the ceiling. "All my life I worked by the ovens and pulled from them bread and rolls and pastries for people to eat, for people to gain strength from. I'm a married man, for more years than I care to remember; I have children, I have grandchildren, and soon I'll have great-grandchildren. Never was I in trouble, not with the police, not with my bosses, not even with my wife. I'm a good man. Yes, I will say it. I'm a good man. But I am bothered by one question, one question eats away inside me, and for it I don't have an answer. What have I learned during my life? What knowledge have I acquired that gives me a minute's peace? I was born a baby and I will pass away a baby. This disturbs me. Something here is not right. Is it possible to live for so many years and pass away a baby?"

He lit the broken half of his cigarette, inhaled a lungful before jackknifing over like a hand puppet, his head bobbing on his knees in another paroxysm of coughing.

"Jesus Chris', Harry!" George's teeth were back in his mouth.

"Go out in the hall an' do y'fuckin' coughin'. I'm gettin' the landlady after y', I mean it, Harry!"

A beat or two of silence, then: "A man has to learn something from life. He can't pass away a baby. But what I can't figure in my mind is what he's supposed to learn. What? What?"

Then silence again and I would fall asleep.

One day a week, as a rule on Saturday, my mother and Poppa came down from North Hollywood to have lunch with me in the cafeteria. They were both radiant; their happiness seemed to increase in ratio to the size of my mother's stomach. Now that I knew the countermen, I could pile their plates high with food and see to it that their checks were punched for a cup of coffee.

"What do you do after work?" Poppa asked me, shaking a puddle of Tabasco on his sirloin steak.

"I practice."

"And after you practice?"

"I go to the movies or read in bed."

"I will have my eyes on you, Eddie. There is much danger in Miami for a young boy. Remember."

"I spoke to your father last week," my mother said.

"Did you? I was going to . . . How is he?"

"Oh, he's fine. I asked him for a divorce."

"What did he say?"

"Not much. Just whoopeeee!"

"I, too, asked my wife and my six kids," Poppa said.

"What did they say?"

Poppa answered me in Spanish.

"I don't know what that means, Poppa."

He threw his short arms into the air, kicked up his short legs, and yelled, "Vhoopeeeeeee!"

It was a good summer for me. I liked working in the cafeteria; I liked sitting on the stone wall on the beach in the evening, watching the waves tumbling in from the ocean; and I liked playing the dogs at night with George Brenner.

But perhaps what I liked best was staring at girls; not talking to them, of course, not dating or flirting with them, but merely staring at them, their rumps, their hips, their breasts, etcetera, etcetera. No novelty here, admittedly, except that until that summer, as I said elsewhere, I had no interest in girls. Now all of a sudden, with no provocation on my part, I carried between my thighs a constant erection, a permanent protuberance that made sitting awkward and standing even more so. It was, to say the least, an embarrassment. It crippled my stylish walk and destroyed the neat creases in my trousers. I was forced to keep a hand in my pocket, at all times, and hold onto it for dear life. When one hand tired, I switched it to the other hand. And this went on twenty-four hours a day. Even in my sleep I'd be switching it from hand to hand. I guess from a sense of guilt it would occasionally shrink within itself, like a well-fed snake, and I would have both hands to myself. But this happened rarely.

It was near the end of August that George and I really got hot at the racetrack. We hit the quinella, had the winner across the board in the fourth, and were ahead by three hundred dollars after the fifth. By now I knew something about betting the dogs. Standing beside George at the rail, I went over the scratch sheet with him, watched the odds on the board, and scrutinized the dogs to see if they were erratic, sickly looking or squatting on the field to make a ca-ca. George's handicapping was, on the whole, objective, but he would never bet a dog who made a ca-ca before the race.

In the sixth we bet a hound named No Regrets, two hundred to win at four-to-one. I made the mad dash to the window, placed the bet, and returned to George's side. It was only during a race that George let himself go. He talked to the dogs quietly, soothingly, encouraging them to greatness, and once they were out of their boxes and bounding wildly after the mechanical rabbit, he hooted them on, shouting and hollering for all he was worth. At the end of the race, win or lose, he retreated back into himself and buried his nose stoically in the scratch sheet.

No Regrets ran away with it and our winnings were nearly a thousand dollars. We had never come close to winning that amount before, going ahead maybe forty or fifty dollars at the most.

George chewed on his teeth. There was nothing in the seventh race that grabbed him. We sat at the bar and had double ryes and ginger ale. We were feeling terrific. This was the first time we sat at the bar and had a drink during the races. We watched the idiots running back and forth to the windows.

"I'm gonna beat 'em tonigh', Eddie. I got a fas' bitch in the eight'. But y'don' have t'bet more if y'don wan'."

"We're partners, aren't we? Two more drinks here, bartender!"

"Eddie, for y'own good, I ha' t'tell y', don' trus' me. I'm a gambler. Y'don' trus' a gambler. Take y'winnin's an' go get y'self a steak an' a blow job."

"Look, George, we're in this all the way."

"Y'mean tha'?"

"Yes, I do."

"Nobody ever trus'ed me before, Eddie."

"I trust you, George."

"It's har' t'fuck a guy who trus's y'."

"I know. But I trust you. I'd trust you with my life."

"Y'trus' me wit' y'r life?"

"Yes, partner."

"I hope I don' fuck y', Eddie."

"That's up to you, George."

"Okay, here wha' we do. We put the roll on Bobbie Bee, 'cross the board. If we win, I'm gonna go over t'the Sout' Sea. They got a poker game. I play till two in the mornin'. Win or lose, I quit. Fif'y-fif'y. Okay?"

137

"I'm with you, George."

"Can y'see if Bobbie Bee is takin' a crap?"

"He isn't, George. And it looks like he didn't go all night."

"Okay. Here's the roll. If y'run y'r ass, y'can jus' make it."

I ran my ass and I just made it.

We left the track with our hearts in our mouths and approximately thirty-six hundred dollars in cash.

I sat at the bar of the South Seas Saloon, waiting for George to be done with his poker game. The place was almost without light and smelled of rotting vegetation. The muffled voices of hotel workers and hookers scurried in the corners and climbed the walls to the low ceiling where a blade fan took them for a ride. With one hand I slowly sipped my rye, and with the other I held on to a week-old erection. I was high but not drunk. I smiled at everyone who happened to glance at me. They didn't know it, but at that very minute I was in the back room gambling with my eighteen-hundred-dollar winnings.

At midnight Vicky, the Amazon waitress with the doll's face and spaghetti nameplate, came in with an Hawaiian-shirted cabbie. She moved toward me as if we had prearranged the meeting.

"Fancy finding you in this shithouse," she said. "Eddie, Hal. He's from Memphis and he pushes a cab sixteen hours a day to support an invalid wife, a girl friend and several illegitimate children. Hal, Eddie. He's from Brooklyn, a classical musician and a busboy at the cafeteria."

I released my erection and shook Hal's hand.

"How'd it go tonight at the track?" Vicky folded her rear end over a bar stool and made the bar stool disappear.

I put my hand back into my pocket, gripped my erection by the throat, and shifted it into neutral. "Good. Very good," I said. "George is inside gambling with our winnings. It could be a big night for us. Can I buy you and Hal a drink?"

The idea struck Vicky and Hal as a sound one and, after I bought them a drink, Hal bought Vicky and me a drink, which led Vicky to buy Hal and me a drink, which led to some confusion. Hal said he didn't know what he was doing sitting in a bar drinking with me when Vicky had promised him they'd have one drink together and then go to bed, so he could get a decent night's sleep.

Vicky said that she had not promised to go to bed with Hal, but that she had said that if he guessed her weight correctly, she would consider going to bed with him, so he could get a decent night's sleep.

"I bet I can guess your weight," I said.

"All right, Eddie. This arguing is beginning to upset me. The person who comes closest to guessing my weight between you and Hal goes to bed with me, so he can get a decent night's sleep."

We marched out of the saloon and walked in single file up the street to a drugstore, stopping at a scale near the souvenir section.

"Eddie," Vicky then said, "whisper in my ear how much you think I weigh."

I whispered in her left ear, "A hundred seventy and a half pounds."

"Hal?"

He whispered in her right ear.

"You have made your choices. And now we will let the scale speak for itself." She inserted a coin, stood on the scale, and bowed her head, shyly, shutting her eyes. "What did you say, Hal?"

"Two hundred pounds."

"Eddie said two hundred and twenty pounds," she lied. "Now what does the scale say, Hal?"

Glumly, "Two hundred an' twenty-nine pounds."

Vicky opened her eyes. "Eddie wins. Goodnight, Hal."

I admit I was scared as I walked with Vicky to her place. But I had to do it. I had to know how it was done, in case it came up for discussion in the future. I shifted my erection into drive and looped my arm halfway around Vicky's waist — that's as far as I could loop my arm around Vicky's waist. I was debating whether or not to tell her I was a virgin, when she said, "I wasn't going to sleep with Hal, Eddie. I knew he couldn't guess my weight. No one ever guesses I weigh more than two hundred pounds."

"I'd never guess you weighed more than two hundred pounds," I said.

"That's because I don't show most of my weight. Most of my weight is in my thighs."

Gulp. The debate was over. I decided to say nothing, as always. I prayed that she wouldn't hurt me, like Buffy the K. My body shivered in the humid night air. Vicky opened a padlocked gate and we entered a backyard in which there were a number of tacky bungalows. I trailed after her into one of them, trying to stop myself from shivering.

The truth is I didn't want to get laid anymore. I wanted to lie down somewhere and get a decent night's sleep. If questioned in the future I could say, "Of course I've been laid. What a question." Besides, I didn't have to get laid tonight, did I? It wasn't a law. I could get laid another night, with an older woman who was married and tired after cleaning the house all day. And I didn't have to do it with Vicky, a woman who weighed two hundred and twenty-nine pounds and probably got laid every night by cabbies and pastry makers. This was really too much to ask of a serious young horn player.

Slyly I shifted my erection into reverse and started moving toward the door.

"Eddie?"

"Yes, dear?" I was shivering so hard that my voice came out in a mousy squeak.

"I like you. I liked you from the beginning."

"Thank you very much." Squeak.

Good God, she was taking off her clothes, everything!

I hunched my shoulders and wilted against the door, in the darkness. The rest of the small room was lit by a thimbleful of moonlight that filtered through the gauze-curtained window over the bed.

"Do you have asbestos, Eddie?"

"Asbestos?" Squeak. Squeak.

"You don't play with fire, sweets, unless you have asbestos."

Leave me alone, you dirty, filthy woman!

"Here, sweets, put this on and come to bed." She held out a flat condom. I snapped it from her hand and caught a whiff of chili con carne. I tried not to look at her, but I couldn't help watching as she fell back on the mattress and lifted her legs to remove her bloomers. You have to believe me now. I'm not exaggerating. That girl covered the bed completely, making the bed disappear. In the moonlight she appeared to be suspended in air, a huge colossus of flesh from which two giant columns rose like some ancient, totemic statuary. I quickly glanced away. I didn't want to see Vicky naked. I didn't want to see any woman naked. But I especially didn't want to see Vicky naked.

"Are you bashful, sweets? Don't you want me to watch you get undressed?"

I was getting angry, really angry at her for bugging me so much. All right, I said to myself, tearing off my clothes. You asked for it; you're gonna get it. Oh, boy, are you gonna get it. I'll show you. I'll screw you until you're deaf, dumb and blind. I'll show you. I'll show you.

Once undressed I had trouble slipping on the condom. The damn thing had an air bubble at the end of it and there wasn't enough left over to cover my erection. I peeled it off, turned it inside out, blew into it, and tried to slip it on again. But now that it was unrolled, I couldn't get it back on. I struggled to force it on. All right, you bitch, you just wait, you're gonna get yours, you're gonna be sorry you ever started up with The Beast of Brownsville, you're . . . just as soon as I get this . . . you're gonna . . .

It was then that I came, with the condom hanging like a night-cap on the tip of my drooping penis.

Vicky saw the problem I was having immediately. "Eddie, you didn't. Couldn't you wait?" She laughed easily, without rancor, and with a towel she wiped me dry, depositing the soggy condom in a condom disposable spittoon. She moved over an inch. "Lie down, sweets."

I did as she asked, lying beside her on a millimeter of mattress, stiff as a mummy, grinning contentedly at the moon in the window.

"You have to go to sleep now." She pressed me to her. "I'll wake you in about fifteen minutes."

"Do I have to go to sleep now?"

"It's the only way you'll get hard again."

"Do I have to get hard again?"

"You have some sense of humor, let me tell you. Now go to sleep, sweets."

"Goodnight, Vick."

"Goodnight, Eddie. Sleep well."

I must have fallen asleep because the next thing I remember was Vicky nudging me awake.

"Eddie?"

"What's wrong? Is it time for me to go to the cafeteria?"

"It's time for us to make love, sweets."

"Am I hard?"

"Look for yourself."

"Oh, boy. Ohhh, boy. This is hard. This is really hard. This is the hardest it's ever been, Vick." I grabbed my penis and jerked it into neutral.

"How do you wanna do it, Eddie?"

"Oh, I don't know. How do you wanna do it, Vick?"

"Let's do it by ear."

"You want it in your ear?"

"No, no."

"It's okay with me, Vick. I'm ready to go."

"Why don't you get on top of me?"

"On top of you? Way up on top of you? All the way up on top of you?"

"Come on, sweets, let's do it."

I climbed up her side like a gnat climbing up the side of Mount Kilimanjaro. Once on top of her I flopped down on a waterbed of undulating, flabby flesh. I bounced up and down several times for the sheer fun of it, and then set to work. I was surprised at how effortlessly I got into her. I started pumping, singing to myself, Zippity-do-da, zippity-day, my, oh, my, what a beautiful day . . .

"Stop it! Stop it!" Vicky screamed.

"Am I hurting you?"

"Hurting me? You're in my belly button!"

"Is that your belly button I'm in?"

"What do you think you're in?"

"Wow, you have some belly button, Vick. You're a terrific woman."

"Let me put it in for you, Eddie. You'll never find it by yourself."

"Thank you very much."

"It's not as complicated as you're making it. We could have ourselves a lot of . . . Eddie?"

"Yes, dear?"

"You're soft."

"I'm soft?"

"It went soft in my hand."

"Does that mean I have to go to sleep again?"

"Let me talk to it."

"Good idea. I'll listen."

"Hello, there, little fellow," she said to my penis. "Are you having trouble?"

My penis didn't answer her.

"My, my, you're a handsome little fellow. You don't have to

143

be shy with Vicky. Vicky likes you. Vicky wants to see you grow up and become a big, strong man. Don't you want to grow up and become a big, strong man?"

My penis shook its head.

Vicky's patience was fading fast. She grabbed my penis and rubbed it between the palms of her hands as if trying to start a fire in a pile of leaves. I watched her with interest, expecting my penis to go up in smoke any second. It didn't. Instead it pulled itself together. Cautiously Vicky took her hands away, held her breath. And there it was, my big, strong man, fully revived and hopping up and down on its one stiff leg.

"It's hard, Eddie! It's hard!" Vicky cried, clapping her hands.

I clapped my hands, too, and yelled, "Bravo! Bravo! Grandioso! Grandioso!"

I'm not saying it happened, but I could have sworn I heard church bells ringing outside the window.

"Keep it like that, sweets. I'll get on top of you."

Squeak. "On top of me? Vicky, you can't . . ." Squeak. Squeak.

But there was no stopping her now. She fell on me like an avalanche, burying me under tons of fat and bone and muscle and a rump that proliferated into eight double rumps.

"Oh, sweets, I love you. I do love you, you're the tops," she wailed in my ear, putting me into her, which was like putting an inchworm into the Mississippi River. "Push, sweets, can you push?"

"Ahhhhh . . ."

"Oh, you're nice, you're a nice fellow. Oh, this is nice, isn't it, sweets?"

"Ahhhhh . . ."

"I'm coming, sweets. I'm coming. Can you help me? Can you contribute anything? Move? Shake? Breathe on my neck? No? That's all right. I can do it myself. Are you still with me, sweets? Are you there? Talk to me so I'll know you're there."

"Ahhhhh . . ."

"Shhh! Someone's coming. Don't move."

Don't move? Was she kidding me? I couldn't move if my life depended on it. But I could hear what was going on.

Someone did come in. Footsteps echoed in the small room, halted at the bedside. "Is Eddie Davis a guest in this house?" The voice was Poppa's.

"You're trespassing on private property. Be nice enough to close the door behind you," Vicky mumbled, speaking over my head into the pillow.

"They told me at the saloon that I would find my son Eddie here. You have the name Vicky, is that not so?"

"There are hundreds, maybe thousands of Vickys in the Miami Beach area. Why don't you stop annoying us? Can't you see we're in the middle of something?"

"Allow me to look at the gentleman who is beneath you. If he is not my son, I will go and you will not see my face again."

"Is he your father?" Vicky mumbled down to me.

"Ahhhhh . . ."

"Wait outside. If he turns out to be your son. I'll send him out to you."

"I wait. But I am not a man who waits too long. That is my reputation."

Footsteps, and the door slammed shut.

Poppa was standing at the gate. As soon as I approached him, he walked away so that I had to run after him.

"I will go with you to your room, Eddie. You will go back to New York tonight. Am I clear?"

"Yes, Poppa."

"I feared for this. Your mother will know nothing."

"Yes, Poppa."

"Take your hand from your pocket."

I did so, after a quick jiggle and a shift into drive.

"I, too, was wild as a young man. Always it was the broom. Day and night it was the broom. The broom ruled my life. I had no restraint. It was the cause of my marriage to Anita at too young an age. It is not the cause of my marriage to your mother."

"I understand, Poppa."

"Buy yourself a bottle of iodine and when the broom becomes too much for you, cover it with iodine. It will kill it like a mongoose."

"Yes, Poppa. Good idea."

As we rounded the corner, I saw George duck out of the doorway of our rooming house. He moved straight toward us, walking rapidly, his head swinging from side to side. In his arms he hugged my French horn.

I grabbed Poppa by the arm and pulled him behind a car parked at the curb.

"Eddie, what are you . . . ?"

"He's stealing my horn," I whispered to Poppa.

"Who is?"

"Him. George."

"Why do we hide if he steals your horn?" Poppa whispered back to me.

"It's embarrassing. He's my best friend."

Poppa bolted from behind the car and chased after George, shouting and dragging me along with him.

George didn't try to run. He pushed the horn at me. "Wha' I say, Eddie? Wha' I say?" he asked me, his false teeth clattering painfully in his mouth.

"I don't know, George. What did you say?"

"Didn' I sa t'y' not t'trus' me?"

"Yes, you did, George."

"Did I lie t'y'? Tell me if I lie t'y'?"

"No, but . . . what happened to the winnings?"

"I los' it, Eddie. I los' it. Why didn' y'listen t'me? Y'shoulda listen," he yelled at me, and tore the plates of false teeth from his mouth, hurled them viciously against the stone wall on the beach, smashing them to bits.

He then turned on his heels and walked back alone to the rooming house.

146

nine

When I returned to the apartment in Brooklyn, I couldn't believe the changes that had taken place during my absence. Every room was wallpapered, painted, refurnished with collector's pieces of Victoriana and art deco; étagère cabinets displayed carnival glass, pewter plates and embalmed exotic birds; on the floor there were Persian rugs, and the windows were framed with richly colored drapes and valances. Books, prints and museum publications were stacked high on a mirrored coffee table, and the television set had been replaced by a hi-fi unit of stainless steel and teak.

The most striking change, however, was my father himself. That he was going through some kind of metamorphosis was quite apparent. He looked years younger than when I had left him, his complexion was perceptibly lighter and softer, and he had permitted his hair to grow down to the nape of his neck. Even his clothes seemed to fit him better, and he had somehow managed to rid himself of a slight stoop that had always made him appear obsequious. For the first time I had to acknowledge that my father was a fairly handsome man, tall, lean, dimple-chinned. I couldn't remember, as was the case with my mother, why I had been ashamed of him.

Anyway, it was an awkward reunion for the both of us. After

a dinner of avocadoes and chicken mornay in sherry with wild rice and sprouts, we sat down in the living room and drank a Kahlua cordial. I filled my father in on my trip and we laughed at the stories I told him about my mother's pregnancy, her relationship with Angel Medina and my adventures at the racetrack. Then I tactlessly brought up the subject of Peter Scharf. Where was he? Had they gone hiking in the mountains? My father's face darkened; his cheerfulness dissolved. Curtly he said that Peter had reenlisted in the marines and that I was referring to a chapter that he would prefer closed forever. There were words under the words which I interpreted to mean that my father would let me live my life without interference, if I would let him live his life without interference. I wanted to ask him what was happening, in his head, but of course I didn't. I said nothing.

It wasn't a bad arrangement, though. I had no complaints. The apartment was empty a good deal of the time and I could practice whenever and wherever I liked. My father prepared dinner once a week, gourmet meals that we enjoyed together, but he ate out the rest of the week and I did the same. I knew that he continued to bowl with The Alley Cats and that he was now with a barbershop quartet called The Bensonhurst Bluebirds, but what else he did with himself I had no idea.

I attended the Conservatory for the next three years, living with my father. I can't say that any of those years was particularly eventful. I discarded my marine jacket and wore exclusively a black corduroy suit with suede elbow patches, a red silk handkerchief knotted under a cotton shirt and a brim-down, black velour hat. To complement all of this, I put aside my pipe and sported a long South American cheroot. For pocket money I worked at the Post Office on 34th Street during the Christmas holidays, as a waiter in an upstate hotel during the summer holidays, and at a variety of part-time jobs, selling, clerking, packing, delivering, etcetera, etcetera.

And I practiced. I played my horn. I rehearsed with an amateur orchestra in Forest Hills, with the Conservatory orchestra, and with Mario Dinato's quintet. For recreation I'd go to concerts, usually alone, to the movies, a public dance occasionally, a party occasionally. Saturday nights I'd be at a bar near the Conservatory, drinking rye and ginger ale, smoking cheroots, and talking shop with the other students.

They had a ceremony of sorts when I received a Certificate of Graduation from the Grand Army Plaza Conservatory of Music, and my father attended. Afterward he invited me to an elegant restaurant on Fulton Street. I should mention that he had left his job as an upholsterer the year before and was now working as a fabric consultant for Bramwell's on Second Avenue, in the city. (I'll also mention that there wasn't in him a trace of his former miserliness. In fact he threw his money around as if there was no tomorrow.) He ordered for the both of us a delicate mousse of fresh salmon as an appetizer, a Suprême de Volaille en Papillote as the main dish, and a bottle of dry white Pouilly Fuissé. While we were waiting for dinner to be served, he opened up and told me things I didn't want to hear. He was frighteningly solemn and there was no play in his voice.

"Eddie, I've put off speaking to you until this evening because I would never do anything to disrupt your musical career." He brought his lean, mournful face as close to mine as he possibly could and held my eyes tenaciously with his own. "I'm going away this summer and I'll be gone until September. When I come back . . . Eddie, your mother is happily married, you have your musical career, but I . . . I want the right to have a life, too."

"Sure, Dad. Go away. Have a good time. Boy, this is terrific wine. It's a terrific restaurant. We should eat here more often."

"Eddie, when I come back I may not be the same as I am now."

"Where are you going, Dad?"

"Sweden."

"Terrific. I'll keep the apartment clean."

"I won't be coming back to the apartment, Eddie."

"Terrific. Where are we moving to?"

"I've already rented an apartment in the city, nearer to where I work, and you're welcome to stay with me, the door is always open to you, but . . ."

"Listen, Dad, don't worry about it. I've been thinking of getting my own apartment, anyway. It's a terrific idea. We'll each have our own apartment and we'll visit each other."

"I'd like that, Eddie, but you may not want to be seen with me."

"Ah, here comes the mousse! Why don't we eat and discuss this at a future date? I'm starving."

My father agreed, reluctantly, but I could see that he was relieved by the postponement. I gorged myself, stuffed the food into my mouth without tasting any of it. On one level I must have suspected what he was going to tell me and yet, I swear to you, consciously I didn't know anything. And I didn't want to know. (As always.) You have to remember that this was during the fifties and what he was thinking of doing wasn't exactly an everyday occurrence. Perhaps a brighter young man would have guessed the truth and would have discussed it intelligently with his father: Dad, I'm not concerned about myself or mother, but isn't it going to be uncomfortable for you? at work? with the bowling team? with The Bensonhurst Bluebirds? Or, Dad, why do you have to go to such extremes? Why can't you stay in the closet and be what you want to be on weekends like everybody else?

Remember, though, we're talking here about the skinny horn player. He couldn't talk his feelings, even if he knew what they were.

(Do you still think I was exaggerating when I told you I once lived inside myself?)

My father went off to Europe and I found an apartment, a room, really, on Greenwich Avenue in the Village, one flight above a White Tower hamburger joint. I also found a job in a bookstore on University Place, thirty hours a week with a take-home of about forty-two dollars. As for my music, I did the following: I joined Local 802, I started lessons with Mr. Hubner at the Carnegie Hall Annex, and I auditioned for several out-of-town orchestras. I bought two more corduroy suits, one tan and one olive green, for day wear, and I picked up a secondhand tuxedo (which could be worn with my black velour hat), for evening wear; in addition I gave up the cheroots and returned to my pipe, now smoking a navy-cut Cavendish blend purchased at a tobacconist's on 8th Street.

I hung out with no one, I was into no scene, participated in no political, social or artistic goings-on. After practice, work, a lesson, or a visit to the union hall, I would put on my tuxedo, bow tie, velour hat, clamp a glowing pipe between my teeth, and make the rounds. I went to Louie's, Julie's, the Cedar Tavern and San Remo's, of course. Habitually I stood at the end of the bar, drank tap beer slowly, puffed on my pipe, and grinned at any one who looked my way. I had a secret and it wrapped me in a cozy little cocoon of conceit. One day they would hear me play the horn. One day they would recall the evening they had seen a skinny, tuxedoed young man with a pipe in his mouth standing at the end of the bar, and they would kick themselves for not having taken advantage of his accessibility. A couple of hours and more than a couple of beers later, with a pleasant buzz in my head, I would walk the silent streets back to my room above the White Tower and dream of playing with the Philharmonic.

I wrote to my father regularly and received a few picture cards from him, the last postmarked Paris and informing me that he was coming home shortly. In all my letters to him I wrote my new address and phone number, but fall came and went and I hadn't heard a word from him. I dropped in at Bramwell's, the fabric house on Second Avenue. I was told that my father no longer worked there and no one knew where he was. The man I spoke to didn't snicker or act in any but a respectful manner.

I did hear from Perry Reese. He phoned one night.

"How did you get my number?" I asked him.

"Your father gave it to me."

"You saw my father?"

"Several times. Eddie, come on over. This is important."

"How is my father? What did he . . . ?"

"I'll expect you at nine. Take down my address. Your father sends you his love and lots of hugs and kisses."

Perry Reese had also moved to the Village. He lived on West 12th Street, in a four-storied building with a garden in front and a brass-hinged oak door. I was disappointed. I was hoping he lived in a tenement and was on welfare. While I was at the Conservatory, he had transferred to New York University and was now going for a law degree. I rang the buzzer and the buzzer rang back. I walked into a well-lit corridor and walked up a flight of stairs. Before pushing a second buzzer, I brushed off my tuxedo, shined my shoes against my pants-leg, and tightened my bow tie.

"Come in! It's open!" It was Perry's voice and it came from somewhere inside the apartment. I went in, passed through a large living room with a fireplace and a kitchen with farmhouse table and chairs. "In here!" Perry's voice brought me into the bathroom.

Son of a bitch! He had planned it like this! He had deliberately and cunningly planned it so that I would find him sitting in a tub of water with a girl on her knees, soaping his scrofulous back!

"I'm glad you could come," he said, rubbing a sudsy sponge in his armpits. "I was afraid you'd be defensive."

"Why should I be defensive?"

"We'll talk about that later. Eddie, I want you to meet my wife, Raquel."

Son of a bitch! What the hell was a twenty-two-year-old snot-nose doing with a wife? And living in an apartment of more than one room while still going to school?

"Perry talks about you all the time," Raquel said, lifting her face to me. Son of a bitch! She was beautiful! And underneath her terry robe, I could see her nice, round, milky boobs. Son of a bitch!

"Raquel's an actress," Perry said, wringing out the sponge. "She's doing a pilot for a new TV series. Why don't you take Eddie into the living room and give him a drink, hon? I'll join you in a minute."

I sat on the Hepplewhite sofa and swallowed the brandy as soon as it was in my hands. Raquel refilled the snifter, then sat down in a Hepplewhite chair, threw her naked legs over its arm, and lit a cigarette.

"It must have been an awful experience for you and Perry," she said.

I put on a tragic mask, thinking that it befitted the event she was describing, an event of which I had no knowledge.

"He's told me stories about you two growing up in the slums of Brooklyn that were the most horrifying things I ever heard," she explained. "It's a miracle that you two escaped without permanent injury."

"Yes, it was tough. Very tough." I swirled the brandy in the snifter and downed it to eradicate the "horrifying" memory.

"Were you with Perry the summer Bummy Margolis shot at him with a magnum revolver?"

"No, I was away that summer. In a P.A.L. camp for children with scurvy."

"Horrifying. What you two have been through . . . It's no wonder Perry says you're like a brother to him."

"We're closer than brothers, Raq. Sometimes when I have cramps, I feel that somehow, somewhere, Perry has cramps, too. It's spooky." The liquor must have been working on me. I wanted to pick the painted toenails off her feet and chew on them.

"Perry admires you enormously. He says you're a fantastic horn player."

"Perry doesn't lie," I lied.

Which brought Perry into the living room, sparks flying from his teeth and polished head. I have to admit the kid had style: his face was perpetually tanned (later on I learned he used a sunlamp daily); he wore turtlenecks, Viyella shirts, chinos, twills, belted jackets and jodhpurs (later on I learned he bought his clothes from a mail-order house in Maine); he had curly, yellow hair, almost perfect features, and a smile that could cripple you. Add them all together and you have my "brother," a number one son of a bitch!

In a polite but firm tone of voice, he asked Raquel to wait in the bedroom and sat down on the sofa beside me. He carefully unwrapped a stick of gum and slipped it into his mouth, like a communicant taking the holy wafer. He did nothing spontaneously: every word and action was performed, acted out, an elaborate dramatization of some internal script of his own creation.

"Can we be brutally frank with each other, Eddie?"

"Why did my father call you and not call me?"

"If you want to go crazy and bang your head against the wall, go ahead and do so. I'm not going to stop you."

"Did you see my father?"

"Yes."

"Why did my father see you and not see me?"

"Here's the bottle of brandy, buddy. Drink up. Take a big swallow."

"What did my father look like?"

"After you take a big swallow."

A big swallow. Choke. Choke. "What did my father look like?"

"Gorgeous."

Another big swallow. Choke. Choke. "He did?"

"Eddie, you may not be aware of it, we've never spoken about it explicitly, but you are my oldest and, emotionally, because of our common childhood, my closest and dearest friend."

"We are?"

"Yes, we are. That I should be placed in this fiduciary position by your father attests to the indisputability of what I'm saying."

"What do you mean my father looks gorgeous?"

"Eddie, I'm not worried about your father. Your father is happier than he's ever been. I am worried about you, buddy. After I tell you what I'm compelled to tell you because of my fiduciary position, I want you to make an appointment with my doctor."

"Your doctor?"

"Doctor Zamichow. He's a brilliant psychiatrist and he'll give you the sort of help you'll be needing for the next dozen years or so."

"What's gonna be wrong with me?"

"Your father . . . Your father, Eddie, is searching to find his way in a jungle of alternate life styles."

"When he went to Sweden did he . . . did he get out of the jungle?"

"No. He saw some doctors there and they spoke, but he hasn't reached a decision yet."

"He's still my father?"

"Yes. He has been taking hormones, though."

"I was going to ask you that next."

"He's been taking them for a number of years."

"They must have cost him a fortune."

"They did. You could say he's going through a period of exploration and experimentation."

"May I ask, Perry, the nature of his exploration and experimentation? Or is that asking too much?"

"I can't answer all your questions."

"Because of your fiduciary position?"

"Yes."

"You don't have to explain. Go on, please."

"I can say that outwardly your father has blossomed into an

entirely new entity with an entirely new personality and an entirely new set of goals and values."

"But he's still my father?"

"Yes, although he has given himself an entirely new name."

"What's my father's new name?"

A pause. "Phyllis."

Another big swallow, from the bottle this time. Choke. Choke. "Phyllis?"

"Phyllis Deedee, that's double-e double-e."

Well, there it was. Something to think about for the rest of my life. I'm not sure how I felt when I first heard the news of my father's search for "an alternate life style." Numb, yes; angry, yes. But perhaps the overriding feeling was one of annoyance. What did I need this for? Why couldn't he have disappeared, lived in Europe, and left me out of it? Why was he (and everyone else I knew) always dragging me away from my horn, distracting me with their hang-ups? What did any of it have to do with me?

"He'll phone you, buddy. He wants to leave you alone for a while to digest what's happening. He says that he wants only what's best for you. If you choose not to see him again, he understands."

I picked a flake of tobacco from the satin lapel of my tuxedo, put on my black velour hat with the brim down, and I walked to the door without saying good night, without saying anything.

I didn't hear from my father that fall or winter. He phoned at the beginning of spring.

"Eddie?"

"Yes?"

"Guess who?"

I recognized my father's voice at once. It wasn't high-pitched or effeminate. It was my father's voice. Maybe a little huskier, tremulous, but I assumed that that was due to nervousness. The problem was that I didn't know what to call him. Dad? Phyllis? Miss Deedee?

So I said, "Who is this, please?"

"It's your father, Eddie."

Oh, my father, of course. "How are you, Father? Are you all right, Father?"

"Eddie?"

"Yes, Father?"

"Don't call me father."

"What should I call you?"

"What everyone else calls me."

"What's that, Fa . . . Sir?"

"Phyl. Eddie, you know why I didn't phone sooner, don't you? I wanted to but . . . Are you all right? How's the music going?"

"Terrific, Phyl. I had a recording job this winter and I played twice with a military band, for money, in Parsippany, New Jersey, and . . . Phyl?"

"Yes?"

"You weren't hospitalized this winter, were you?"

"No. I still haven't decided."

"You haven't?"

"The prospect frightens me."

"It does?"

"Don't try to influence me, Eddie."

"I'm not saying anything."

"The decision is entirely my own."

"It is, Da . . . Fa . . . Phyl."

"Don't be disrespectful."

"I'm not, honest. When can I see you?"

"Do you want to?"

No, I thought, but I said, "We can't go through life never seeing one another again, can we?"

"Do you know Delaney's on Sheridan Square?"

157

"Sure."

"I'll be in the rear booth, under the fire-exit sign, tonight at ten." And the phone clicked dead.

Oh, boy. Ohh, boy, was I sick, was I shaking, was I ready to throw up. I could have killed my father and done a better job of it than Oedipus. How dare he! How dare he burden me with his lunacy! How dare he jeopardize my career and my future because he hadn't had the moral guts to decide what the hell he was thirty years ago, before he married my mother, before he impregnated her with a horn player! How dare he!

I was filled with self-pity, reeked and stank with self-pity. Why me? Why? Why was I chosen to carry this cross? Wasn't the road ahead treacherous enough? Weren't the odds against me high enough? Was it a test? Was that it? Was I still being tested by some superior authority and/or Nelson and Amanda? That had to be it! Otherwise it was too cruel and gratuitous to make any sense. Yes, I was being tested, I concluded. This was my cross, my special cross because I was special. I was probably destined to be the first famous French horn player whose father was on the brink of womanhood!

I got into my tuxedo, knotted the bow tie, stuck my hat on my head, and went off to meet my father and procreator, Phyllis Deedee, double-e double-e.

I entered Delaney's. It was almost pitch-black inside. Amber wall lamps seemed to have no purpose but to illuminate their own opaque shades. With my hands groping in front of me, I moved blindly to the rear, passing a number of bent, shapeless shadows at the bar. I saw the fire-exit sign, but there was no booth nearby. I stood under the sign and puffed my pipe, nonchalantly.

"Here, Eddie. I'm over here," my father's voice called from the darkness.

I moved to the voice, bumped my shin on a bench, and sat down, slowly raising my eyes to the figure sitting opposite me. I could vaguely make out a cloche hat with an impenetrable veil falling down from its brim and a single strand of pearls shining luminously in the darkness. I could see nothing else.

"Hi, Phyl, how's it going? It . . . It's pretty dark in here, isn't it?" I laughed stupidly, feeling around the table for an ashtray. My hand accidentally landed on my father's hand; he withdrew it as if he had been touched by a leper.

"I'm sorry, Eddie." His voice was a trifle higher than on the phone, but it was still husky, tentative, like a voice that hadn't settled into its own chromatic scale. "I'm sorry for this and for everything," he said. "If it's any consolation to you, I'm very, very happy, happier than your mother even."

"Dad . . . Phyl, you don't have to go into it." That wasn't what I wanted to say either. "You have your life, I have my life, mother has her life."

"I believe I understand her now, Eddie."

"You understand Ma?"

The veil floated up and down. "I can sympathize with some of the things she had to deal with. Her life with me wasn't a bed of roses."

"It's all in the past. We don't . . ."

"Is she really happy with the Cuban cigar maker?"

"He's in the motel business, Phyl. And she is happy. I spoke to her recently. She had a son, you know."

"I'm glad for her. What's his name?"

"Jesus."

"Jesus?"

"She calls him Jimmy, though. For religious reasons."

"You didn't tell her anything about . . ."

"No, no. You didn't want me to, did you?"

"Absolutely not."

"Do you mind if I light my pipe, Phyl?"

"Please, don't."

"Can I light it under the table?"

"If you have to. I'm very uncomfortable, Eddie."

"I know. So am I. I'll only take a minute." Under the table, I lit my pipe and in the match's flare I saw the bottom half of my father. Oh, boy. Ohhh, boy. My stomach did a flip-flop. The legs weren't bad, one folded over the other, hairless and shapely in sheer nylon stockings. But the large feet in the open-toed pumps! Oh, boy. Ohhh, boy. I blew out the match and popped up again, thankful now for the darkness.

"So . . . What have you been doing with yourself, Phyl? Read any good books lately?" My voice sounded high-pitched and effeminate.

"I have a wonderful new job, Eddie, and a wonderful apartment in the city and . . . I am indebted to you for creating an interest in me for music. I'm with a new quartet, The Lollipops. We travel around the country and enter singing contests. We came in fourth in Philadelphia last month and . . . But what about you? What was that about getting work?"

"I am. There are a couple of things happening, good things. I'm really encouraged."

"I want you to take this, Eddie." He pushed three one-hundred-dollar bills at me.

"Phyl, you don't . . . I have . . ."

"Please. I'm not a miser. When I was married to your mother, I suppose I hoarded my money as I hoarded my true nature. But money means nothing to me anymore. I want you to have it."

I took the money rather than argue with him. "Thanks. Can we have dinner together one night?"

"Soon. I think we should go about this very slowly and not hurt each other. If an emergency arises, call this number." He wrote it on a napkin, no address, and handed it to me. "Short of an emergency, I prefer that you wait until I contact you."

"Whatever you say, Phyl."

"Eddie, do you remember my instructions to you when I pass away?"

"Yes, Sir. I go up to the teller's window at the Brownsville Bank for Savings and I say to Mr. Arthur, 'Hello, Mr. Arthur.

My dad spoke to you about me before he passed away, unexpectedly. I'm four-nine-two-dash-eight-three-six-four."

"That's it."

"Is anything ... ?"

"No, it's just that I withdrew all the money."

"You ... ?"

"There isn't a penny left."

"There isn't? For my future?"

"I may need it for medical expenses."

"Oh."

"In case I decide to have the operation."

"I see."

"It's really a series of operations."

"I see."

"It's not as simple as people are led to believe."

"I couldn't do it."

"I'm not asking your opinion, Eddie."

"I wasn't ..."

"It's my life to do with as I please."

"I wouldn't ..."

"And don't be smart with your father."

What the hell were we talking about?

"It's an incredibly complicated series of operations. What they do is utilize one's own sensitized tissues to create an entirely new and organically functioning ..."

"Phyl, why don't you take the three hundred dollars? I have no use for it, really."

He took the money rather than argue with me. "Thank you. I may need it. Do you have a date tonight?"

"No, I'm free ..."

"Unfortunately, I have a date. I must go now. I'm late. I do like your tuxedo, Eddie. Try wearing pastel shirts. They can be very effective." And with a rustle of silk and nylon, he was up and out before I could get a decent look at him.

ten

Well, it was bound to happen. This week the manager of the Geneva Hotel requested that I drop in and have a chat with him. It's hard to believe that I've been here since August 8th. It's now the first week of November. I'm forty-five years old.

Happy birthday, Eddie.

In a letter slipped under the door, the manager, Mr. Raymond, complained of (1) my refusing to allow the chambermaid into the suite; (2) leaving the phone off the hook so that I couldn't be reached by him or other members of his staff; (3) disturbing the regular routine of the hotel with my horn playing and on occasion shouting and dancing to the displeasure of my neighbors; (4) my paying a reduced rate, which was no longer acceptable to him.

Lately, I admit, I have been letting myself go. I seem to have lost interest in "keeping up appearances." I spend the greater part of the day practicing the horn, going for six, seven hours at a stretch, often merely fingering the valves when I have no breath remaining in me. Evenings, after my walk, I pick up my dinner in a brown paper bag and bring it back with me to the hotel. It's weird but I haven't bumped into anyone I know. Where is everyone? Where are the people I used to work with? socialized with? dealt with? It's as if I never lived in this city.

No matter. I'm determined to call no one, see no one, give the horn all the energy and concentration I have. I thought I'd be ready by now. I'm afraid I have a way to go yet. No matter.

Well, there was just no avoiding Mr. Raymond. This morning the hall porter, Mr. Alfred, stood in the corridor and rang the buzzer for I don't know how long.

"Mr. Davis, Mr. Raymond is waiting for you downstairs! Mr. Davis, we know you're in there! Are you ill, Mr. Davis? Open up, please. Open up this door!"

He stuck a key in the lock and rattled the knob. Luckily I had the chain on, and he eventually went away. But I have to put a stop to it.

Before seeing Mr. Raymond, I had my hair cut, my beard trimmed, my nails manicured, and I got into the only pressed suit I have left, a Bergdorf Goodman chalk pinstripe. I knocked on the manager's door in the lobby and entered a carpeted office. Mr. Raymond was a Humpty-Dumpty figure of a man, with gold-rimmed specs and hair parted and plastered to his egg-shaped head. He jumped up from behind his desk as soon as I closed the office door.

"Ah, Mr. Davis! Ah, sit down, sit down." He motioned me into a chair and patted his hands together, as if he was making a snow-ball.

I didn't sit down and that unnerved him. He stared at me uncertainly. "Ah, don't you want to sit down, Mr. Davis?"

"I'd rather not."

"You're not . . . annoyed with me, are you?"

"Yes, I am. I'd like to speak to your supervisor."

"My supervisor? I . . . I don't have a supervisor."

"You don't? What kind of hotel is this?"

"Mr. Davis, uhhh, I'm the manager of this hotel and, uhhh, I'm only accountable to the Board of Directors."

"Then I'd like to speak to the Board of Directors."

"That . . . That would be impossible. What, uhhh . . . What is your complaint?"

"One, the service here is deplorable; two, I'm being harassed and badgered by the staff; and three, the supposedly clean linen I get from the chambermaid is bespotted by spirochetes!"

"By, by . . . what?"

"Spirochetes! Sperm! Semen! Come! It's disgusting! I have a good mind to check out this afternoon!"

"Ah, yes, Mr. Davis, that's what I'd like to discuss . . ."

"But I can't check out this afternoon."

"Why not? Ah, we can facilitate . . ."

"I'm in the middle of a project that is of the utmost importance. I'm not permitted to say any more. Can you see to the linen, Mr. Raymond?"

"Ah, yes, I . . ."

"Then I'll hold off speaking to the Board of Directors. Thank you."

(Why couldn't the skinny horn player have inherited a little of my aggressiveness? Why was he always so serious, so vulnerable, so incapable of asserting himself and taking control of his own life? Sometimes I have no pity for him at all.)

I met Jennifer née Koussevitzky, no relation to the conductor, at a party given by Perry Reese. I wore, during those days, double-breasted gangster suits, dark shirts, light-colored ties and a greenish felt fedora that had a six-inch brim. I had moved from the room above the White Tower to a railroad flat on Rivington Street, and I was working as a clerk for a stationery firm. I continued to play with several nonprofessional groups, substituted briefly in the pit of a musical at Jones Beach, marched in Queens and Staten Island with the Sons of Italy band, and I took courses in composition at the New School for Social Research. Along the way I switched back to Sir Walter Raleigh pipe tobacco.

It was on a Friday night, in the summer, that I was invited to Perry's party. He had many such parties but most were given exclusively to further his business relationships. Although he had finished law school, he never practiced law. The previous year he had divorced Raquel and was now sleeping with, among others, a forty-year-old attorney for Associated Artists Representatives, Karen Morrison; she had succeeded in getting him a job at A.A.R. as an agent in their television department.

In those days I suffered from the disability of always being early. I couldn't help myself. If I started out late, I was early. So naturally I arrived early for Perry's party, even though I had walked twice around the block, browsed in a bookstore, and had a scotch in a neighborhood bar.

Perry was still showering and Karen Morrison was giving instructions to a student bartender and a sachet-smelling serving maid. I graciously offered to spread Gourmandise on the sesame wafers, and my offer was graciously accepted. In the kitchen (wearing my gangster suit and green felt hat, which I never took off, not even indoors, this to conceal for as long as possible my dwindling supply of God-given hair), I sat at the farmhouse table and performed my chore diligently, rewarding myself with a tumbler of scotch after each third sesame wafer properly besmeared. Guests arrived in pairs, in foursomes, in droves; the noise coming in from the living room was deafening, but I was, too, yes, anxious, uptight, unsure of myself, to leave the kitchen. Perry stuck his polished head in and waved for me to join the party. I raised my scotch and drank to his undoing. I was by now besmearing rabbit pâté on my fingernails. Inwardly I carried on the following conversation.

Boy, this is some party.

Boy, it's a terrific party.

Boy, I'm having fun. Are you having fun?

Boy, I'm having more fun than you are. You don't know how to have fun.

Whatta you mean, I don't know how to have fun? I'm having fun.

So why don't you laugh? Why don't you sing? Why don't you go in and meet a girl and take her home and make love to her in the bathtub with the faucets turned on?

You wanna see me meet a girl and take her home and make love to her in the bathtub with the faucets turned on?

Yeah.

Okay. Okay. Watch me move. Watch me go and do my stuff. Here I go, hot to trot, watch me move and do my stuff. Hot to trot. Do my stuff. Watch me trot and do my stuff!

A bit unsteadily I went into the living room, pressed myself between the packed groups of strange people, and reached the window at the other end of the room. Once there I realized that I didn't have a drink. So I pressed myself between the packed groups of strange people and I had the bartender fill a glass for me. Then I pressed myself between the packed groups of strange people and returned to the window. I looked out. It was too dark to see anything. I looked at the groups of strange people. They all looked strange to me. I looked out the window again. It was still too dark to see anything, but nobody knew it, so I continued to look out the window and pretended that I could see something.

"Why don't you take off your fucking hat!" Those were the first words Jennifer née Koussevitsky spoke to me. She was seated in a chair, penciling beards and mustaches on faces in a fashion magazine as she drank from a can of Budweiser beer.

I knew I had to pick my words carefully or I would lose her. "What do you do for a living?" I asked her.

"None of your fucking business," she answered, and was about to return to her doodling when I came back with, "I'm a French horn player. I was born in Brooklyn, New York. My name is Edward Davis and I'm twenty-nine years old. I've never been married."

"No shit," she said.

But I went right on, pushed merrily along by the booze. "Tell me this, Miss, I'm curious, what do you think of the music of Charles Ives? I'm thinking of his Second Piano Sonata in particular? No thoughts? Cat got your tongue? Oh, I forgot to ask you. Have you read Camus's *Plague*, Sartre's *Nausea* or Kierkegaard's *Fear and Trembling*? No? Cat still got your tongue? Oh, by the way, can I get you another can of Bud or would you prefer a cold bottle of Schlitz?"

I could see that my line was working. She stared at me for a full minute before speaking. "Why don't you take that fucking hat off?" she yelled at me again.

"I'm sorry, Miss. I can't take my hat off."

"Why not?"

"Because if I take my hat off, my head'll fall off!" And I broke in half, spilling laughs over the both of us. Oh, God, I *was* funny, I *was* hilarious, I *was* intelligent, I *did* keep myself phsyically clean, and why couldn't she just rub my penis for a few seconds and let me go home and dream of playing with the Philharmonic?

"You're drunk," she said curtly, putting a Vandyke beard on Frank Sinatra.

"You're wrong there, Miss. I did have a drink or two, but I'm nowhere near my capacity. I have an insatiable capacity. I can sit down with anyone in this room and in my present condition drink them underneath the proverbial table."

"Bullshit," she said.

"Why is that what you said, Miss?"

"Do you drink beer?" She raised her eyes to mine as she opened a sack of Bull Durham with her teeth and tapped out a cigarette for herself.

"Yes, I do. I'm a very good beer drinker. I majored in beer drinking at the Conservatory."

"Sober up. I'll meet you in the kitchen in twenty minutes. I'll match you beer for beer and whip your ass."

167

"I think I'd like that, Miss. I think I'd like that very much." I tipped my green fedora and walked off, stiffly, left the apartment and sat on the stoop to sober up and psyche myself for the beer drinking contest with Jennifer née Koussevitzky.

Let me describe her for you, please. Her skin was dark, tawny, the color of Nestlé's cocoa; her nose was small, flat, with somewhat wide nostrils; she had incredibly lovely, ebony-bright eyes, and her short, ink-black hair hung neatly in bangs on her forehead; her teeth were large and slightly bucked, which made her full, fleshy mouth deliciously appealing; she was built as thin as a rail, but it was a model's thinness, the hip jutting forward, her walk easy and feline, her teenybopper's breasts coming alive with her body's least movement.

When we first met she smoked (tobacco sprinkled her clothes and her fingers were faintly nicotine-stained), drank (beer only, out of a can or bottle, starting at dinner and downing about a dozen glasses by bedtime), cursed like a truck driver, and dressed like a construction worker, bundling herself in coveralls, baggy pants, denim shirts, army-and-navy seconds, ankle-high hiking boots and frayed sneakers; she rarely wore a dress or skirt, never put on makeup or gave a thought to her appearance.

For the longest time all I could learn from her was that she had gone to private schools, had a bachelor's in art from Brandeis, worked briefly and without enthusiasm as a model, and that now, at the age of twenty-six, earned her living as a window designer for a company called Starlight Designs.

Well, I was as ready as I ever would be for Jennifer née Koussevitzky, but the booze was still buzzing in my head. I rose from the stoop and went back into the apartment. She was waiting for me at the kitchen table, a pyramid of beer cans in front of her. There were almost as many guests in the kitchen as there were in the living room. I assumed, correctly, that she had told them about the contest.

I sat down, punctured the first can with a flourish, wiped my mouth with my jacket sleeve, and drank the beer down thirstily without lifting the can from my mouth.

I received a round of applause, stood up, and curtsied.

Jennifer raised a can of beer to her mouth, wedged it between her buckteeth, and drank it down neatly.

She received a louder round of applause, stood up, and bowed.

More guests squeezed into the kitchen. Before downing the second can, I looked up to see Perry shaking his head unhappily. Karen Morrison was having conniptions. I was feeling terrific. Like a million bucks. As we drank, we wisecracked, told jokes, bantered back and forth like a pair of old vaudevillians. How perfectly beautiful she was! How perfectly beautiful everything was! Sitting there and drinking with Jennifer, surrounded by a crowd of spectators, their peals of laughter encircling our heads with tinseled halos . . . It was perfect, absolutely perfect!

I remember saying, "I want to put a née in front of your Koussevitzky, Jennifer."

I remember her saying, "I'd rather you put a knee in front of my knish."

I remember saying, "You know, I was so poor as a kid that if I didn't have an erection I had nothing to play with."

I remember her saying, "You poor thing. Did you hear that? The kid had nothing to play with!"

Laughter. Joke. Laughter. After a while I stopped drinking beer and I drank Jennifer, wallowing my tongue in her, filling my mouth and stomach with her, bloating myself with her skin and eyes and long-ribbed body.

I know what you're waiting to hear. That she drank me under the proverbial table, that I passed out or threw up or, in one way or another, made a fool of myself. Well, you're right. I did all three but not in that order: first, I made a fool of myself by pouring a can of beer into my green hat and putting my green hat on my head; then I threw up in the bathroom, took a shower, and greeted everyone in my underwear; then I passed out.

I gave away my gangster clothes and I started dating Jennifer. I got into the habit of asking her what she'd be wearing and I'd try to come as close to her outfit as I could. On one date I'd be wearing Lee coveralls, a lumberjack shirt with sleeves rolled to the elbows, a pair of heavy construction boots and a Panama straw hat; on another date I'd have on khaki pants with cuffs rolled to the ankles, a Mexican serape, basketball sneakers and a pendant earring. We were matched, duplicated, xeroxed, and not only in clothes. We evolved preferences and attitudes distilled from each other's fantasies.

I was in love with Jennifer née Koussevitzky, but I rarely if ever said I love you. I said to her, Marry me. I said to her, Love me. I said to her, Be with me for the rest of my life.

Ah, but you should have seen the skinny horn player in the Panama straw hat in the throes of love! How he carried on! How he preened himself and crooned love's sweet tune and skipped and flew down Rivington Street with a bunch of pushcart daisies in his hand! If he had a date for eight, he'd be walking around her block at seven. If she said phone when you get home, he'd phone on the way home, from a drugstore, a delicatessen, a sidewalk booth, a bar, a hotel lobby, etcetera, etcetera. If they were going to a restaurant for dinner, he'd be there a week ahead of time to reserve a quiet corner table and introduce himself to the waiters so he'd be recognized when he showed up with her. If she said she was working and couldn't meet him, he'd be in her office anyway, chin in hand, waiting until she was done, and then he'd walk her home, his arm wrapped around her like a vine, grinning from ear to ear at buildings, at fire hydrants, at cars and at trees.

He played the horn for her and there were tears in her lovely eyes and she said, "Promise you'll never give up music, Eddie," and he was too grateful to say, Thank you very much, and there were tears in his eyes, too. She brought all kinds of food and delicacies to his apartment, baklava, bratwurst, St. John's bread, ravioli, Greek salads, sour tomatoes, and they sat in the middle of the mattress on the floor (there was no bed in the room) and they ate and talked and listened to strings and woodwinds and horns.

How he loved to watch her eat! watch her put food in her pink mouth and chew it between her large, white teeth and swallow it with an expression of absolute bliss. How he loved to watch her guzzle beer and chain-smoke from her sack of Bull Durham and pour forth a string of obscenities in a mock-tough snarl that was free of all vulgarity. How he loved to study her, the tawny texture of her skin, the symmetry of her long, thin fingers, her knees, her shoulder blades, the dark, musty down at the nape of her neck.

"How can you love me?" he once asked her.

"You're beautiful," she answered.

"No, I'm not. I'm singularly unattractive."

"No, you're not. You're beautiful."

"Is that the only reason you love me? Because I'm physically beautiful?"

"No, you have humor and intelligence."

"Is that the only reason you love me? Because I have humor and intelligence?"

"No, you're an artist. You have sensitivity and imagination."

"That's true. That happens to be true," he said.

And yet (and here's the hitch, my friend), she wouldn't sleep with him. This after a year or so of being together, day and night, night and day, hands and lips rubbed raw from constant friction. Of course our horn player practiced his touch-and-come technique (a technique that he had developed over the years which made it possible for him to reach orgasm by merely touching or standing in close proximity to a member of the opposite sex), and always, if required, she stroked him to quiescence. But

171

that was it. The line was drawn. No penetration. Not even a quick, lousy, catch-as-catch-can coitus interruptus!

"Why not? Why not? This is the sixties! You're driving me crazy, for cryin'-out-loud! You're not a virgin. I know you're not a virgin. Are you a virgin?"

"Don't be a putz, Eddie. I've been wooed, screwed, and tattooed all over the place."

"Then why not me? What am I, an orphan?"

"I'm motivated by my experiences, Eddie. Every time I get involved sexually with someone the relationship deteriorates. I don't want it to happen to us. I don't want us to lose what we have."

"Okay, fine. I'll buy that. But what am I supposed to do? I have a raging, living animal here, tell me what to do with it and I'll do it!"

"We can do touch-and-come or I'll whack it for you."

"No! Don't whack it for me. Don't do me any favors. If I want it whacked, I'll whack it myself!"

"Don't be like that. Let me . . ."

"Leave it alone! Get your hands away! Take them away! Jeez, this is incredible. I finally meet a girl I can talk to and I can't get laid. Go figure life. Go ahead and figure life."

"I wish I could help, Eddie. I really wish I could," she'd say, resting her beautiful face on my chest.

And they would lie like that, on the mattress on the floor, night after night, Jennifer in her panties and the young horn player in his Gimbel's underwear, both of them staring dumbly at his erection as it climbed slowly up toward the chandelier.

"When was the first time?" I asked her one night.

"I was thirteen."

"When was the second time?"

"I was thirteen."

"How many times did you get laid when you were thirteen?"

"Between fifteen and twenty."

"Didn't you go to school when you were thirteen?"

"Yes, mornings only."

"Are you lying to me?"

"Yes, let me whack it off."

"Take your hands away! Take them away! Jen, in all serious-ness, you asked me to forgo certain prerogatives that every lover has. All right, I'm willing to go along with that, tem-porarily. The least you can do is level with me."

"What do you wanna know, lover?"

"When was the first time?"

"I was seventeen, the last year of high school. I went away for a weekend with . . ."

"No names, please. Did you go away with him for the whole weekend?"

"Yes."

"Friday and Saturday nights?"

"Yes."

"Was he seventeen?"

"Yes."

"Did his parents go, too?"

"No."

"Where did you go?"

"A ski resort. Bromley."

"He had money at seventeen to rent a room for the whole weekend at a ski resort?"

"Yes. He was independently wealthy. Don't forget, Eddie, I went to a private school. All the kids there had money."

"How was it?"

"The campus was nice but I hated the faculty."

"Not the school! Not the school! I'm talking about . . ."

"Oh, it was all right. I came."

"You did? You had an orgasm?"

"Uh-huh."

"The first time you were penetrated by a human penis you had an orgasm?"

"Uh-huh."

"Was it a multiple?"

"It was like fifty firecrackers going off one after the other."

"Did he hurt you?"

"No. He was very sweet. As I was coming he fanned my face with his jockey shorts."

"I see. Tell me more."

"More what?"

"More dirty stories."

"Eddie . . ."

"Did you ever sleep with a jock at college?"

"Yes. A linebacker from Cornell."

"Are you lying?"

"No. His name was . . ."

"No names, please. Was he an extra big jock or was he just your normal, run-of-the-mill, linebacker jock?"

"Your extra big jock."

"Was his thing as big as mine?"

"No."

"Are you lying?"

"No. His thing was three inches bigger than yours."

"No names, please. Did you go on top of him or did he go on top of you with all that excessive weight?"

"None of your fucking business."

"Don't get uptight now, Jen. This is very beneficial for the both of us. I told you everything about my sex life, didn't I?"

"Was that everything?"

"Yes."

"Just the fat lady with the condom disposable spittoon?"

"Yes."

"Were you lying?'"

"No. Now go on, please."

"Go on where?"

"Tell me more dirty stories."

"Eddie, will you . . ."

"Did you ever live with a guy?"

"Uh-huh."

"This is interesting. For me this is getting interesting. How many times did you live with a guy?"

"Once."

"For what extended period of time?"

"Two months. A beach house in Malibu."

"Where you in love with him?"

"No."

"Have you ever been in love with someone you slept with as much as you're in love with me whom you never slept with?"

"No. I never slept with anyone I love as much as you."

"Thank you. Now this . . . this man you went to bed with for a period of two consecutive months, how was it? I mean, compared to the innumerable others?"

"It was the best."

"It was the best, wasn't it?"

"Uh-huh."

"May I ask in passing, and since we have the whole night ahead of us with nothing to do, what to your mind constitutes being the best?"

"He was intelligent and he had a sense of humor."

"He made you laugh?"

"Continually."

"He sounds a little like me, doesn't he?"

"Yes. As a matter of fact, when I first saw you at Perry's, that's who I thought you were."

"You thought I was him?"

"Uh-huh. There's a strong physical resemblance, too."

"That is funny. Does he by any chance look like Franz Kafka?"

"Definitely."

"How do you like that? There must be thousands of Franz Kafkas walking around in this world and we never bump into each other."

"He had the biggest . . ."

"No names, please. Can I ask you one more question, Jen?"

"The last one."

"If we're so much alike, why did you live with him in Malibu for two consecutive months and you won't give me two consecutive seconds in my own apartment on Rivington Street?"

"It's ironic, isn't it?"

"I would say so."

"I love you so much more than him it's absurd."

"I would say so."

"Let me whack it for you."

"Take your hands away! Take them away! You're not to touch me, ever! I don't want you ever to touch me! Now get up and make me a hero sandwich with ham, turkey, Swiss cheese, tomatoes, pickled peppers and Gulden's spicy brown mustard."

"Yes, sweetheart, and after you eat I'll give you a rubdown and massage your feet."

When we were going together Jennifer née Koussevitzky was determined to become the best window designer in the country, and I respected her for it. She could work twelve hours at a stretch without being conscious of time; she could lose herself in her work and block from her mind every other concern and/or distraction. At the beginning I'd stand on the curbstone outside a department store and watch her decorate a window. With pins and paint and junkyard debris, she'd create a montage that caught the eye of the most harried New Yorker and glued him to the sidewalk. She borrowed freely from what was being done in art, fashion, textiles, photography, and weaved the whole into a bold, outrageous cartoon of city life.

At the end of the day her genius remained, as it were, in the office. She dressed abominably, without flair or real style; she cut her own hair and scissored her own fingernails. And as could be expected, wherever she lived was a shambles, furniture hastily and cheaply bought, no curtains on the windows, no carpet on the floors, plants brown and seared from lack of attention. She didn't enjoy giving parties or having people over for dinner. She wouldn't hear of owning a domestic animal. In fact she was an avid vivisectionist.

On West End Avenue she shared an apartment with a Japanese girl, Sono Something-or-other, who was shacking up with a kid from New Delhi, Jaya Something-or-other. They were both biology students, working for doctorates at Something-or-other college. We didn't spend much time in Jennifer's apartment because whenever we were there, they'd be in the bedroom. We were forced to sit in the living room and watch them take turns moving from bedroom to bathroom, then back to bedroom again, wiping their hands scrupulously dry with a towel, as if to continue some delicate and vital piece of dissection. I'd fume and Jennifer would giggle, and once I ran out of the apartment almost in tears.

Nonetheless, it was in Jennifer's living room, while Sono and Jaya were marching between bedroom and bathroom, that I asked Jennifer to marry me.

She started to tremble, visibly tremble, her lashes fluttering over her lovely, ebony eyes. She sat down on my lap and hugged me tightly. "I want that more than I ever wanted anything," she said in a breathless voice, kissing me on the mouth with all her might.

I swallowed the lump in my throat and began trembling, too. "So do I, swee . . . sweetheart. But I have to say, you know my circumstances, you know my situation, I have no money, no assets, no prospects for the future. I also have to say, in all fairness to you, that I have no intention of changing my profession."

"If you gave up music, Eddie, I'd cut your balls off," she said angrily.

"Thank you, swee . . . sweetheart. It'll be rough, but the rent for my place is thirty-five a month and if we cut down on the food bill and electricity, we should be able to get by on what I make."

"I have money, darling. I can . . ."

"Not a penny, do you hear me?"

"You can be so . . . Eddie, I don't think it's a good idea."

"What isn't a good idea?"

"Our getting married."

"What are we talking about? I thought you loved me. I thought you wanted to marry me more than anything!"

"I do. I do. But . . . Why do we have to get married? Why can't we just live together?"

"Live together? You want us to live together? Without getting laid?"

"That isn't . . ."

"I can do it, Jen. I'm not saying I can't do it. I've been in training for it since I met you!"

"Eddie, if we live together, that's different, that's an emotional commitment. We can get laid, then. We can fuck each other to death, honey. We can take showers together and every night I'll go down on you."

"No!"

"Why?"

"Because I'm not taking showers with a woman who isn't my wife. It's out of the question."

"I love you, Eddie."

"Then marry me or deny yourself my body."

"Okay."

"Okay what?"

"I'll marry you."

A pause. "Are you sure?"

"Yes."

A long pause. "Are you positively sure?"

"Yes."

A long, long pause. "Are you positively and emphatically sure?"

"Yes."

"Even though I might never make a living as a horn player?"

"Yes."

"Even though I might end up in the gutter and take you with me?"

"Yes. I love you. I'll always love you. Even in the gutter."

"Thank you."

"Eddie?"

"What?"

"Let's not have any children."

"Okay."

"No joking now."

"I'm not joking. I don't want children. And the truth is I don't want to get married either."

"Then why . . . ?"

"Because I want to be with you for the rest of my life. There's a lot I have to teach you."

"Let me whack you off."

"Take your hands away! Take them away! You're not whacking me off again until we're married and that's final!"

eleven

For months Perry had been after me to (1) see his analyst; (2) have lunch with him at La Côte Basque; and (3) work as his assistant at Associated Artists Representatives to learn the ropes and then to join him in starting an agency of our own. I didn't treat any of his offers seriously prior to my proposal to Jennifer. But the prospect of being both broke and married didn't augur much in the way of marital bliss, so I went for number three. Paradoxically, I cared for, thought of, esteemed the mighty buck more than Jennifer did. And this even after we had all the money we wanted and/or needed. I was the one to say, "Isn't that too expensive? Shouldn't we do some comparison shopping?" Jennifer was the one to say, "Fuck it. Let's buy the mother."

I joined Perry at A.A.R. But not for an instant did I think I was giving up the horn. I was merely . . . rearranging my priorities. I would earn a living during the day and still manage to practice evenings and weekends. When the hours were actually counted, I wouldn't be spending any less time on the horn.

Jennifer's reaction couldn't have been better. She was furious. She wouldn't see me. She called me every name under and over the sun. I was a traitor, a coward, a middle-class whore. She didn't want to marry a man who didn't have a backbone, who used marriage as an excuse for quitting, who sold out the first chance he got.

Patiently, I explained my position to her. You're wrong swee... sweetheart. I am and I always will be a horn player. But how can you be sure I won't benefit by having a steady nine-to-five job? How can you be sure that being with people, confronting practical situations and practical problems, won't be good for me? I want to support my wife, I want to have things, a dollar in my pocket, a herringbone topcoat, an apartment I'm not ashamed of, a weekend in the Hamptons. Is that sick or healthy? Infantile or mature? Cowardly or realistic?

She bought it, begrudgingly, and I was invited to dinner at her parents' to discuss our marriage plans.

(I should point out here that there wasn't a word of truth in the skinny horn player's argument. He didn't want to work from nine to five and support a wife. He didn't want a herringbone topcoat. He wanted to keep on going just as he had been. But he was afraid he'd look foolish if he didn't do "what was expected of him." He said nothing he felt and therefore it was easy for him to spin a tale based wholly on fictitious feelings.)

Mr. Hyman Koussevitzky, a retired furrier and self-taught scholar of religious philosophy, and his wife, Miriam, lived in a huge, sunless apartment on Riverside Drive, near Columbia University. They had married late in life, in their forties, I believe, and Jennifer was the sole offspring of their union. I had met them a couple of times before the evening of the dinner, but I had exchanged no more than a hello and good-bye with them. They were fiercely proud and passionately devoted to one another. Mr. Koussevitzky's eyes bulged out of his gaunt, wrinkled face (probably due to an overactive thyroid); dropping from his chin was a stalactite of a goatee, and a wild bush of white hair sprouted from his rather gnomelike head. He wore dark suits, vests with an entwining gold watch chain, pale, square-knotted ties, and, archaically, mustard-colored spats on unbelievably shiny patent leather shoes. He carried a beechwood cane, but refused to lean on it.

His wife was in many respects his female double. Thin, gaunt, and wrinkled, she was invariably in dark, ankle-length caftans with masses of antique jewelry; she also wore, invariably, a hand-wound lavendar turban that spiraled high above her grim, humorless face.

They moved, stood, and sat together, stiffly, rigidly, spoke and acted as if they were descended from a long line of royalty.

After a greeting and a polite remark about the weather, they led us into the dining room. The table was big enough to accommodate a dozen guests and the distance that separated the four of us was ludicrous. In front of me was a dish of chopped liver garnished with slices of oil-dipped horseradish. I debated whether to ask Mrs. Koussevitzky if she had made the dish herself when a small, plump, round-shouldered old woman shuffled in from the kitchen with a steaming cauldron of matzo-ball soup in her hands. I looked across to Jennifer. She smiled and pushed her hobnailed shoe into my crotch under the table.

"Esther, this is my fiancé, Edward Davis," she said to the old woman, and to me, "Esther has been with us since I was a baby. She really raised me, not my mother."

"Eat your food," Miriam Koussevitzky said sternly, sitting ruler-straight at the end of the table.

"So you are the gentleman," Esther spoke with the sing-song inflection of the East European immigrant. "Tell me, you are perhaps a Jewish boy?"

"Yes, Ma'm. By birth."

"Dot I like. Dot's the first good news we have from the polar regions." She carelessly ladled out the soup, splashing it over the damask tablecloth. "I have two children of my own," she said, "vun is vit the government in Vashington an' the udder vun is living vit a bum in Poughkeepsie. Tell me, young man, vot is it you do for a living?"

"I'm a musician. And I'm starting a job with an international entertainment agency."

"Dot I like. Two jobs is alvays better dan vun, especially in dese times vit inflation an' vars in the Orient an' who knows vot else dere doin', the lunatics. But I'll tell you vot I want from you, young man. I vant you should make from my Jenny a Jewish voman. A Koussevitzky she has t'be, but she doesn't have t'be a shiksa."

"I'm not sure I understand . . ."

"My parents are non-observers," Jennifer interpreted for me.

"That will do, Esther," Mr. Koussevitzky's voice cut through like a razor.

"Votever you say, your highness," Esther answered him sarcastically, and before shuffling into the kitchen, she said to me, "Vatch out for dot vun," she jerked her chin toward the furrier; "dot vun is a killer. An' the udder vun," she jerked her chin toward Miriam; "dot vun is a regular Hitler."

We ate the rest of the meal with a minimum of conversation. After the soup we had stuffed capon and glazed carrots with prunes and triangular cinnamon-sprinkled dumplings that were absolutely delicious. No one enjoyed the meal more than Mr. Koussevitzky; his face softened, his eyes retreated into their sockets, and he savored each mouthful as if it contained a madeleine memory of his youth. I imagined that he tolerated Esther's rudeness because of her cooking and that he would have tolerated anything to guarantee her continued employment in his home.

Tea and noodle pudding were served in the living room. I was too intimidated to light my pipe. Mahogany bookcases lined the room and on the wall behind a cluttered, kneehole desk there were innumerable testimonials, awards, certificates and photographs of Mr. Koussevitzky and some eminent scholar or other. He sat on the sofa with his wife, holding her hand in his, the beechwood cane clasped between his knees. They looked royal indeed, what with his goatee and spats and her turban rising like a crown on her wrinkled brow. Esther sat on a folding chair by the door. I waited for the furrier to dismiss her but he didn't. He spoke to me quietly, with echoes of czarist Russia in his voice.

"As is the custom nowadays, Jennifer has not asked my wife and myself to give an opinion of you, Edward, so there is nothing we can say in that regard. However, as to the wedding itself, Jennifer has expressed the wish that she be married by a maharishi of the Buddhist faith who is a personal friend of ours. Are you in agreement?"

"Frankly, Sir, I was hoping we'd go off to Atlantic City and elope, but . . ." I hawked a laugh, turned to each of them, and smiled. No one smiled back at me. "Yes, Sir," I said at once. "It's perfectly all right with me. A maharishi of the Buddhist faith. It sounds perfect."

"The ceremony will be held at the Park South Hotel and we will have a catered meal afterward."

"It's not kosher!" Esther shouted at me. "Tell him you're not gonna put a piece of food in your mout'!"

I took my cue from the others and ignored her.

Mr. Koussevitzky went on, "Your parents are both living, Edward?"

"Yes, Sir."

"Then I think it proper that my wife and I meet with them and discuss the guest list."

"I vant my two children dere and the bum from Poughkeepsie," Esther said.

And I said, "What did you say, Sir?"

"I said I think it proper that we meet your parents."

"Oh, you don't have to meet my parents. They can't come anyway."

"Your parents can't come to their son's wedding?"

Esther asked, "Is this for the reason I suspect, dot they live in this house like goys?"

"Is that what you're saying?" Miriam glared at me, leaning forward to catch my answer.

"No, no, not at all, that's out of the question," I said. "It's just that . . . You know my parents are divorced and . . . You see, my mother's in business, out of town, she's on the road. And my father . . . my father . . ." Oh, boy. Ohhh, boy. "He . . . He . . . My father . . . I sure would appreciate another noodle pudding, Mrs. Koussevitzky."

Now it was their turn to ignore me.

"Perhaps you can translate for us what it is your fiancé is trying to tell us," Mr. Koussevitzky spoke to his daughter.

"I never met Eddie's parents," Jennifer said, and turning to me asked, "Would you like to speak with me privately, sweetheart?"

"Yes! Precisely! Excellent idea! Is there a private room where we can speak privately? There is? Terrific! We'll be back in a jiff. Don't anybody move." And out we went.

Jennifer poured me a glass of plum brandy in the dining room and I told her about my father. God, how easy it was to talk to her! She listened, staring down at the floor, her arms crisscrossed on her thighs. Not once did she interrupt me or make me feel that I was telling her anything out of the ordinary. When I was done, she came to me and covered my face with kisses.

"I want to meet your father, Eddie. And your mother."

"Yes, I would too. We'll meet them together. But now do you know why they can't come to your wedding?"

"Our wedding, sweetheart."

"Of course. That's what I meant."

"Let me talk to my parents. If it'll make you miserable having a wedding, we don't have to have a wedding. Your feelings count as much as anyone's."

"You're so wise, Jen; so wise. How did a college graduate get to be so wise?" I kissed her teenybopper breast. "Look, about your nice parents, we don't have to tell them . . ."

"We can't deceive them, honey. Don't worry. They're very liberal. They were Communists in the thirties."

185

"Okay, if they were Communists, okay. But what about Esther? She wasn't a Communist in the thirties, too, was she?"

"Yes, she was. She was a member of the Pelham Parkway branch. Leave it to me, honey. I'll take care of everything. Do you want me to whack you off before I speak to them?"

"No. Let's wait until we get married. I'm too nervous now."

"Have another drink. I won't be long."

She left me alone with the bottle of plum brandy. I lit my pipe and sipped the brandy. Was I lucky. I was the luckiest person in the world. To have a woman like that in love with me, a woman who was at this very moment speaking to her parents and Esther, all of them former Communists, and telling them that my father was on the brink of womanhood . . . doing that for me . . . I wasn't good enough to lick her construction boots, and that was the truth.

She came in shortly, nodded reassuringly, and we went into the living room. As we entered, I heard Esther whine, "*Oi vey, oiii iz vey.*" I didn't pay her any attention. I was tempted to go down on my knees before the Koussevitzkys, but Jennifer looped her arm through mine and we stood side by side in front of them.

"In my advanced years, I have come to believe in the spiritual nature of man, Edward," Mr. Koussevitzky began; he chose his words carefully, his voice reverberated in the huge room with chilled, Siberian cadences. "I have come to believe in monotheism and pantheism, in Protestantism, Catholicism, Judaism, Moslemism, Sufism and the anthropomorphic gods of the American Indian. There is design, purpose and meaning to the universe. I accept with all my heart the wheel of reincarnation and the commandments of Moses and the sanctity of the crucifixion on Calvary. It is not for us to sit in judgment but to be judged. I open my arms to your mother and her Cuban husband who is in the motel business. I open my arms to your half-brother born of their marriage and given the name of Jesus. I open my arms to your father who has . . ." Here the furrier faltered and turned to his wife, his eyeballs popping out like agates in his bony head.

"Oi vey, oiii iz vey," Esther whined, rocking back and forth in her folding chair.

"Tell him what we've decided, Hyman," Miriam said to her husband without looking at me; her lips were puckered as if she had just bitten into a sour tomato.

"Yesss. Yes. I do open my arms to your father who has . . . who has his karma . . . who has in the search for his divine soul . . ." Here he retracted his eyeballs, drew the lids over them, and appeared to be in deep meditation.

"It wouldn't be right to have a wedding and not have your parents there," his wife continued for him, still not looking at me. "My husband and I . . . we think it best . . . that you and Jennifer go . . . go marry in Atlantic City."

"Yesss," the furrier picked it up from there, his eyes popping open, his cheeks suddenly swollen. "They are your parents and it is your duty to . . . Darling," he turned to his wife and pressed his forehead to hers, "should we . . . do we offer them . . . his father . . . an invitation to our . . . home?"

A giggle escaped from between Miriam's puckered lips; she clamped it off immediately, squeezing her face into a ball of wrinkles. "That is for Edward to decide," she said, and pressed her forehead harder against her husband's forehead so that they looked like a pair of old rams engaged in mortal battle.

"Yes, Ma'm, I will. I'll make a decision," I said hurriedly. "We have to go now. We had a terrific evening. Thank you very much."

Neither one moved. As Jennifer and I were leaving, Esther stopped me at the door and asked, "Vot is he, a canary?"

For what it's worth, Jennifer met my mother a number of times, in New York and Miami, but she didn't meet my father. In fact, by mutual ploys and stratagems, I never saw my father again, and to this day I don't know what his preference was or what his sexual orientation is. I would be less than honest if I didn't admit that I remain somewhat embittered, but on one level or another I do wish him well.

Several things should be mentioned about our honeymoon (spent in an oceanfront hotel at Atlantic City): one, Jennifer cried for the first time since I knew her, not out of unhappiness, but because she was afraid something would go wrong between us; two, I was surprised at how completely passive she was in bed; there wasn't a trace of aggression and/or kinkiness in her; she didn't (ever) use obscenities while making love, and if I didn't initiate or communicate to her my desire for . . .

An hour ago I was interrupted by a knock on the door. It was Mr. Raymond, the roly-poly manager of the hotel. I would have cleaned up a bit if I had known he was going to barge in. The suite was a mess. Piles of dirty laundry and soggy towels lay on the Aubusson rug. Room-service trays with stale food on them were stacked on the upholstered chairs, and empty Coke bottles were all over the place. Because of the extremely cold weather I hadn't opened a window in weeks, and there was a decidedly foul odor throughout the suite. But what I felt most uneasy about was the clothes I had on, the unpressed, stained pants and the soiled shirt from which I had frivolously ripped off the collar. I seem to have lost all interest in uniforms.

Mr. Raymond had psyched himself for the meeting. "Ah, Mr. Davis, I . . . I have too much to do, too much to do to be up here discussing these matters with you." He shoved the bridge of his gold-rimmed specs on his piggly-wiggly nose. "You must, ah, vacate these premises at once, at once, uhhh, do you hear?"

"Mr. Raymond . . ."

"Don't you, ah, Mr. Raymond me! It's not to be discussed." He had worked himself into a conniption, his right cheek twitched, and he kept smacking his hands together to shape his imaginary snowball. "You, ah, have been told and told repeatedly, the, ah, noise, the music, the disorder, you've made a toilet of our most prestigious suite, a toilet, Mr. Davis! Now do you remove, ah, yourself from these premises of your own accord or do I proceed to . . ."

"Mr. Raymond?"

"Ah, yes?"

Tactfully, "I fully appreciate your predicament and I sympathize with you."

"You do?"

"Unfortunately . . ."

"Mr. Davis, I . . ."

"Will you hear me out or will you continue to be rude and hostile?"

"Was I being rude and hostile?"

"You certainly were."

He beamed, flattered by the accusation that he was capable of rudeness and hostility.

"Unfortunately, Mr. Raymond, I can't stop what I'm doing just now. It shouldn't, however, take me more than another month or two to finish."

"To finish?"

"I'm preparing to audition for several symphony orchestras. I may even be required to perform at a concert."

"That's precisely what I . . ."

"I do thank you for your kindness in the past." I pulled out my wallet and stuck five bills at him.

"What's this?" he asked, making the bills disappear before my very eyes.

"Five hundred dollars, for the approaching holidays." I ushered him to the door, my arm draped over his shoulders.

"Yes, yes, uhhh, Mr. Davis, can we say you'll be gone by the first of the year?"

"Word of honor." I raised my hand in a binding oath.

"Do try not to play at night on that . . . that horn of yours," he whispered to me, "and if you have to jump up and down, for whatever reason you do jump up and down, uhhh, jump up and down on the rug, please."

"Word of honor." My hand reached for the ceiling again.

He nodded, anxiously, and left, smacking together his imaginary snowball.

At the beginning I was employed as Perry's secretary, not as his "assistant," at A.A.R. I sat at a desk at the door of his office, taking his calls, scheduling his appointments, proofreading contracts, scripts and so on and so forth. But our plan was, as I already mentioned, for me to hang in there until I learned the business and then for the both of us to leave and start our own agency, dragging along with us all the A.A.R. clients we could steal.

In keeping with my new position, I grew an incredible mustache and spent a bundle on uniforms, buying the smartest plaids, checks, tweeds and solids I could find, top quality, blazers with wide lapels, pleated pants with bell-bottoms, dagger-collared custom shirts, broad, silk ties, belted coats and peacock-feathered fedoras.

The times they were achanging, my friend.

Jennifer and I rented an apartment in a brownstone on East 90th Street, two flights up a Gaudi-like curved, wooden staircase, and into three sunfilled rooms and a makeshift terrace overlooking patches of backyard and a sliver of the East River. We bought a cushioned Voltaire chair on Bleecker Street and took turns sitting in it all afternoon, then made love in it at night; we carried home shopping bags from a Szechuan restaurant and ate the steaming, hot, spicy food in bed out of cardboard containers while watching television, and between mouthfuls and commercials, rolled over and made love; we took bubble baths together and talked of work and acquaintances and dreams, and when we could talk no more, we slid down to the length of the tub and we made love.

(You've experienced it all, haven't you, my friend?)

When he stepped out on the sidewalk in the morning with his longlimbed, ebony-eyed wife in lumberjacket, coveralls and construction boots, the neighbors applauded and schoolchildren threw flowers in front of them; stopping off for a newspaper, the store owner hugged them and invoked a blessing for their well-being and a profitable day; at the bus stop, the passengers disembarked and stood on the curbstone until Mr. and Mrs. Edward Davis were comfortably seated before returning to the bus to gape and gawk at them, the husband impeccably attired and scented, the wife looking like something of a slob, but so vivacious and radiant that they knew immediately why he had deigned to marry her. Mrs. Davis left the bus first, and her husband kissed her on her moist, delicious mouth. The passengers oohed and aahed and the bus driver sang a chorus of "Oh, What a Beautiful Morning," from the show *Oklahoma* by Richard Rodgers and Oscar Hammerstein.

Mr. Davis gets off the bus now, walks briskly to the A.A.R. offices in a skyscraper on Madison Avenue. The elevator ride to the thirty-second floor, a good morning to the receptionist, a good morning to each of the secretaries at her desk, and at last he's at his own desk. He hums: hmmmmm, hmmmmm, opens the mail, answers the phone, puffs on his grained Algerian briar, hmmmmm, hmmmmm, life is cozy, he sings to himself, love my wife, he sings to himself, he hums: hmmmmm, hmmmmm, and one secretary asks him, "Are you Mr. Reese's permanent secretary?" and he answers, "Temporarily. Professionally I'm a horn player," and she nudges the girl beside her and hushes, "He's a permament temporary, can you believe it? He looks like he's president of the company!" Giggle-giggle-giggle. But Mr. Davis hums: hmmmmm, hmmmmm, another day, he sings to himself, another dollar, he sings to himself, and he sings, I'll build a stairway to Paradise . . .

I took lessons on the horn without showing any great improvement, changing teachers periodically, and finding none with whom I was satisfied. My interest in the composition courses at the New School had waned to boredom and I stopped going to them, but I continued to play at widening intervals with marching bands and nonprofessional groups.

It was while marching along Fifth Avenue on St. Patrick's Day with a satin-jacketed band advertising Pete McCallahan's Astoria Tavern, that I heard from a fellow musician that the Cleveland Symphony was sending someone to audition horn players for an opening in their orchestra.

The same afternoon I phoned Cleveland from my desk outside Perry's office. After introducing myself as an A.A.R. agent in the music department, garbling the name of an agent in the A.A.R. music department, I was put in touch with a Mr. Winston Jones. I told Mr. Jones that I had a client, Edward Davis, who was an extraordinarily talented horn player, and that our multibranched company would be eternally in his debt if he granted the said Edward Davis an audition. Without hesitating, Mr. Jones gave the said Edward Davis an appointment for the following Wednesday, at a studio across the street from Carnegie Hall.

I couldn't believe my good fortune or my ballsiness. It occurred to me then that I had the makings of a terrific agent. I cut out early and went home to work the horn. I didn't tell Jennifer, thinking that if nothing came of the audition I wouldn't have to endure the humiliation of her knowing it.

I felt confident. I fantasized giving notice to Perry. "I am not your secretary, Sir! I am no man's secretary! How dare you even imagine such a thing! How dare you!" And of moving to Cleveland with Jennifer. We'd purchase a farm by the river, fifty acres and a weeping willow tree. We'd grow our own vegetables and raise our own little chicks. In the evening I'd drive into town to perform with the orchestra, Mozart, Beethoven and Mendelssohn, and Jennifer would stay home on the farm, baking sponge cake and mending bed sheets by the amber light of an antique pewter lamp.

The morning of the audition I carried my horn with me to the office, placing it prominently on the file cabinet, this for the edification of my co-workers. Perry came in twenty minutes late, as usual, glowing in his cashmere turtleneck, a Colgate smile crackling across his tanned, handsome face, not a spontaneous, unpremeditated bone in his body. He greeted me with his usual, "Did the girl bring in my coffee, Eddie?" Now he knew that there was no "girl" to bring in his coffee, but by saying, "Did the girl bring in my coffee, Eddie?" he was really saying, "I'm not taking advantage of you, buddy; don't forget how nice I'm being to you."

"The coffee's on your desk, Perry. How'd it go with your date last night?" By saying what I said, I was really saying, "I'll never forget how nice you're being to me, buddy. Tell me how much more nooky you had last night than anyone else in the world."

"Too much, Eddie. It was too much," Perry said, which was really saying, "What we didn't do, buddy, doesn't exist."

And that would start off our day on the proper note of self-serving duplicity.

My appointment with Mr. Jones was for noon. At eleven-forty I told the receptionist I was going out to lunch and to take any calls coming in for Mr. Reese. On the sidewalk I strolled leisurely to the address on West 57th Street, my horn in its black case swinging at my side. I was amazed at how absolutely calm I was: no butterflies in my stomach, no cramps, no shivers racing through me. I was on top of it. The worst that could happen is that they'd choose another horn player. But at least I'd have had the chance to be heard. That's all I ever asked for.

I climbed a flight of stairs and entered a small room in which four or five men were seated, golden horns planted on their laps. I sat down and waited, glanced at the expressionless faces of my competitors. I wasn't the oldest; that made me feel even better. And I couldn't help noticing that some of them were dressed inappropriately, wearing sneakers, polo shirts, sweaters and washed-out jeans. That certainly wasn't how one should dress when auditioning for a major orchestra. It was dumb. It showed disrespect. I buttoned my plaid jacket, tightened the knot of my silk, regimental tie. Objectively speaking, I'd have to say that I was the best-dressed person there. That had to count for something.

In an adjoining room a horn player was blowing up a storm, a medley of baroque pieces, I think. He was pretty good. He was more than pretty good. I resented that we had to listen to him before auditioning ourselves. Why lay that on us? Why rub our noses in somebody else's expertise? It didn't seem very fair or professional to me.

Shortly the door opened and the horn player came in, grinning from ear to ear. Trailing him was a bald-headed man, his scalp riddled with freckles, his long, sallow face beaming. He shook the horn player's hand and mumbled flatteringly to him. What was going on here, anyway? Were the auditions over? Had they offered the horn player the job already? Why was this being done in our presence? Was that professional? Was that how a major orchestra auditioned prospective members? I couldn't believe it. It was all being done so grossly.

"Mr. Edward Davis next," the bald-headed man announced, looking around the room with his squinting, myopic eyes.

I jumped to my feet. "Yes, Sir." My voice didn't sound quite right to me.

"Come with me, please."

He held the door open. I walked into a much larger room with nothing in it but a single chair against a wall of windows and three more chairs set against the opposite wall. Two men were smoking cigarettes and chatting quietly.

"Let me introduce myself, Mr. Davis." The bald-headed man closed the door and approached me with extended hand. "I'm Mr. Jones. The two gentlemen there are my associates, Mr. Allentuck and Mr. Cowan. We will make a recommendation to the maestro. A further audition will be required in Cleveland. Do sit down." He motioned me to the single chair against the windows.

The two men extinguished their cigarettes and the three of

them sat down, facing me from across the large room, like three executioners.

Shafts of sunlight crumbled on the bare floor. I could hear the cars and trucks grinding and screeching outside the windows.

"Tell us about yourself, Mr. Davis." I believe it was Mr. Allentuck who spoke.

I should have been prepared, but I wasn't. I had naively assumed that they'd be concerned with how well I played, not in how many credits I had at Pastafazoola University or how many years I had spent kissing some conductor's behind.

"I studied with Mr. Brooks, with Mr. Noonan . . . I was graduated from Grand Army Plaza Conservatory of Music, and I . . . I performed with . . ." This was ridiculous. They were deliberately putting pressure on me. Why? What was the sense of it? On a simple human level, it was inexcusably cruel of them. "I could list the orchestras and ensemble groups I was with, Sir," I said, "but I prefer you hear me play." My voice still didn't sound quite right to me.

"Very well, Mr. Davis," it was Jones speaking. "Please, play for us."

I had arranged a medley of my own, starting with Weber's Concertino in E Minor, for the chords in it, and I knew, given the opportunity, given a degree of tolerance, I could perform more than satisfactorily. But I felt I was being denied these common courtesies. I took the horn from its case. My hands were wet and slippery. The hell with it, I thought. I'll show them. I'll show them. I clamped the horn to my mouth, angrily, and as soon as I blew the first notes I knew I was in trouble, I knew it, no one had to tell me. My tone was flat and wobbly; my lips were like worn strips of rubber, without firmness or elasticity. I had every intention of stopping, of apologizing, of filling my lungs with air and starting over again. But just then I saw Mr. Jones turn and say something to the other two. And they were grinning, the three of them were grinning from ear to ear! I couldn't believe it. How dare they! How dare they!

I replaced my horn in its case and rose from the chair.

An astonished chorus rose with me.

"Mr. Davis, what is it?"

"Where are you going?"

"Why did you stop playing?"

I wanted to say, I am not in the habit of performing when people are carrying on a conversation; I find these conditions intolerable, gentlemen, intolerable!

But I was too angry to speak. And I was afraid that if I did speak I would start bawling. I held it in.

The three of them rushed at me.

"Will you tell us why you're leaving, Mr. Davis?"

"Would you care for a glass of water?"

"Do sit down, please."

I didn't bother to answer them. My head ached. How dare they! How dare they! I stumbled to the door. Mr. Jones wrapped his chalky fingers around my arm.

"There must be a misunderstanding . . ." he began.

I tore my arm free and I walked out, slamming the door shut, viciously.

I stopped taking lessons after that and I practiced less and less frequently. In some bizarre way I was waiting for something to happen, for a sign, a word, a clue as to what my next move should be. I didn't forget I was special, that I was a unique individual, destined for an extraordinary undertaking; and yet I neglected the horn and I was living the most ordinary middle-class life: wife, car, apartment, job, weekly deposits in the bank, etcetera, etcetera. Perversely I couldn't understand why the phone didn't ring, why a telegram didn't arrive asking me to perform somewhere.

I glanced through the mail each day as if expecting a letter from the Philharmonic.

twelve

In time I was given an office and a secretary of my own at A.A.R. Perry and I worked closely together, sharing the same clients, developing the same packages, presenting the same shows to the networks for their approval. We got lucky once in a while and had a project go to pilot and series, but none of them lasted more than a season. It didn't much matter to us, though. We weren't there to improve the financial statement of A.A.R. We were there to make contacts, know who to know, get around, and spread the news that there were a pair of new hotshots in town.

I have to laugh as I write it, but damn if I didn't enjoy being an agent! It was a game to play, and the minute I recognized it as such I could play it with the best of them. To play the game one had to have an intimate knowledge of what everybody in the business was doing, who was in and who was out, who was moving up and who was moving down, who had pull and who was a hat rack. On occasion, lying was permitted, so long as one wasn't caught at it, and a pretense to loyalty automatically gave one a stolen base, two runs and a rib-cracking hug.

But what I didn't know then was that these people took the game seriously. They weren't playing for bottle caps and baseball cards. To them it was a matter of life or death. Looking back I'd have to say that the reason I became as successful as I did was because I played for bottle caps and baseball cards. I didn't, I couldn't treat any of it too seriously. At least not at the beginning.

I had to treat seriously Jennifer's quitting her job at the window-display company some months after our marriage and deciding that it was her legal and moral obligation to keep house for me. Along with this decision came a number of startling changes. She gave up rolling her own cigarettes and only smoked a token filter at rare social gatherings; she gave up her beer guzzling as well and only drank an extra-dry martini at the same rare social gatherings where she smoked her only cigarette; to replace these nasty habits — habits which, I confess, made any woman attractive to me — she nurtured an appetite that would have shamed Attila the Hun; she ate incessantly, stuffing herself at odd hours with fruits, raw vegetables, ice creams, cakes, wedges of cheese, olives, pimentos, anchovies, nuts, pretzels, potato chips, onion rings, cookies, croutons and whatever else was within arm's reach. She didn't, surprisingly, gain a pound; in fact she lost a little weight. I insisted she see a doctor. "What did he say?" I asked her that evening. "I should eat something between meals," she said, and pulled out the popcorn machine from the kitchen closet.

She also started to attend classes at various local colleges and museums, taking courses in gourmet cooking, appliqué sewing, Aztec pottery, home economics, interpersonal relationships and the indoor growing of the avocado plant.

I thought of asking her: "Why did you change so suddenly?" But I never got around to it.

She was always shopping, cleaning, and cooking: yet the things she bought were inevitably returned to the store where purchased; the apartment remained for the most part unfurnished and always seemed in need of a cleaning; her cooking improved to the extent that the food she prepared was eatable. She refused to find anything humorous in all of this.

Twice a week she played cards with a group of people of whom she said: "The less you know about them, the safer you are."

Somewhere she had snared a mauled, evil-eyed, striped alley cat, which she named Melvin; she talked to him as if he was her best friend.

She became obsessive about having guests over for dinner. Desperately she'd search through our address books. "Let's invite Bertha Klinger over for dinner." "Who's Bertha Klinger?" "Her name is in your address book." "Oh, I think I knew her when I was fourteen." "How about Julie Heller?" "Julie Heller? I'm not sure he's still alive." "I'll get somebody," she'd say. And she would. One evening we had dinner with Mr. Petrokowski, the super, and his wife.

I had no choice but to speak to her.

"Jen?"
"Yes?"
It was a humid summer's night and we were seated opposite each other in the cool bathtub, wearing our Vietnamese gym shorts and playing a card game called War on a board perched between us. I puffed on my pipe and Jennifer was biting noisily into a crisp McIntosh apple. A paper bag loaded with apples was on the rim of the tub behind her. Melvin, her charcoal-striped cat, sat on the sink and watched us with his evil green eyes; one of his ears had been torn off in a street brawl and he habitually scratched its nubbly stump, purring meanly as he did so.

"Jen, I never really discussed this with you, but how come you quit your excellent-paying job?" I had decided to run through my entire list of complaints.

"I hated it," she answered with vehemence, brushing aside the curtain of bangs from her forehead.

"I thought you liked your job." I put down a jack of hearts and she whisked it away with a queen of diamonds.

"I hated everything about it," she said in the same tone of voice. "I hated dressing the dummies. I hated working nine-to-five. I hated seeing the same people day in and day out. I don't know how you can stand your job, honey."

"Well, I guess one of us has to work for a living."

"Why? We have enough money to last us for a year."

"And after a year?"

"Fuck it. Who cares? We'll probably be dead by then."

"But if we're not, we still have to eat, don't we?" I snapped up a three of spades with a five of diamonds.

"You're so insecure, it's frightening," she said, crunching into her McIntosh, and soon mumbled peevishly, "I haven't heard you practice the horn in weeks."

"Let's stick to the subject," I responded. "Do you plan to go back to work in the foreseeable future?"

"No. Never. I have a job."

"What job?"

"Making you happy," she said, without smiling.

"Who said I wasn't happy?"

"You don't have to pretend with me, sweetheart," she was smiling now but sympathetically. "You're miserable," she said. "You're the most miserable man I ever met. That's why I love you with such a passion."

"Because I'm miserable?"

"Uh-huh. It's a quality I find irresistible."

"Be that as it may, making me happy isn't a full-time job."

"It is for me," she answered, "especially when you consider I have to make Melvin happy, too." She put down an ace and took away five picture cards of mine.

I glanced at Melvin. His mauled, mean, whiskered face split open in a gaping yawn. He had to be the ugliest cat in captivity.

"That's something else I want to discuss with you," I said, trying to sound casual. "Why are we living with that ugly cat?

I'm scared of cats, you know that. And he's crazy. He happens to be a crazy cat. Every time I walk into the apartment, he grabs my leg and humps it like a dog."

"Melvin isn't your ordinary cat, honey."

"That's what I'm telling you."

"He's more like a son of ours."

I swear, if I had had some place to go, I would have walked out at that point in our conversation. Instead I asked in a squeaky voice, "Melvin? He's a son of ours?"

"We agreed we're not having children, right?"

"Right."

"You don't want children and I don't want children, right?"

"Right."

"Melvin is in effect our substitute child," she said, and tossed her apple core into the toilet bowl; immediately, she plucked another McIntosh from the paper bag behind her. "Now, who do we invite for dinner this Friday?" She bit noisily into the fresh McIntosh, sprinkling us both with its juice. "How about my aunt and uncle from Bensonhurst?"

"I'm not having dinner with relatives anymore," I said decisively.

"How about Perry?" was her next question.

I glared at her, wiping apple juice off my face with a washcloth.

"The trouble with you, sweetheart, is that you have no friends." She took the washcloth from me and wiped off her own face.

"I have friends . . . "

"Name one friend of yours, just one, go ahead."

"Uhhh . . . "

"You're a man totally devoid of friends."

"I have as many friends as you have," I said, indignantly. "Name one friend of yours, go ahead."

"Sono, Jaya, Mr. Petrokowski . . ."

"You call them your friends? The only one you see is Mr. Petrokowski and that's when he's collecting the garbage."

"I'll tell you what. Let's each of us make a friend this week and invite them to dinner on Friday," she proposed as she lifted my last card and then shouted jubilantly, "I won! I won! You owe me a walnut-fudge sundae and a package of Pepperidge Farm molasses cookies!"

Hearing of my defeat, Melvin was so overjoyed that he leaped from the sink onto the board perched between us, dropped into the tub, and started humping my leg like a dog in heat.

I had been with A.A.R. for about two years when Perry, who had married an editor of an artsy-craftsy publishing house, Linda Weigel, and had in rapid succession a boy, Matthew, and a girl, Daphne, and I moved into our own offices on West 55th Street, just off Sixth Avenue. We carried with us from A.A.R. eleven actors, seven directors, one alcoholic playwright and a carton of ashtrays and coat hangers.

As it turned out, we weren't quite the hotshot agents we thought we were. Not being with a large company really cut us down to size. We had no clout, no organizational connections; nobody was around to pick up the bills for us. If we were lucky enough to sign an actor into a Broadway show, the most we could get for him was scale, three hundred at that time. Ten percent was a big thirty bucks. And that was for a Broadway show. What saved us was our alcoholic playwright. He wrote an original screenplay about an alcoholic playwright who in a drunken rage kills his wife, his kids, his in-laws, his next-door neighbors, and sets Bloomingdale's afire by ramming a Getty gasoline truck into its sidewalk windows. We sold the script for a hundred and fifty thousand and gave our alcoholic playwright a case of Chevas Regal for Christmas.

It was also during this period that Perry suggested we concentrate on creating a game show for television that we could produce ourselves. We spent months reviewing every game show on the air, studied, analyzed, and dissected them, and then began to put together several possibilities. It wasn't as simple as you might think. To quote Perry: "A game show has to have tension, suspense, focus, a whole spectrum of entertainment values." The skunk was born to get rich in television. He had a knack for selling, and it had nothing to do with ability, talent, or anything else. It had to do with his physical appearance, his toothy smile, his perennial suntan, his curly lemon-yellow hair and his country wardrobe that smelled of Westport estates and Caribbean beaches. People listened to him, not because he had anything to say, but because he was attractive to look at and emanated rays of sanitized vitality. Socially he was fun to be with, although I found him totally without a sense of humor and for my taste too self-centered. He had, and this I'll grant him, a genuine flair for dramatizing the most trivial events of his life.

Nonetheless, our early efforts as television producers were dismissed out-of-hand by the networks. We hung in there, though, got to know who to know, which minor executive to woo and court, which secretary to send a nosegay to. Still it took us quite a while to come up with a show that a network accepted. The idea for the show was mine. But even then they wouldn't go ahead with it until we brought in a master of ceremonies who met their requirements. The idea to call Jackie St. Claire was mine, too. Jackie had, over the years, achieved a solid reputation as a comic actor. The network was excitedly responsive: "Sign him and we guarantee you a season," they said. "No problem," Perry said. "No problem," I said. It was a problem, believe me.

"I am an actor, not a seller of soups," Jackie said to us over his chateaubriand at The Four Seasons.

"Another round of Gallianos, waiter," I said.

"Jackie, listen to us," Perry said. "Our show can make you a star. You're not a star. You should be a star. But you're not a star. Do a season or two on TV, and you can choose any play you'd like to do, and there'll be money to do it."

"Not to mention films," I piled it on. "You can use national exposure, Jackie. This will give you national exposure. Your name will become a household word."

"I can do without becoming a household word. Why can't I act? Why can't I do Shakespeare, Pirandello, Ghelderode?"

"You can, you can," Perry said.

"You can, you can," I said.

"I am an artist," Jackie said, "an actor. I've learned my craft for more years than I care to remember. Get me a job acting in the classics and I'll do it without qualm or recompense. But this, this game show, this giving out trash and filthy lucre to hysterical women in the midst of menopause . . ."

"It's a brilliant idea for a game show," Perry said.

"Let me explain it to you, Jackie," I said. "You see, we have six contestants. They each sit on a carousel horse that races on an oval ramp built inside a theater. The audience shouts, cheers, goes wild. Don't forget, each member of the audience was given a ticket with a number on it and if it's the number of the winning horse he or she receives a valuable prize. But the winner of the horse race, the contestant, gets to answer three questions on Hollywood celebrities which can win for him or her a bona fide racehorse or twenty-five thousand dollars in cash."

" 'Horse Around,' " Jackie sneered at the title of our show. "How could you! How could you think of me in that manure! Is that my repayment, Edward, for keeping you out of the Korean conflict?"

"Another round of Gallianos, waiter," I said.

"Jackie, listen to me," Perry said. "This is right for your career, take my word for it. Two or three seasons on TV and you'll be a celebrity yourself, a star, you'll call your own shots, you'll have more money . . ."

"I'm not interested in money. If I were interested in money, I would have gone into the diamond business with my father."

"We'll raise our previous offer," I said, glancing at Perry.

"We'll cut you in on profits," Perry seconded the motion.

"With profits, salary and royalties, you'll be earning more than the President of the United States."

"Another round of Gallianos, waiter," I said.

"Jackie, listen to me," Perry said. "Three or four seasons on TV and you'll have it made. Don't be a loser all your life. Everybody's getting into television. Look at the names. Say no and we have ten other actors waiting to do it. You want their names?"

"You wouldn't use . . . ?"

"That's him," Perry said.

"You'd . . . ?"

"He's on top of the list."

"Perry, he's a sweet boy, but he has no wit, no presence. You can't inflict him on . . ."

"You give us no choice," Perry said.

"No choice," I said.

"We don't want him," Perry said.

"I don't," I said, not knowing who they were talking about.

"We want you," Perry said, not to me but to Jackie, "We want your wit, your charisma, your universal appeal. If you turn us down, though, we have to go to you-know-who, and I promise you, Jackie, you-know-who will be a star within four or five seasons on TV."

"Whose idea was 'Horse Around'?" Jackie asked, digging into his rugallah salad.

"Mine," I said.

"Very well, Edward," Jackie said. "I'll do the show. But you'll pay dearly for it."

And he wasn't kidding.

But what was so incredibly ironic was that as soon as the network gave us the go-ahead with the show, Perry started to behave peculiarly. Afternoons he was never in the office. I couldn't believe it. He'd disappear like clockwork at about four and that would be it for the day. I had to do everything myself. When I first asked him what was happening, he mumbled some gibberish about his kids' orthodontics. And it was only after persistent questioning that he told me that his mother was very, very ill, implying a malignancy as the cause; he said he didn't want Linda or Jennifer to know anything about it, and that was why he had been so secretive. Of course I responded by saying that he was not to concern himself with the show, that I would fill in for him. Where could he be reached in case of an emergency? Try Kings County Hospital, the intensive-care unit, he answered, and he was gone for the remainder of the afternoon.

No doubt this arrangement would have continued indefinitely if his mother hadn't phoned the office from a resort hotel in West Palm Beach. She left a message for Perry. She wanted him to know that his kids would be arriving at LaGuardia airport, not at Kennedy, as she had advised him the previous evening.

I hit Perry with his lie the next day. And like the master con artist he was, he ripped right into me. "You know what's the matter with you, Eddie? You think you're the only sensitive person alive! To you other people don't have feelings! To you other people don't fight for a better world!"

"Now what are we talking about?"

"I couldn't tell you the truth, idiot! Are you blind? I have marital problems, damn it! My marriage is up for grabs! When I think of Matt and Daphne . . . You don't have kids, what the hell do you know? What the hell do you know about anything? What do you know about pain and sacrifice and denying oneself for the sake of someone else!" he yelled at me, and looked longingly toward the open window.

"All right, all right, don't get hot under the collar," I said, pacing between him and the open window. "Are you and Linda getting a divorce, is that it?"

"You bet that's it!" he cried, flipping a Hermes handkerchief from his breast pocket and dabbing pearls of perspiration on his bronze face. "Eddie, open up, please, will you?" he begged, drowning me in his baby blue eyes. "Show some compassion, some feelings. I can't get through to you. You're closed inside; you're ungiving and unforgiving. For your own good, visit Doctor Zamichow; don't be too proud to ask for help!" And with that he rushed out of the office.

I didn't see him again for a week.

I told Jennifer what was going on as we lay naked in bed with dishes of Delmonte fruit salad and marshmallow topping resting on our chests; the television set was babbling at the foot of the bed.

"He is eating another woman," Jennifer said at once, passing a marshmallow-dipped finger to Melvin who was sprawled out on the other side of her, his one good ear raised like an antenna.

"What makes you so positive? Did you speak to Linda?"

"She doesn't know anything. He tells her he's been working every night until midnight."

"That's a lie," I said. "I've been working every night until midnight."

"That's what I said. He's eating another woman. She's probably a better lay than Linda."

"That's hard to believe."

"That she's a better lay than Linda?"

"No, that he could lie to her about working late."

"Any woman's a better lay than Linda," Jennifer said, finishing her fruit salad, and relieving me of mine.

"How could he tell Linda he's been working late when I'm in the office every . . ."

"Eddie, I think you should have a mistress, too."

"Now what's that supposed to mean?"

"You don't even have to tell me. Just enjoy yourself."

"Where are you going?"

"To get a bowl of Haagen Dazs pistachio ice cream. Do you want some?"

"No. Stay here. Why are you suddenly telling me to get a mistress?"

"Because I want you to be happy," she replied, looking around for something to eat.

"Will you please stop trying to make me happy? The more you try to make me happy the more miserable you're making me!"

"Honey, let's face it, after a few years of marriage every husband yearns for a mistress. I just wanted you to know that I have no objections, that's all," she answered, finding a walnut under her pillow and starting to crack it open with her strong buckteeth.

"That's the craziest thing I ever heard of," I said.

The walnut cracked between her teeth and she eagerly dug into it with her fingernails. She didn't speak until there was nothing left but the shell which she tossed across the room, aiming at her Ranger knapsack. "Just do me a favor," she then said. "When you get a mistress, keep it to yourself. Be discreet about it."

"Jen, I really don't understand why you brought up this depressing subject."

"I'm not good at sex, honey. You know it and I know it," she said, looking around again for something to eat.

"That isn't true, swee . . . sweetheart. You're very good at sex. You're the best I had."

"I wish you hadn't said that," she replied, wincing. "We both know I give lousy head."

"No, you don't."

"Yes, I do."

"Who said you give lousy head?"

"Everybody. I give the worst head in the world. I don't even like giving head."

"Then don't give head! Who's asking you to give head?"

"It's expected of an intelligent woman nowadays." She found a rubber band on the night table and began chewing on it. "Let's not talk anymore," she said, turning to the television set. "Look, there's James Cagney. He's gonna get his balls blown off any minute."

"Will you stop watching television? We're discussing something here! And get Melvin off the bed, will you? Why does he have to be in bed with us?"

"Don't raise your voice, honey. Melvin had a very rough day. He tried to hump a fire hydrant. It nearly killed him."

"He hates me. That cat hates me. He always looks as if he wants to sink his teeth into my Adam's apple."

"That's because you don't show him any affection."

"I have enough to do without showing a cat affection."

"You have one offspring, the least you can do is show him affection," she mumbled under her breath.

I let it pass. "Jen, listen, maybe our sex life is a little dull, a little mechanical. Why don't we do something different for a change?"

"Like what?"

"Don't you have any ideas?"

"I ran out of ideas on our honeymoon."

"How about polymorphous perverse?"

"Do we have to wear costumes?"

"Jen, if you don't . . ."

"What do you mean by polymorphous perverse?"

"I mean having sex without using our sex organs."

"I thought we were doing that."

"Go on, just . . ."

"You wanna do polymorphous perverse, let's do polymorphous perverse. How does it work?"

"How do I know? You think all I have to do all day is sit in the office and think about polymorphous perverse? I'm trying to get a show on the air!"

"Why don't we try, ahhh . . . Why don't we try putting maple syrup and maraschino cherries on the Haagen Dazs pistachio ice cream."

"Then what do we do with it?"

"We eat it. In soup bowls."

"If you're not gonna be serious, Jen, let's . . ."

And suddenly she was serious. "I haven't heard you practice the horn in I don't know how long, Eddie. Did you give up?"

"I didn't give up."

"Why don't you find a teacher and . . ."

"I don't need a teacher. I had enough teachers. After the show gets on, I'm leaving the agency. I'll be on the horn full-time."

"Is that a promise?"

She held my face so that I had to stare at her. "I said so, didn't I?"

She spit out the rubber band. "Ask me what I did today," she said, solemnly, lifting ugly Melvin onto her chest and hugging him. "You never ask me what I do. Don't you care?"

"Maybe you should find another job, something to keep you busy . . ."

"Fuck you!" she screamed, dropping Melvin to the floor. "I'm not getting a job! I have a job! I'm gonna make you happy if it kills me, Eddie Davis, if it kills me I'm gonna make you happy!" And she reached for my penis and shook it fiercely, like a Las Vegas gambler rattling dice at the crap table.

"What do you want me to say, Jen? I'll say whatever you want me to say," I said, arching my spine and taking aim at the dying avocado plant by the radiator.

"I want you to make love to me." She lay back on the bed, lidding her ebony-bright eyes. "But you have to do me a favor, hon."

"What's that?"

"Don't take too long. There's a Gary Cooper movie on next."

I was standing at the rear of the network theater when Perry came in and stood beside me. He looked terrible. His face was drawn, his eyes puffy, and his yellow hair hung limply around his filigree ears.

"I have to talk to you, buddy," he whispered to me. "Let's go for a drink."

"Tom Sullivan's coming."

"Who's Tom Sullivan?"

"We don't have insurance to cover the show," I fumed quietly. "He's from Century. Several companies have already turned us down."

"Tell him he'll get five percent of the premium on the Q.T. One drink, buddy. It's the last thing I'll ask of you."

"How do I know you're telling me the truth this time?"

"If I'm lying, may God strike me dead."

I followed him out of the theater and into The Ginger Man. We sat at a table and I waited for him to drop dead.

"Okay, buddy, the truth. I have been seeing someone and . . . It's been hell for me, sheer, unmitigated hell. I . . ." He couldn't go on. He caught the eye of a waiter and ordered scotch-and-sodas for the both of us and a hot roast beef sandwich and mashed potatoes for himself.

He asked for my understanding and went to the men's room; when he came back to the table he continued.

"Okay. I . . . I've been having an affair. I fell in love, head over heels in love. I've been . . . I don't want to live anymore, Eddie. I want to die and be done with it!" Instinctively he glanced about for an open window to jump out of, but just then the waiter carried over the drinks and the hot roast beef sandwich, and he decided to eat instead. "I know how unfair I've been to you," he said, smothering a slice of roast beef in the thick gravy and forking it into his mouth. "You were doing all the work while I was having the most fantastic sex a human being can have," he said, cutting another slice of roast beef.

"It was really good, huh?"

"Beyond words and description. So gratifying that I often thought I had transcended into a state of Nirvana."

"What did she do to you?"

"You name it, she did it," he admitted with a grin, attacking his mashed potatoes.

"I'd appreciate it if you told me in detail what she did to you. Jennifer and I have been discussing this same subject recently."

But he was on his own track. "Eddie, I can't leave Linda and the kids."

"Why not?"

"I can't afford it."

"If the show runs five or six seasons, you'll have enough."

"Do you know what it costs to maintain two households?"

"No."

"Then don't talk, please. I have to break it off with Pinky."

"Pinky?"

"Pinky, Pinky, Pinky," he recited tunefully. "Womanhood is thy name."

"Womanhood?"

"Goszinger. Pinky Goszinger. What a woman, Eddie. What a woman. But how do I do it? How do I break off with someone who has given me so much pleasure?"

"Why don't you send her a telegram?"

"You can be such a heartless son of a bitch. Where are your feelings? Don't you have a soul?"

"Sorry."

"Pinky deserves more than a telegram from me. That's why . . . buddy, you do this for me and I'll work on the show twenty-four hours a day. I'll do your work and my work. I'll see to it that the show's a hit and we become millionaires."

"What do I have to do to become a millionaire?"

"The only decent way for me to break off with Pinky is to take her to Acapulco for a week."

"Are you sure that's the only decent way?"

"Positive. I can wine and dine her and break it off gradually without hurting her."

"Where do I come in?"

He slid an ice cube from the bottom of his glass into his mouth and sucked on it thoughtfully. "Be my beard," he said, pinning his baby blue eyes to mine. "Cover for me if Linda asks any questions. I'll tell her I'm traveling around the country, digging up contestants for the show."

"Okay," I nodded in agreement. "Now let's go to the theater. Tom Sullivan's . . ."

"I can't go with you, buddy."

"Why not?"

"I have to go home and pack. I'll catch you in a week."

I went back to the network theater to meet Tom Sullivan. He was on the stage, talking to Ben Snyder, our chief electrician. Near them there were six hand-carved and gaudily painted carousel horses set on six portable monorails that encircled the auditorium, rising steeply to the balcony before descending again. As I walked down the aisle toward the stage, Jackie St. Claire flapped his arms at me as if trying to bring in a jet on an aircraft carrier. He was seated next to Oscar Libin, a writer I had hired to write his opening monologue and to furnish him with whatever additional material he might need.

"Edward, you must give us a minute. I don't think I can take any more of this," Jackie blurted out in a barely controlled, quivering voice.

Oscar moved over a seat to make room for me.

"Only a minute. Tom Sullivan's . . ."

"You speak to him, Oscar," Jackie pleaded with the writer. "If I speak to him, I'll explode. And don't keep anything from him," he cautioned. "Someone has to tell him in public what everyone is saying in private."

"Mr. Davis, we're in a crisis situation here," Oscar advised me, very softly, very earnestly. If I had to make a comparison, I'd compare Oscar to a giant brown bear: he was grossly obese, slovenly, dressed in a dirty safari outfit; two lugubrious eyes were pasted on his snub-nosed face which was almost hidden behind a haystack of brown hair; his voice was faint, almost inaudible, a wistful sigh that was wholly without resonance. You'd have to be a fool to be intimidated by him.

"What is it, Oscar?"

" 'Horse Around' is an abomination, Mr. Davis. It's a crude, sadistic notion that is offensive to anyone above the age of twelve years."

"I'm not going to do it, Edward," Jackie hissed at me. "I am not doing this show and I will not say another word!"

"What did you tell Jackie, Oscar?" I played the work-weary producer and spoke as feebly as Oscar did.

"I know it's none of my business, Mr. Davis. I know you hired me merely to do some writing for Mr. St. Claire. But I'd like to be as helpful as I can."

"I'll break my contract!" Jackie exploded, stretching his red-coiffed head atop his giraffe's neck. "I'm the one who has to confront those cameras! I'm the one who has to do this bat dung! I will not say another word!"

"I sincerely believe, Mr. Davis, that Jackie's talent is too immense to be wasted on a game show." Oscar was softly knocking nails into my millionaire's coffin. "I recommend, with humility, that you discard the 'Horse Around' show and inform the network that if they want Jackie St. Claire, they give him an hour dramatic series based on the life of Mahatma Gandhi."

I couldn't keep my voice feeble any longer. It rose to a shriek. "Mahatma Gandhi? A television series?"

"He preached a doctrine of nonviolence," Oscar droned on, feebly. "It was through his efforts that India gained her independence and . . ."

"I know who he was," I interrupted, and to Jackie, "You wanna do Mahatma Gandhi opposite Mary Tyler Moore?"

"I'll be stupendous as the Mahatma Gandhi," Jackie answered, tucking his legs under him and conjuring a beatific expression. "I'll shave my head and I'll wear a pristine loincloth."

"He'll be devastating," Oscar stuck his two and half cents in. "He's assured an Emmy and a *Time* cover for his performance."

"You didn't write any of this, did you?"

"Merely an outline, the first thirteen shows." He removed a pile of papers from his Hunting World canvas bag and gave them to me. "I'd be grateful if you read what I've . . ."

"He'll read it," Jackie huffed, unfolding his legs and losing his beatific expression. "He'll read it or the draft board will learn of a certain producer who was too preoccupied with his musical career to answer his country's call to arms."

"I'll read it," I said, pushing my way to the aisle. "But let's keep this to ourselves. I don't want to jeopardize anything until we have the network's approval, okay?"

Jackie looked to Oscar before speaking. "Very well, Edward, but we insist on having an answer within the week. And don't stall us. I'm familiar with your tactics."

They stood up and ambled out of the theater, the giraffe mincing along, the bear trudging forward, moving off together as if they were about to board Noah's Ark.

Another headache was waiting for me on stage.

"I can't give you insurance on the show, Mr. Davis." Tom Sullivan, the insurance salesman, was a lanky young fellow, dressed nattily in a three-piece Brooks Brothers suit. He wore taps on his wing-tipped shoes, his arms dangled loosely at his sides, and one expected him to shuffle into a snappy dance routine of "Sunny Side of the Street" at any minute. "You've built a roller coaster here," he said, kicking the support ramp with the toe of his shoe. "Look how high the rails are. Somebody falls, you've got multiple fractures, lacerations and at best compound concussions."

"That's impossible. We've taken every precaution. Is there any chance of an accident, Ben?" I turned to our chief electrician who was sculpted on a chair, a Yankee cap angled jauntily on his stubbled, jowled face.

"No chance, Mr. Davis. We checked and double-checked. It's as safe as a merry-go-round," was Ben's predictable reply.

"If my company insured this operation, the premium would be prohibitive." Sullivan slapped his thighs, whirled around and started to walk away.

"Let's give it a try," I said, throwing my leg over a sleek piebald and strapping myself in.

"You're not getting me to ride those horses," he answered, picking up his attaché case from the floor.

"Five bucks says I beat you," I said. "Take any horse you want."

"Is it rigged?" He glanced at the carousel horses with the eye of a connoisseur.

"It's operated by a computer. No one can predict the winner," I assured him.

Sullivan tossed aside his attaché case and in a single leap jumped over the rump of a midnight stallion with a ruby-ornamented saddle. "You wouldn't up the ante to ten bucks, would you, Mr. Davis?" he asked, strapping himself in.

"You're on. Okay, Ben. Let 'em ride!"

"Let 'em ride!" Ben shouted to someone offstage, refusing to budge from his chair.

There was a pause, a whirring of motors, and then all six carousel horses glided smoothly under a rising peppermint-stick barrier to the piped music of the *William Tell* Overture. Two riderless horses took the lead. Sullivan and I were right behind them. We couldn't have been moving more rapidly than if we had been walking, but the screeching of the new rails and the shouts from the stagehands who had mysteriously crawled out of the woodwork seemed to push us ahead at a much faster clip. Sullivan had apparently forgotten his concern for safety; he was now hooting his midnight stallion on, kicking his tapped heels into its wooden rump. I yelled for him to be careful as we climbed the steep incline to the balcony. The last thing I wanted was an accident. I could hear the stagehands placing bets on the outcome of the race, and my belief that the show had great commercial possibilities was noisily affirmed. As we came down from the balcony, my piebald inched passed Sullivan's stallion. I crossed the finish line a mare's nose in front of him.

Victoriously I jumped off my horse, anticipating an enthusiastic ovation. But the stagehands had mysteriously vanished back into the woodwork. The chief electrician remained glued to his chair, peacefully nursing a Macanudo cigar.

"Didn't I tell you it was safe?" I pounced on Sullivan. "That's ten bucks you . . ."

Something was wrong, though. Sullivan sat rigidly on his carousel horse, his hands digging into his hips, his boyish face torn in a pained grimace.

"Sullivan, what . . . ?"

"My back," he groaned pitifully. "I can't move. Call an ambulance."

"But how . . . ?"

"I must have wrenched it. Coming down from the balcony. Didn't I tell you it was dangerous?"

"Come on, cut it out. You didn't . . ."

"I said I did, didn't I?" he yelled at me. "Who's your insurance company, Davis?"

"You're my insurance company."

"Not until there's a written policy. Are you saying you're not covered by insurance, Davis?"

I admit, for a second there, I was in a sweat. "Ben, did you see him hurt himself? How did he hurt himself?"

"You got me. I thought it went like gangbusters," the electrician answered, without budging from his chair.

"Call an ambulance!" Sullivan yelled. "The pain is unbearable!"

"Okay, okay, take it easy." It was then that Perry's suggestion popped into mind. "Ben . . ." I pried the electrician loose from his chair and whispered to him, "Go to the bathroom and wash your hands," and said loudly enough for Sullivan to hear, "Get an ambulance over here. It's a matter of life or death."

"Got ya, Mr. Davis," he grinned, winking at me and mysteriously vanishing into the woodwork.

"The ambulance is coming," I said to Sullivan. "Is there anything else I can do?"

"Morphine. Do you have morphine?"

"I'm afraid not on me."

"The pain is excruciating, Davis. How come you don't carry a general liability policy?"

"I thought you'd handle it for us. Is there any way I can ease the pain?"

"What are you driving at?"

"Can't we settle this amicably?"

"What are you driving at?"

"If Century gave us a policy on the show, we intended to give you something for your trouble. On the Q.T."

"What are you driving at?"

"Three percent of the premium," I said.

"Where's the ambulance? The pain is crippling me!" he yelled out at the top of his lungs.

"Five percent of the premium. I can't go higher."

"Get me down," he said quietly, wrapping his arms around my neck. "You're beginning to talk horse sense."

"Did you ever study acting?" I asked him as we left the theater.

"A year with Uta Hagan and two years with Lee Strasberg," he answered, grinning from ear to ear.

thirteen

This winter has been a real bitch, the coldest within, as they say, living memory. I haven't been getting out. I usually have dinner brought up so as not to lose any time on the horn. They make a creamy pea soup here and the most wonderful veal cutlets. Frankly, the meals at the Geneva are almost as good as the ones I used to have at Mrs. Hinkey's.

When I do get out, after dark, the streets are practically deserted. It's spooky. I haven't bumped into a single soul I know. I shaved off my beard. Too much trouble trimming it. I now practice the horn seven, eight hours a day.

Last night, Thanksgiving evening, I went down. The raw, bitter wind whipped at my clothes, sent snow flurries swirling around my ankles. My Burberry was inadequate and I wasn't wearing a hat. But I had to have fresh air, and I couldn't abide the thought of eating turkey alone in the hotel. How bleak and gray the city was! No one was out. Towers of concrete stood sullenly and vacantly on the sidewalks. Like forlorn beggars with their hands in their pockets. Where was everyone? Was the entire city at home eating turkey?

As I walked along with the cold nipping at me, I heard a horn bellowing in the wind. Immediately I remembered the young horn player seated against a tree in Central Park. And when I reached Third Avenue I saw, in a recessed alcove at the entrance of the Bowery Savings Bank, a group of musicians, a brass quartet of golden horns. And the young horn player with the purple beret was with them! I flew across the gutter, feeling giddy and foolish, but I was unable to stop myself.

There were no spectators, no audience. Still the quartet played, something of Telemann, I think. There were two trumpets (one trumpeteer was a young lady), a trombone and a horn. They were in their teens, bundled in goosedown parkas, woolen caps, mufflers and fingerless gloves. They sat on rickety crate boxes and had metal music stands; a bruised tin derby with some coins in it was on the ground in front of them. I no longer felt cold. The wind collapsed at my feet. It was as if the sun had suddenly broken through the slate-gray sky. How unselfconsciously they played! How arrogant they were in their young conceit! The horns echoed gloriously within the bank's alcove and tumbled in brassy waves over the empty streets. Ostentatiously I plucked a twenty-dollar bill from my Tiffany clasp and dropped it into the tin derby.

When they were done with the Telemann, I said, "That was terrific, really terrific," and to the young horn player, "We met in the park, remember?"

He shrugged, disinterestedly, but his cheeks flushed crimson. How thin he looked! And how ridiculous in his flapjack purple beret, with his hair long and stringy, and his hatchet-sharp face jutting out like a pinocchio carving.

How can I help you? What do you need? I thought.

But I asked the others, "Do you guys go to school?"

"A couple of us do," the trombone player answered, thumbing the spit valve of his horn and shaking it.

"Thank you for being so generous," the trumpet lady said, nudging her companion to remove the bill from the tin derby, which he did.

"I know this sounds outrageous but . . . I have my mouthpiece here. I'm a horn player, too. Would you mind very much if I sat in on the next one?" I said this to my young counterpart.

He wasn't at all pleased about it. He began to say no, but the word clotted in his mouth and he handed me the coils of gold, relinquishing his chair with an unfriendly scowl.

"What would you like to play?" I was asked by one of them.

I glanced through the sheet music. "Let's do the Bach Chorales." I started to feel anxious, uneasy, and wondered why I had gotten myself into this fix. I wanted to leave, but the opportunity to play with them, on the street, in the open, was too much of a temptation. I had the distinct feeling that I was living a fantasy of mine or reexperiencing a dream.

I blew a few notes, grateful for the hours I had been practicing lately. The trombone player scanned our faces and we took the beat from him. I fell behind several bars, caught up, ran ahead several bars, blew perhaps a bit more energetically than I should have, but we were soon playing together, the Bach, Four Dances by Praetorious, the Sander's Suite and a Maschera Canzon.

My friend, I don't know how it ended or how I got back to my hotel room. But I do know that I practiced for hours afterward, practiced until I couldn't stand it anymore, practiced until the people upstairs knocked madly on the ceiling. I do know that I got up from my chair and began to dance, began to swing and shake and jump, to jump higher and higher, higher and higher, and to sing, yes, to sing!

And I do know that I went to bed and that I slept like a baby, dreaming of playing with the Philharmonic for the first time in many, many years.

The giraffe and the bear dropped in one day to have it out with us.

"Did you think we'd forget, Edward? We didn't forget. And since you didn't extend to us the courtesy of a phone call, you can accept this letter of resignation for what it is, a letter of resignation." The giraffe threw a sheet of paper on Perry's desk.

"I am not doing the game show," he announced with finality. "I consider our contract null and void, and I am not saying another word!" He fluttered his eyelashes, stretched his neck, and sniffed up at the chandelier.

"What's all this about?" Perry asked me as if he didn't know. I had told him weeks ago that Jackie wanted to do the life of Mahatma Gandhi instead of "Horse Around." In fact I had given him the pages of Oscar Libin's outline, which he had thrown into the wastebasket without reading them. I hadn't read them either.

I went over it again for him. "Well, did you tell the network," he inquired petulantly. "The idea has merit. I think Jackie would be dynamite as the Mahatma."

"So do I," I said, not wanting to be in the minority. "I've been trying to set a meeting with Vogel, but you know how he is."

Perry exhaled a sigh of incalculable weariness. It was evident that having me as a partner was a burden to him. "My apologies, Jackie," he murmured contritely. "I've been traveling around the country, searching for contestants. I didn't know . . . Why don't you keep the letter of resignation until after I meet with Vogel?"

"I know I can trust you, Perry. I wouldn't say the same for you-know-who. But 'Horse Around' is going on in two weeks. I want to give you ample time to find a replacement for me."

"We have plenty of time," Perry answered him. "I'd like to talk to Oscar about the outline for the Mahatma series."

"Did you read it, Mr. Reese?" The bear hadn't moved from the door. He stood there, shaggy head embedded between sloping shoulders, still wearing his dirty safari outfit, his Hunting World canvas bag hanging at his side.

"What can I say, Oscar? Tell him what I said, Eddie?"

"The best thing he's ever read, including *Death of a Salesman*," I replied dutifully.

"We'll be working on the Mahatma outline with Oscar for the remainder of the day." Perry slipped the letter of resignation into the giraffe's pocket and opened the door for him. "You go home.

Relax. What's good for your career, Jackie, is good for our career."

"Thank you, Perry." The giraffe clasped his hand, arranged a meeting with Oscar, and pranced out of the office, without saying a word to me.

"Did you like all of the outline, Mr. Reese?" The bear took a tentative step into the room, but no more than that.

"Tell him what I said, Eddie."

"The best thing he's ever read, including Strindberg and Ibsen," I replied dutifully.

"You know what happened, don't you, Oscar?" Perry stared at the bear as if trying to get him to dive through a flaming hoop.

"What is it, Mr. Reese? I didn't . . . I haven't heard . . ." The bear was at a loss for words.

But Perry wasn't. "What does a bungalow at the Beverly Hills Hotel, per diem expenses in excess of actual expenses, and a fat contract to do a screenplay on the life of Mahatma Gandhi mean to you?" Perry asked him.

It was on occasions such as this that I had to admit that I was no match for Perry Reese.

Oscar's legs gave way under him and he plopped into a chair, holding his shaggy brown head between his stubby paws. "I . . . I can't believe it," he said, faintly, his eyes widening with bearish bewilderment.

"Tell him what I said, Eddie."

Thanks a lot, buddy. "It's true, Oscar. Perry and I thought so much of your Mahatma idea that we've been talking to a top studio exec. There's an element of risk here, of course. The contract hasn't been finalized . . ."

"Don't be your usual pessimistic self," Perry warned me.

"You tell him," I tossed it back at him.

"It looks good, Oscar, very good," Perry said. "We want you to fly out to L.A. this afternoon, check into the Beverly Hills Hotel, and get to work on the screenplay. It's stupid to waste Mahatma Gandhi on a TV series."

The bear started to shiver, perceptibly, his teeth clacking in his mouth. He took the canvas bag from his shoulder and clutched it to his chest for warmth. "Jackie . . . I told Jackie we'd do it together for t-t-television. I c-c-couldn't . . ."

"He doesn't want to do the screenplay," I said to Perry, a note of relief creeping into my voice.

"Then let him not do it!" Perry shouted, banging his manicured fists on the desk. "There's no copyright! We'll get someone else to write the damn thing!"

"Don't, p-p-please," the bear protested, getting up from his chair, his blubbery body shaking like a fur coat caught in a hurricane. "I have to do this screenplay. You fellows don't know how long . . . the years . . . forced to do t-t-television crap. Films, movies, the cin-cin-cinema, that's been my goal since I was a boy . . . living in the Bronx on Davidson Avenue, no heat, corn soup and banana sandwiches every night. You have to let me do it!"

He could have been sobbing under his haystack of hair for all we knew. Perry moved to the door and swung it open. "It's yours, Oscar. Get on that plane and send us the first draft by the fifteenth of the month," he ordered, pulling on Oscar's arm.

"Mr. Reese, I don't have enough money . . ."

"Do you have an American Express card?"

Oscar grunted unintelligibly.

"Well, that's what it's for, buddy." A hefty tug and Oscar was out in the hallway. Perry slammed the door shut behind him.

With the bear out of the way, we were able to deal with the giraffe. We phoned Jackie's agent and prophesied a seven-digit lawsuit if his client failed to fulfill the terms of his contract. The agent was unduly sympathetic and told us not to worry (whenever you're told not to worry, worry): Jackie was a professional, he told us, and professionals don't renege on their professional obligations, which made sense to us. But a week before we were to do the show, taped at the network theater, we received a call from a Doctor Something-or-other advising us that his patient, Jackie St. Claire, had come down with an intestinal flu, and was in no condition to perform for at least a month. There followed a series of meetings, renegotiations and visits to Jackie's apartment on Central Park South. During these visits Jackie sat aloofly and imperturbably in a tasseled, shantung dressing gown, knobby legs crossed, dabbing at his red snout and refusing to speak directly to us.

Not until an hour before the start of the show, with the theater jammed with network bigwigs, media people and once-upon-a-time celebrities, did we know whether or not Jackie would appear. We did have a no-talent hanging around in the alley if worse came to worse and we had to use him. I stayed out on the sidewalk for as long as possible. Jennifer was with me, wearing her evening attire of housepainter's coveralls, khaki officer's shirt, navy stocking cap and construction boots. Linda Reese was there also. In my meanest moments I couldn't have wished for Perry a wife like Linda. She was, I suppose, physically appealing: short, shapely, turquoise-tinted eyes, heftily boobed and haunched, bedecked in the best of everything, not a visible cell tissue unpreened or unattended. Beneath the goo there lived a nervous, neurotic, ambitious woman who had a tongue as finely honed as a machete. She'd hack at one's eardrums until nothing was left but strips of shredded flesh. She claimed to have an encyclopedic memory and answered any question thrown at her with unhesitating certainty and unfailing inaccuracy. Her two bratty kids were with us also, scrounging through a garbage can for discarded treasures. I was trying to think of an excuse to break away when Perry ran out to tell us that Jackie had arrived.

"Did you see him?"

"The stage manager saw him."

"Should we ... ?"

"Let's wait until later."

We all tramped into the theater, the wives and kids taking seats

225

downstairs while Perry and I went up to the control room to pace behind the technicians. Dan Bradley, our publicist, was giving a pep talk to the audience and they responded with enthusiasm. The six carousel horses and the ramp built inside the auditorium were so novel a concept that the very air was charged with a sense of adventure, and as soon as Jackie hopped into view and began his monologue, cracking a string of one-liners and radiating an eager, joyful conviviality, we knew we were home free.

Afterward there was a party at the Proof of the Pudding. The network bigwigs hung onto us as if our destinies had become inextricably entwined; they pounded our backs, pumped our hands, praised and hallelujahed us; they even started negotiations right then and there for three more game shows. Everyone was riding high.

It was after Perry had told Oscar Libin on the phone that the film studio had lost interest in the life of Mahatma Gandhi, that there was a volcanic eruption of applause and yelps of bravo. With that as a preamble, Jackie swept into the restaurant, his roseate head bobbing like a buoy on his elongated neck, a camel's-hair coat draped cavalierly over his shoulders; an entourage of apprentice lackeys trailed in after him.

He moved straight to us, barely acknowledging the applause. There was no guessing from his expression what his feelings were. He raised his arms for quiet, circling the floor as if he had just been declared yo-yo champion of the world.

"Ladies and gentlemen," he announced in his hoarse actor's voice. "I want to go on record as saying that the success of our show is due solely to the labors of these two geniuses. Their faith in me, an unknown off-Broadway thespian, and their uncompromising devotion to the principle that television does not have to be shallow or sophomoric in order to be commercial, are virtues that compel me to state publicly my eternal affection and everlasting gratitude to them."

Applause-applause-applause.

Maudlinly, he hugged and kissed Perry, then hugged and kissed

226

me, hissing into my ear, "We're even now, Edward Davis. Don't expect another favor from me for the rest of your life."

It would be misleading to say that Jennifer was indifferent to the skinny horn player's success, but her reaction, initially, was so blasé, so demeaningly nonchalant, that he was confused by it. He frequently said, as though to himself, "I did it. I'm a success." And she frequently said to him, as though to herself, "Why aren't you happy?" He didn't understand her. He couldn't follow her line of thought. What was she getting at? he wondered. What had one thing to do with the other? Why wasn't she congratulating him, telling him how wonderful he was, how he had won out against impossible odds? Why wasn't she adding up the weekly statements and saying, "My God, we're rich! You did it, sweetheart, you did it! You're really special; you're really a unique human being!"

But he got none of that from her, and he refused to ask her why, as was his way. Besides, there was plenty to keep him busy. A corporation had to be formed, lawyers and accountants retained, negotiations with the network pursued. Strike while the iron is hot, he sang to himself. Grab it while you can, he hummed to himself. Take the money and run, he laughed to himself while running to the bank in his rainbow-colored sneakers and custom-tailored sweat suit. And not only did he and Perry contract to do three more game shows for the network, but a couple of pilot sitcoms and a variety special as well!

He may not have been happy, but he was having fun. That money was divisible by fun was a mathematical equation that had never honestly occurred to him. He was a babe in the woods. He experimented with his shekels. He tipped waiters, cabbies, porters and chambermaids an extra 10 percent, and he was dumbfounded by the deluge of friendly faces and gestures of obseqiousness that poured down on him like manna from heaven. It didn't cost that much to be loved, he realized. He enjoyed himself. He traveled first class. He had a uniform for every occasion. He bought art books for the coffee table, something he had always wanted to do. People he knew changed. His doctor scolded him when he didn't keep an appointment for his annual checkup. His dentist sent him a Water Pik for his birthday. And the more he earned the harder it became for him to spend money. Business associates wouldn't allow him to pay for his meals. He received gifts from strangers. His mother stopped calling collect.

He came to believe that everything was a game, that if he could posture the appropriate attitude, evoke the appropriate tone of voice, he could get by with his life and attain a degree of contentment.

Secretly he admired his "buddy," Perry Reese, and tried to emulate him.

In time Jennifer reintroduced the matter of my horn playing, the promise I had made to return to it once the show was on the air. In my opinion, she had changed, too. She seemed to derive some kind of weird satisfaction out of making me feel guilty or emotionally uncomfortable or, on a less complicated level, inconveniencing me. For example, she insisted that during the week we have dinner at home, even though I usually didn't get home until after nine and it would have been much simpler and pleasanter for us to have dinner at a restaurant. And on weekends, I had a list, gulp, of chores to do: it was my responsibility to get my shirts from the laundry, my suits from the dry cleaner's and my shoes from the repair shop; it was also my responsibility to accompany her to the supermarket and personally carry the bags of groceries through the streets, up the stairs and into the apartment; and it was left to me to screw in electric bulbs, grease door hinges, tighten faucets, calk tubs, unplug drains, etcetera, etcetera. Of course all of this could have been done by the super (the other chores by a delivery boy), but she wouldn't hear of it. Don't ask me why.

The horn, yes.

We were having dinner at the kitchen table. Jennifer was stark naked. Jennifer was always stark naked. As soon as she came into the apartment the first thing she'd do was peel off her clothes and walk around stark naked. It was a new habit of hers. Frankly she didn't look that great stark naked. She was too bony, her breasts too spiked, and I had already seen her stark naked countless times so that there was no legitimate reason for her to walk around stark naked. I wanted to say to her: Sweetheart, I find you infinitely more attractive fully clothed, especially when we're having dinner. But I said nothing. I didn't want to depress her.

Anyway, we were eating at the kitchen table; that is, Jennifer was eating, I was pretending. She scooped the food into her mouth, a watery stew with hard potatoes and soggy carrots; her head was bent over, her shoulders curved around the dish as if defining her territorial prerogatives. When she ate a meal, she didn't talk. Blissful sighs and moans escaped from between her large, masticating teeth. She became completely absorbed in the sequential steps of the digestive process; her face shone with an intense, euphoric concentration. Should the need arise, she belched with uninhibited vigor, and offered no apology.

Melvin, her ugly cat, was curled in a charcoal-striped bun on the washing machine, staring at me with his evil green eyes. He hadn't humped my leg in weeks, not since I had sent him skidding across the room with a beautifully executed soccer kick, and I knew he was scheming to even the score.

After swallowing the last morsel on her dish, Jennifer rose from her chair to get a coconut, an ice pick and a hammer. She put the coconut on the table, stabbed it with the ice pick, and then started to bang at it with the hammer. The dishes bounced crazily on the table.

"Would you like me to do that?"

She shook her head, wiping the jet-black bangs from her forehead. "I can do it, honey. Would you like coconut chips or would you prefer grated coconut on the chocolate pudding?"

"I'm full, thank you. How . . . How did your day go today?" I had learned enough to ask her that question every evening.

"Good. I won over eighty dollars playing three-card monte," she answered, banging away at the coconut. A salt shaker rolled off the table and crashed on the floor. "Leave it. I'll sweep up later," she said as she continued to hammer at the coconut.

"That reminds me, Jen. I received a phone call this afternoon from a Mrs. Miller. She's a neighbor of ours. I think she lives across the hall."

"I know her. She's a nosy bitch. She's worse than that degenerate couple on the ground floor who have an open marriage. What did she want?"

"She was complaining about the people who come to play cards with you. She said they were from the Mafia. She intends to tell the landlord."

"Let her go fuck herself where she breathes," was her neighborly response, and she swung the hammer down on the coconut as if it was Mrs. Miller's head. Shards of coconut whizzed through the air, hitting the walls like buckshot pellets. One piece caught me an inch below the eye.

"Oh, my God, what did I do?" Jennifer screamed; the hammer flew out of her hand and landed on top of the gas range, shattering our Pyrex coffeepot.

And with that as an excuse, Melvin jumped off the washing machine and went straight for my leg. He got in one hump before I slammed him against the bottom of the table.

"Will you take your cat!" I yelled at Jennifer, holding a towel to my eye. "What's going on here? Everything's breaking, he's humping me and you blinded me with a coconut shell!"

"Leave Daddy's leg alone!" She shooed Melvin out of the kitchen, then pressed my head against her spiky breasts and said, "Let me see it, darling, please. If you're blind, I'll blind myself, I swear. Do you feel better?"

Fortunately there was only a slight scratch under my eye. Jennifer washed it, dabbed some iodine on it, and with her arm around my waist led me into the bedroom.

"Can you see all right, honey?"

"Half and half."

"Don't talk. I'll do the talking. Do you want something to eat?"

"I thought we just had dinner."

"We didn't have dessert and an egg nog I have cooling in the refrigerator. Don't talk. I'll get it for you in a minute. I'm glad this happened tonight, darling." She lowered the window shades and started to undress me. "It shows how much tension there is in this apartment. You bring the tension home with you from the office. When are you quitting the agency?" She asked this with a casual, matter-of-fact tone.

At first I didn't know whether she was serious or not. Could she be serious? Did she really want me to quit the agency? I was earning close to five thousand a week! What if we connected with another show, with another two shows? Did she have any idea what that added up to? What was she talking about?

"Honey?"

"Yes?"

"I asked you when you were quitting the agency," she repeated, tucking me into bed.

"Soon," I mumbled.

Her voice became strident, pitched a bit too high. "Didn't you say you were quitting when you got the show on? Didn't you say you were going back to the horn? Didn't you promise me that?"

"There's no hurry."

"There is a hurry. There definitely is. You've been working twelve, fifteen hours a day. You're away every other week. We have no life together. We have no home, no family . . . I know you don't want children. I'm not talking about that. I'm talking about having a family life, of doing things together, and spending time together. Is this what you want, Eddie, what we have now? If it is, I don't know why you wanted to get married. I don't know the reason for our getting married."

Most of what she said I couldn't follow. The words rushed out of her, gushed out of her as if they had been scorching her tongue for a long while. She sat on the edge of the bed, her ebony-bright eyes glistening tearfully in the dark room.

I pretended to be thinking.

"Honey, I know you've been miserable these past few years," she went on, taking my hand in hers. "You'll always be miserable unless you go back to the horn and give it everything you have. Isn't that what you want? Isn't that what you always wanted?"

Go back to the horn! She had to be kidding. Close to five thousand a week! Five thousand! How many horn players wouldn't cut their throats to be in my shoes! What was she hassling me for? Why didn't she say, "You did it, sweetheart. No one thought you could. They had you pegged for a loser. But you did it. You're wonderful, you're marvelous, how I love you!"

"Perry depends on me . . ." I began.

"Fuck Perry!" she blurted angrily, releasing my hand. "You don't owe that degenerate anything! You made the show a success. He should be kissing your ass in front of Macy's." I could hear her heart pumping away, her breath fluttering like butterfly wings in the darkness. "Honey, you're not a lousy TV producer; you're more than that, much, much more. Remember what you told me your friend the hunchback said to you about your music? He knew and I know, believe me. Are you gonna quit? Tell me you're gonna quit."

"It'll take a few months. I can't just . . ."

"That's all right. Are you quitting in a few months?"

I mumbled a sound that could have been construed as a yes.

"Thank you, sweetheart," she said, kissing me with her salty mouth. "You won't be sorry. When you're playing the horn again, we'll be happy. I know we will, even if it's only the two of us and Melvin. I'll get the dessert now and we'll watch a little television and then we'll do something we never did before."

232

"What's that?"

"We'll have a late night snack of pastrami and macaroni salad."

She must have been counting the months. It was on a Saturday that she brought up the subject of my leaving the agency again. But I was prepared for it. Some weeks before I had signed a deed to a town house on East 73rd Street and as soon as she asked me if Perry knew I was quitting, I took hold of her arm and told her to come along; we grabbed a cab and rode downtown. At a solid, vermilion door, I gave her the keys to a narrow, four-storied brick building with white, glossy trim. She fumbled with the keys; the expression on her face was puzzled, but amused, not the least critical. She unlocked the door and we entered the house. The V-slatted parquet floors had been waxed and buffed to a mirrored sheen; the walls had been freshly painted. Sunlight streamed in through the curtainless windows. Everything glowed and shimmered. And in the middle of the bare living-room floor, I had spread a picnic tablecloth on which I had placed an ice-filled bucket with a bottle of Moet in it, and two crystal champagne glasses. I poured the wine and handed a glass to Jennifer.

"Welcome home," I said ceremoniously, pecking at her cheek.

"Is it ours?" Her eyes were as wide as sweater buttons as she took it all in.

I nodded, feeling enormously pleased with myself. I couldn't have hoped for a better reaction from her. "It's not paid for yet but . . . Let me show you around."

Taking the bottle of champagne with us, we toured the house, stopping in every room, examining every closet, every fixture, as we climbed up and down the four flights of stairs.

"It's too big," Jennifer kept saying. "We don't need this much space. What are we gonna do with six bedrooms? Eddie, it's too big, really. Can't you give it back?"

"In twenty years, after we pay the mortgage," I got a laugh out and guided her to the cedar-paneled basement.

An old pool table with vintage accessories was set equidistantly from the cedar walls.

"I bought it from the previous owner," I informed Jennifer, spilling the last of the champagne into our glasses. "Do you like it?"

"It's beautiful, it is, but what are we gonna do with it?"

"We'll have to learn how to play pool."

"That's not such a hot idea." She ran her hands over the table's smooth, taut felt, then shook her head, thoughtfully, scraping her lower lip with her large, protruding teeth. "Well, I guess there's one thing we can do with it," she said, and before I could chalk a pool stick, she peeled off her clothes, scrambled on top of the table, and sank her hands and heels into the four corner pockets.

I stripped and made love to her, begging my body to give her pleasure.

We lay on the pool table for hours, maybe for days.

I thought of saying, I love you, sweetheart.

Outside it started to rain. We covered ourselves with my jacket.

The champagne was gone. Jennifer found a package of fig newtons in her pocketbook and we finished them, drinking water from the sink.

She said, "You worked hard for this, honey. You deserve it."

"Thank you," I said.

"It must have cost a fortune."

"My accountant said it's a wise investment."

"But with the mortgage payments and . . ." A frown clouded her face. "Eddie, did you tell Perry you're quitting?"

"I will," I answered, swallowing a lump in my throat.

"Do you know how many months it is since you promised me you'd tell him?" She scrambled off the pool table and started dressing. "You haven't done anything about it, have you?"

"I told you there was no hurry." I sat up and put on my jacket. "Jen, I have a contract with the network to fulfill. You knew about the contract. I can't just walk away. They can sue me for every penny..."

"Bullshit! That's bullshit!" she screamed at me. "You lied to me, didn't you? You had no intention of quitting!"

"I didn't lie. I am quitting. I..."

"Stop it, Eddie, stop it!" She was crying now, the tears sliding down her cheeks and forming huge puddles at her feet. *Don't lie to me anymore. Please. Don't lie to me!*"

She stood still for a moment, her thin chest heaving convulsively, crying from deep inside herself.

Then, biting wretchedly on her lower lip, she grabbed her pocketbook and ran upstairs. I heard the vermilion door slam shut behind her.

My friend, if I had been around at that time, do you know what I would have done to the skinny horn player? With one hand I would have held him by his scrawny neck, and with the other I would have bloodied his nose, his mouth, blackened his eyes, pummeled and punched him with my fist until he lay on that pool table in a helpless, sniveling heap.

I would have done just that, if I had been around at that time.

I wouldn't have talked to him or explained anything to him.

It would have been useless.

He was unapproachable; he couldn't be reached; he was incapable of changing.

I realize now that he, too, has become a distraction, an obstacle, a burden to me.

The memory of him nibbles at my dreams like a rat on a piece of cheese.

Why do I go on writing about him?

Is it to "entertain" myself when I'm not practicing the horn?

I don't believe that anymore.

Perhaps I do so, as a holy man prays, in the hope that I can exorcise him, once and for all, from my earthly flesh.

fourteen

Moving into the town house on East 73rd Street was a mistake. Jennifer was right. It was too big for us. It had too many rooms, too many staircases, too many nooks and crannies. The furniture we owned was lost in vast areas of emptiness. When we spoke to one another, our voices echoed hollowly and falsely against the freshly painted walls.

We rarely went down to the basement.

We didn't learn how to shoot pool.

The pool table buckled, sagged, fell forward on its knees like some mortally wounded animal.

Whatever Jennifer was thinking she didn't tell me. She buried her thoughts and never mentioned my quitting the agency or my horn playing again. She made no effort to furnish the house. It was as if it didn't belong to her. I had no idea what she was doing with herself. When I asked her she said, "I'm looking for the silver lining." I couldn't get a handle on where she was at. She borrowed five thousand dollars from me and went to Las Vegas with Melvin, her ugly cat. "To make money at blackjack, for personal reasons," she said, tight-lipped. When she returned, she wouldn't tell me what had happened. "You'll get your money back with interest," was all she said.

And always I had the feeling that she wanted me to say something, but I didn't know what she wanted me to say.

The point is I couldn't talk to her.

I didn't know what game we were playing and consequently I didn't know what was expected of me.

I said nothing.

(The skinny horn player said nothing and I am no longer responsible for what he did or didn't do.)

The following year I arranged, as an investment, to buy eleven acres of land in Manchester, Vermont. I recall signing the necessary papers at a midtown real estate office and arriving home earlier than usual. In the foyer I picked an umbrella from the rack and waited for Melvin to come charging at me for his evening hump. I made it easier for him by pushing my leg out and pointing my shoe at the ceiling. Behind me I firmly held the umbrella, ready to whack him a couple of good ones.

I waited in vain. No Melvin. Somewhere upstairs a typewriter was clattering raucously. I returned the umbrella to the rack and climbed to the fourth floor. In an atticlike room Jennifer was seated at a white Formica desk, typing away. She was wearing a prisoner's coarse shirt, nothing else. On her lap was a box of Tootsie Rolls and Tootsie Roll wrappers littered the floor. Neither the desk nor the typewriter had been there the previous evening.

I pecked at her cheek. "How . . . How did your day go today?" I asked her by rote.

She waved me toward the door, as if to say, Can't you see I'm working? Why are you interrupting my work? Do I interrupt your work when you're working?

I started to leave, waved back to her, as if to say, I'll meet you downstairs when you finish your work, and added, aloud, "Where's Melvin?"

She pounded the typewriter without answering me.

In the living room I poured myself a scotch, neat, and turned the pages of my coffee table art books. The truth was that things were going from bad to worse between Jennifer and myself. A lot was left unsaid. A lot was said that wasn't meant. There were words under the words and they hurt and gave pain. I thought she was being narrow-minded and inconsiderate. She hadn't had my experiences. She hadn't lived my life. How many years had she spent in a cold-water, roach-infested tenement? How many meals had she missed?

Who was her father? Who? Was he *my* father?

And more, plenty, plenty more. Where did she come off with that holier-than-thou crap! Didn't she have enough insight to know why I was doing what I was doing? It was no mystery, not even to me. I had needs, too, damn it! I had to have someone say, and I didn't care what motivated it, let it be for producing a lousy television show, "Eddie, you're indispensable. We couldn't have done it without you." Did I ever get that playing the horn? Forget the money, how about a kind word? encouragement? being sought after? And it was for the both of us I worked twelve, fifteen hours a day, wasn't it? Did she have any doubt that I loved her, that I wanted to grow old with her? shrink with her? hobble arm-in-arm with her into a nursing home?

Didn't that count for anything? Faithfulness! Devotion! Commitment! For cryin'-out-loud, in all the time I had been married to her I hadn't even looked at another woman! And talk about opportunities! Opportunities? I could have balled every night in the week! I could have been making it with the most gorgeous, the most luscious, the . . . What's the difference. But just the same, didn't that count for anything? Why was she always angry with me? Why did she put down my achievements? Because I wasn't a horn player? You have to be kidding. What was it then? What did she want from me, for cryin'-out-loud!

She finally came into the living room, sat at the other end of the sofa, placing the box of Tootsie Rolls on the coffee table.

"Hi. How did your day go today?" I repeated in case she hadn't heard me upstairs.

238

"We have to talk," she began, dully, unwrapping a Tootsie Roll and tossing the crushed wrapper behind the sofa.

"You first," I said, smiling. "Where's ugly Melvin?"

As she chewed on the candy, she unwrapped another. "He's dead," she replied, dully.

"Dead? When . . . ?"

"A week ago Friday." Pause. Chew-chew-chew. "You didn't know, did you?" She stared at me, her face grave and impenetrable.

I shook my head.

"He was at the vet's for two weeks before that. You must feel relieved." There was no bitterness in her voice; it was as if she was delivering a prepared speech.

"No, Jen, I'm not. I . . ."

"Let's not talk about him."

"Just one question."

She allowed it, reluctantly.

"What did Melvin die of?"

"A fur ball. Cats die of fur balls, but I think it was something else. I think it was a lack of affection and . . ." She forced herself not to continue. "Let's skip it," she said. "I'm going back to work. You're not against my working, are you?"

"No, no . . ."

"I spoke to Linda Reese. She's very enthusiastic about it."

"About your going back to work?"

"About the book I'm writing."

"You're writing a book?"

"I started this morning. Linda's publishing company can't give me an advance, but they want first refusal." She kept shoving Tootsie Rolls into her mouth, like a kid trying to find out how many would fit in there. "Are you interested in knowing what my book is about?" she asked.

She spoke so intensely that I felt frightened for her. I wiped off the Tootsie Roll juice dripping down her chin with my handkerchief. "Yes, yes, I am," I answered hurriedly. "What is your book about?"

"Hookers," she said. "It's tentatively titled *Private Interviews With Public Hookers*. I'll be using a pseudonym, Felicia Travis. I don't want people saying I achieved anything because I'm the wife of a successful producer. What do you think?"

"Think?"

"About the subject of my book."

"I think it's been done already."

"Are you saying I shouldn't do it? Are you discouraging me from having a career of my own?"

"No, no, I think it's a terrific idea. I'm very enthusastic. I'm more enthusiastic than Linda who doesn't know her ass from her elbow."

"Okay. That's all I wanted to hear."

"Jen, how ... How did you get into hookers?"

"One of the women I played cards with was a hooker."

"Oh."

"You realize I won't be able to cook dinner for you in the future, don't you?"

"That's all right."

"Nor shop nor furnish the house nor do any of the things a wife is supposed to do."

"That's all right."

"You won't be depressed if it turns out I'm more successful than you are, will you?"

"No, no, not at all. By the way, I bought some land in Vermont and I thought we'd go up there this weekend ..."

"I can't. I have interviews with hookers in Newark, New Jersey this weekend. I'm giving it everything I have," she said, and went back to her typewriter, taking the box of Tootsie Rolls with her.

An army of hookers began to trudge into our house on East 73rd Street. Jennifer tape-recorded their sordid histories, typed from the tapes until the wee hours of the morning. She blocked everything else from her mind and worked with a resolve that was truly admirable. Perhaps I would have shown more interest in what she was doing if the hookers she interviewed had been of a better class, let's say call girls who got a hundred dollars a throw. But incomprehensibly, at least to me, she chose the dregs, the lowest of the low, hookers who would have had difficulty giving it away at a naval training station. I don't know where she found them. Scarred, bruised, decrepit hags with blistered feet and scabby faces, many without visible boobs and others with boobs flapping down to their knees like gunny sacks. She sat with them in her "office," the atticlike room on the fourth floor, hour after hour, totally engrossed in what they had to tell her. Occasionally, when using our Finnish rowing machine on the third floor, I couldn't avoid overhearing their muted dialogue.

"Did the John fuck you, Sonny?"

"Uh-huh," Sonny replied. "He ask' me for golden showers."

"What's golden showers?"

"Pee-pee."

"He wanted to pee-pee on you?"

"Uh-huh."

"Did you let him?"

"Nobody pee-pee on me."

"So how did you deal with the sick son of a bitch?"

"I call my girlfriend, Cora."

"She lets them pee-pee on her?"

"Uh-huh. She do anything for a buck. She got no principles."

"I'd like to meet Cora."

"I send her up. You in for a big surprise."

And there were evenings when I came home to an empty house. On the kitchen table there would be a note from Jennifer which contained the address of a whorehouse and instructions to phone the police if the alarm clock rang and she wasn't in bed. There were also evenings when she invited a few of her collaborators to dinner and one Sunday when a whole gang of them dropped in from Scranton, Pennsylvania, and partied through the night. But it was when the lavishly decorated pimp limousines started to sprout like mushrooms along the curbstones of East 73rd Street that I got to know my neighbors on a first-name basis.

After a polite telephone call, a delegation from the Block Association arrived at my office. Mike, Bob, Rhonda, and Corkey introduced themselves and chatted about this and that before getting into it. From their point of view, their grievance had merit. It wasn't a concern for real estate values that had prompted their visit, they informed me, but a concern for the safety of their children. It seems that Corkey's twelve-year-old son was actually propositioned by one of Jennifer's collaborators who, for ten dollars, had promised to sell him a bush. When Corkey refused to give her son the ten dollars for the bush, he went into a violent tantrum that required a prescription sedative and the services of a therapist.

I told them that the matter would be taken care of promptly. And I meant to speak to Jennifer about it, but she was so absorbed in the writing of her book that I decided, rather than to cause her any uneasiness, to sacrifice the chance of conversing with my neighbors on a first-name basis.

During all of this, Perry and I were putting together a variety special to feature Jackie St. Claire, and a sit-com written by our alcoholic playwright. An earlier sit-com of ours went to pilot and bombed ignominiously; there was a little pressure on us from the network, but nothing to worry about: when you tell yourself there's nothing to worry about, start worrying. Anyway, "Horse Around" was running during prime time and contracted for syndication; the bloom was still on the heather and the hoar was still in the wings.

We dissolved the agency and were now operating solely as producers. We dubbed our company Nightingale Enterprises, in tribute to our alma mater, and we moved into more spacious offices in the same building on West 55th Street. We employed a receptionist, a pair of secretaries and a script reader. We were, I suppose, unregenerate chauvinists. Our employees were young, single and, with the exception of the reader, smashingly good-looking: they emitted in their wake whiffs of erotic essences and squishy currents of soft fabrics and succulent thighs. We gave them nicknames. Perry's secretary was Muff, mine was Puff; the receptionist was Bubbles and the reader Rosey Posey.

(Sisters, I go on record as disowning the two of them. Macho pigs! Male vermin! Sexist scum! Uggg! I should mention, however, in defense of the skinny horn player, that Perry did the hiring and the skinny horn player nicknamed only one of them, Rosey Posey.)

The traffic in and out of the office was heavy and continuous. Writers, directors, actors, TV execs, casting agents, independent producers, weirdoes of every ilk and kind sat on each other's laps in the reception room or lined up in the corridor as if we were giving away tax-exempt municipal bonds. The place was in a perpetual turmoil. The phones buzzed, memos flew back and forth, there were meetings, conferences, emergencies at the network theater, trips to the lawyers and/or accountants, etcetera, etcetera. I worked closely with our alcoholic playwright, Steve Mitchum by name, on the sit-com, and with the writers — Oscar Libin was among them — on the variety special. I also read, diligently, the material Rosey Posey brought to me, scripts, screenplays, outlines, novels and news stories that could be converted into grist for the boob-tube mill.

I wanted very much to have another successful show. For the money, yes, primarily for the money, but also to prove to myself that I was capable of bringing it off again, this time through the deliberate exercise of skill and judgment.

I was mesmerized by the possibility of making millions.

All around me I saw idiots raking it in, piling it up, stashing it away.

Why not me? I had infinitely more talent than the rest of them. Who said I couldn't earn a couple of million? Who said I couldn't cash in, get lucky, become King of the Game Show? This was America, wasn't it?

(That was what he had come to. His ambition was to "earn a couple of million." God, dear God, free me of him! tear him from my flesh! There's no sense to it anymore. It's over, past, dead. Let me practice my horn. Let me work on the Weber Concertino. What has any of this to do with me? King of the Game Show? Enough! Enough!)

I was off to a good start. I knew who to know. I had my foot in the door. Besides, I already had several hundred thousand in the bank, and property, insurance policies, annuities, equities . . . I was doing terrifically, terrifically!

Yet I couldn't rid myself of a feeling of imminent catastrophe, of an oppressive anxiety that forewarned me, illogically but persuasively, that I could be declared bankrupt at any moment. I would wake up in the middle of the night, drenched in the stink of my own sweat, my heart thumping away like a dog's tail. I would lose everything. I would be poor. I would blow it and be left out on the sidewalk, staring through the grimy window of a White Rose bar.

I wanted to say to Jennifer: We have to go easy on expenses; we have to economize; we're spending beyond our means.

I wanted to say to my accountant: You're charging me too much for your services; I'm afraid I'll have to let you go.

I wanted people to understand that my possessions were ephemeral, that they could vanish in a twinkling of an eye, that the foreign situation and the domestic policies of our government continually threatened my meager savings.

I thought of talking to Perry about it. How are you protecting yourself, buddy? Got a tax shelter you can recommend? What are they up to down on Wall Street? But the skunk acted as if he was guaranteed a million a year. Money poured out of him.

Dollar bills flowered on his fingertips. Coins dripped from his nose. His eardrums manufactured certified checks. He owned a house in Scarsdale, a co-op on Park Avenue, a ski chalet in Aspen, several imported cars, supported a cook and a maid, and walked around with his hands in his empty pockets, whistling "Raindrops Keep Falling on My Head." The man was totally devoid of imagination.

I said nothing to no one.

But I knew that I had to earn more money, a lot more money, or I would never know a minute's peace.

I worked hard, too hard. I was good at the creative end of producing; Perry was unbeatable in selling to the networks whatever I threw at him. I wouldn't go so far as to suggest that he didn't work as hard as I did, but he certainly was out a great deal more than I was, and he certainly wasn't cutting into his long weekends or missing the chance to get laid because of a business engagement. Jennifer was right about him, too. He was a degenerate. He had to cheat on his wife. He had to dip his polished shlong into every pretty girl who said hello to him. He rationalized his gluttony by saying, "I can do without sex, Eddie, but I can't do without love." Can you believe it? I wondered how the man could live with himself, how he could go home after whoring with one of his girlfriends and face his wife and kids. The energy he expended in concealing the truth from his family and in scheduling his myriad liaisons would have been sufficient to power a fleet of submarines across the Atlantic, both ways.

Somewhere in the warped recesses of his warped mind, he had drawn a line, and he didn't try to make, rape, or penetrate any of our employees. "You don't dirty in your own backyard," was his explanation for this heroic moral decision. After working until seven or eight, we'd all go to a nearby pub and unwind by sipping booze and gossiping about one thing and another. I enjoyed this hour or two. I liked getting high and I liked gabbing with Muff, Puff, Bubbles and my favorite, Rosey Posey. They'd talk about diaphrams, abortions and orgasms with good-natured candor. I could forget, for the moment, how much money I was losing by not being more successful.

Steve Mitchum, our alcoholic playwright, would usually join us. He was a garrulous man in his late forties with mottled, veiny cheeks; he had shaved off the few hairs that survived at the rim of his scalp, and his head was as bald and clean as a new balloon. I never saw him drink more than a single glass of wine, and yet he was always drunk or was always playing at being drunk, I really couldn't tell. He'd do anything for a laugh: drop his pants in public, turn over a pitcher of water on his hairless head, introduce himself to strangers, and carry on like a raving lunatic. Perry would delight in provoking him into the most outrageous behavior, and we'd all be rolling on the floor, our bellies cramped with laughter.

Then we'd pack it in when Perry went off to meet his date for the evening and I was required by the laws of matrimony to be at home for the ten o'clock news which began with the stern reprimand, "Do you know where your children are tonight?"

But as I said, frequently Jennifer wasn't at home. There'd be her note on the kitchen table with instructions to phone the police if the alarm clock rang and she wasn't in bed. It happened that one night the alarm clock did ring — it was at three in the morning — and she wasn't in bed. I immediately dialed the police emergency number. The line was busy. I re-read Jennifer's note. The instructions were there, but no address of a whorehouse where, presumably, she was doing her investigatory work. I phoned the police again. The line was still busy. I phoned Perry at his Park Avenue co-op. He hadn't heard from her, he told me, yawning luxuriously into the receiver. Linda must have grabbed the phone from his hand.

"I knew it, Eddie! I knew it" she screamed hysterically. "It's just what I expected! We're coming over!"

"I have to go to the police station. What do you mean you expected . . . ?"

She hung up on me.

I dressed and rushed out of the house, leaving the key in the mailbox for them. It was too late to get my car or a cab, so I ran along Fifth Avenue to 85th Street and into Central Park. Hidden in the depths of the park was a police station, the only one I knew in the neighborhood. Can you imagine what it was like running into Central Park at three in the morning? Can you imagine what it was like being mugged in Central Park at three in the morning while running to a police station to report your wife missing? Don't. You probably have enough nightmares as it is.

I entered the park and sprinted past the Metropolitan Museum. There were no cars in either direction on the transverse. A gossamer moon grinned behind a veil of clouds. Trees leaned against each other and dozed quietly on both edges of the roadway. All I could hear was the clapping of my own shoes on the asphalt. I regretted not taking a weapon with me, a knife or a baseball bat. On the curbstone, near the bushes, I spotted an iron bar used for changing tires. I bent over to pick it up. Suddenly I was embraced from behind, jerked off my feet by a muscular arm, and pressed possessively to a perspiring, manly chest.

"Don't move or I'll knock the shit outta you," a voice crooned mellifluously in my ear.

I didn't move. I stared up at the sky, dangling on my assailant's arm, trying to spot the Big Dipper. My wallet was torn from my pocket and I was rudely dropped to the ground. Unwittingly I turned to see a pair of dark shapes dashing into the bushes. They were of adult size, wearing Hawaiian shirts with Oriental surfers imprinted on them.

At the station house, where I shortly arrived, panting and lapping for breath, there was a young police officer, in shirt-sleeves, playing backgammon under a green-shaded bulb. He looked like

247

a high school kid to me: his auburn hair was well brushed and neatly parted, and he wore a pair of tortoise-rimmed specs.

"My wife! My wife! She's missing!" I shouted at him. "And I was just mugged in the park by a couple of men wearing Hawaiian shirts!"

He stared at me as if I had no business there. Cautiously he moved an ivory checker on the backgammon board before shaking the dice in a leatherette cup.

"My wife! My wife! She's missing! And I was just mugged in the park by a couple of men wearing Hawaiian shirts!" I shouted at him again.

Spilling the dice on the table, he asked coolly, politely even, "Do you know how to play backgammon, mister?"

"What's going on here?" I yelled at him. "The city's falling apart! Crime's rampant! Taxes are sky high! Can't a private citizen get any attention!"

"You're having a bad night, huh?" He moved a maroon checker ten places.

"The worst. I just hope my wife is all right. She told me if she wasn't in bed when the alarm clock rang to get in touch with the police. But your line was busy and she forgot to leave me the address of the whorehouse."

At last he seemed interested. He angled his chair toward me. "What whorehouse?" he asked.

"Where she does her research work."

"In a whorehouse?"

"She's there practically every night. She goes under the name of Felicia Travis."

"No offense, mister, but what do you do for a living?"

I soaked my handkerchief at the water fountain and sponged my face with it. "I'm a television producer," I said. "Did you ever watch 'Horse Around'? That's my show."

"Hey, Clifford, come in here," he called out. "This man says he's a television producer, his wife's in a whorehouse, and he was just mugged in the park!"

"Have you been drinking, mister?" Clifford stood in the doorway of an adjacent room. Behind him I could see a switchboard flashing. He was younger than the high school kid, his hair was well brushed and parted, he was in shirt-sleeves, and he was chewing on a wad of bubble gum.

"Look, fellows, I don't have time for this. You can verify everything I said by phoning my attorney, Mr. Samson, at 555–2368."

"What's your name?"

"Edward Davis."

Clifford glanced at his fraternity brother. "What do you think, Darcy?"

"Check it out?"

Clifford nodded, cracked a series of masterly bubbles, and returned to his switchboard.

"What was that you said about muggers, Mr. Davis?" Darcy put on his blue cap, a gesture, I suppose, to signify that we were now officially engaged.

"They were wearing Hawaiian shirts with Oriental surfers on them. They grabbed me in the park and took my wallet. Can I ask you a question, officer?" There was an embarrassing tremor in my voice. "Why do you have a police station in the middle of the park? Aren't you setting up the private citizen for the benefit of the mugger?"

Darcy went into himself, weighed at length the pros and cons of my complaint. He appeared incapable of reaching a satisfactory explanation.

"He's Edward Davis, all right," Clifford called from the switchboard. "I'll get on the muggers. Did you say they were Oriental, Mr. Davis?"

"No, I did not. I said the surfers on their Hawaiian shirts were Oriental."

"How do you know that?"

"They had slanted eyes."

"On their Hawaiian shirts?"

"Yes."

"Were the muggers black?"

"I didn't say they were black, did I?"

"Were they Hispanic?"

"Did you hear me say they were Hispanic? Where are you getting your information from?"

Clifford came into the room, blew a bubble to affirm his civil service status. "What were they, Mr. Davis? Let's cut the kidding around."

"I couldn't see their faces. It was too dark and their backs were to me."

"But you saw the faces on the Hawaiian shirts?" Clifford was losing his temper. I could tell because he was blushing.

"Yes. The shirt faces were Oriental. There was a gossamer moon. I could see the faces on their shirts by the light of the gossamer moon."

"Do you believe him?" Clifford looked to Darcy who took a raspberry lollipop from his pocket and stuck it into his cheek.

"Check it out?"

Clifford nodded and bubbled his way to the switchboard.

"Look, I don't care about the muggers," I said to Darcy. "What about my wife? She's in danger, not the muggers."

"How did you get into television, Mr. Davis?" Darcy leaned forward and spoke in a whisper so Clifford couldn't hear him.

"Television?"

"I'd like to get into television myself," he murmured, the lollipop stick wagging in his mouth. "This job is a dead end for an ambitious person."

"That's it, Darcy. I'm not answering any of your questions until you find my wife."

"Couldn't we have lunch together and talk?"

I didn't answer him.

"Don't get upset, Mr. Davis. Here, fill this in." He handed me a mimeographed sheet. "We'll get out a call on your wife."

I did as he asked, quickly, delineating a description of Jennifer

— "artistic, impulsive, accident-prone" — and gave the sheet back to him.

"You go home now," Darcy said. "If your wife shows up, phone us."

"How do I get home? You don't expect me to walk through the park again, do you?"

"No chance of us having lunch?"

I didn't answer him.

"Can you tell me why?"

I didn't answer him.

"Would you like me to phone a cab for you?"

"No. I've had it with you," I snapped at him, and shouted to his fraternity brother at the switchboard, "Clifford, please call a cab for me. I'm not talking to Darcy anymore!"

fifteen

At the vermilion door on East 73rd Street, Perry and Linda Reese were waiting for me. Morning sunlight seeped over the rooftops. I told them about the muggers and my experience at the police station. Linda pushed a manila envelope under my arm as I dug for the key in the mailbox. Even at this hour she was preened and plucked to waxy perfection.

"What's this?" I asked her.

"Jenny's manuscript on hookers."

"She finished?"

"Weeks ago."

"But she's still out interviewing . . ." I dropped the thought like a hot potato. "Is the book any good?"

"The worst piece of writing I've read in my nine years as a senior editor," she replied, mercilessly. "Did you read it?"

I shook my head.

"No wonder she ran away."

"Ran away? What are you talking about?"

"Let's go inside. I have a lot to tell you."

In the living room I said, "All right, let's hear it. I'm tired and I'm hungry; I'm anxious and I'm depressed. Where's Jennifer?"

"Don't crossexamine my wife," Perry said, without humor, as

he searched through one of Jennifer's pocketbooks for a clue to her whereabouts.

"I can defend myself," Linda said to her husband, as she searched through a chest of drawers in the foyer, examining each piece of Jennifer's clothing, especially the labels.

"He can speak to you in that tone of voice when I'm not here, but when I'm here he's going to have to use another tone of voice," Perry persisted.

"Will you mind your own business and let me . . ." Linda began.

"He feeds on dissension," Perry interrupted. "Darling, I know him like I know the fingers on my hand. He's jealous of what we have. Don't let him belittle what we have by speaking to you in that tone of voice."

"Were you belittling what we have?" Linda raised her turquoise-tinted eyes to me.

I slumped into the Voltaire chair. "Linda, please. I don't want to get into it. I'm tired and I'm hungry; I'm anxious and I'm depressed. Jennifer . . ."

"I think we should get into it, Eddie. It's relevant to what I have to tell you about Jennifer."

"Linda?" Perry moved to his wife, wrapped his arms around her slim Weight Watchers' waist, and sent a shower of sparkles down on her bleached head. "I love you," he said, convincingly.

The skunk was doing it all for my benefit!

Linda ran her tapered finger along the ridge of his jaw. "No one can take away what we have, Perry. Don't you know that?"

"I'm afraid. When I see what's going on in this house between Jenny and Ed, I become so terribly afraid." He brought her to him and held her tightly.

"Why don't you go to bed, darling? You've been up all night. Let me speak to Eddie alone."

"I am tired and hungry," he said. "I am anxious and depressed. Will you call me if you need anything?"

"I'll be fine."

253

He kissed her hard on the mouth, tilting her to the side like a tango dancer, then he came toward me, "Eddie, there's a lot I have to say to you, but it'll have to hold until I get some sleep. Just let me say this: next to my wife, next to Daphne and Matt, you mean more to me than anyone else in the world. We grew up together; we lived in the slums of Brooklyn together; we faced Bummy Margolis together that summer he shot at me with his magnum revolver . . ."

"Who's Bummy Margolis?"

"Don't be sarcastic, I'm warning you," he said, warningly. "I can forgive you, Eddie, for never saying one word of thanks to me for bringing you into the field of television, for training you to be a top-notch agent and producer, for seeing to it that you earned more than a decent living. Did I ever ask you for one word of thanks?"

"No, you didn't."

"And I don't want a word of thanks from you, let's forget it. But what I cannot forget or forgive is that you never, in all the years I have known and loved you, you have never, not once, invited me or my family to your house for dinner. That I cannot forget or forgive!"

And with that he was out of my house.

Linda went back to examining Jennifer's clothes. "If I had to conjecture, Eddie, I'd conjecture that Jenny is with her parents."

I pounced on the phone, got their number from the operator and dialed it. Miriam Koussevitzky answered. I didn't know what name to use when speaking to her. "Mother" snagged in my throat. "Mrs. Koussevitzky" implied she was a stranger. "Miriam" implied she was a friend. I called her "Ahhh."

"Ahhh?"

"Eddie?"

"Yes, Ahhh. Is Jennifer there?"

"Jennifer?"

"Your daughter, Ahhh."

"She isn't here, Eddie. She hasn't been here for five minutes since she married you."

"Well, if she drops in, Ahhh, please tell her to call me. And, Ahhh . . ."

"Yes?"

"My regards to the others."

I got rid of the phone. "She isn't there," I said to Linda.

"I suspected as much," she countered at once. "She's no doubt in Scranton, Pennsylvania."

"What would she be doing in Scranton, Pennsylvania?"

"She has friends there. You have not provided her with the barest emotional necessities. She's been threatening to leave you for years. It disturbs me to tell you this to your face."

"But you don't think she's in danger."

"That's possible. I wouldn't exclude any possibility. She's in desperate straits." Linda went down on her haunches, pulled a box of mismatched sneakers from under the chest of drawers and poked at them. "Poor Jenny. Amidst such apparent wealth, such dire poverty. What she hasn't been through. I don't know how to tell you this, Eddie, but let me try."

"Please."

"It isn't that you haven't been a good husband; it isn't that you haven't been a faithful husband; it isn't that you haven't been a financially generous husband. It's just that you've been a selfish, rotten person. Do you want me to go on?"

"Please."

She came into the living room, sat on the sofa, and threw a shapely nyloned leg on her knee, giving me a tunnel-visioned peek at her panties. "You do know Jenny has been seeing Doctor Zamichow, don't you?"

"Who?"

"Doctor Zamichow. Perry's psychiatrist."

"Why has she been seeing him?"

"Because you refuse to have children."

"Children?"

255

"She's been driving herself crazy trying to keep your marriage together. And yet you act as if you knew none of this."

"What are you talking about? How could I know anything if she didn't tell me! How long has she been seeing Doctor Zamichow?"

"It must be two or three years now."

"Did she tell Perry?"

"Of course. He arranged it."

"Then why didn't she tell me?"

"That's what Doctor Zamichow advised her to do. In fact he asked to meet you, but she wouldn't have it. She wanted it to come from you."

"Wanted what to come from me?"

"The desire to have children. Didn't it ever occur to you that that's what she wanted?"

I guess I shook my head.

"Eddie, you're pathetic. You're everything in a man I despise. Do you want me to go on?"

"Please."

"Do you know what you need?"

"No. Tell me."

"A wife like me."

The phone rang and I grabbed it, gratefully.

"Mr. Davis, Patrolman Darcy Benson here."

"Did you find my wife? Where is she?"

"I'm sorry, not yet, but we did catch the muggers in the Hawaiian shirts."

"Is she in Scranton, Pennsylvania?" Linda was buzzing in my ear.

I waved her to be quiet. "What about my wife?" I shouted into the phone.

"We have a call out for her. Your description of the Oriental faces on the Hawaiian shirts was uncannily accurate. Can you come down and make an identification? We have your money and credit cards."

"Not until you find my wife. Were they black?"

"No, they were Hungarian. Mr. Davis, can't we have lunch one day this week? I have an idea for a television soap . . . "

I hung up on him. I couldn't see straight anymore. My head started to ache. "Linda, go home. Leave me alone."

Evidently I had offended her. She hit the ceiling. "Go home? I confided in you, Eddie Davis! I revealed confidences to you that I was pledged to secrecy by your own wife, and you're throwing me into the street? Oh, are you lucky I'm not your wife; are you lucky! I'd be on your back every minute! I'd show you! I'd . . ."

I must have flipped my lid. I remember kicking over the coffee table and when the phone rang again, tearing it from its socket and splattering it against the wall.

It was then that Jennifer came into the living room, stark naked and yawning, her face lined with pillow creases.

"What the fuck is this? I'm tryin' to sleep and you guys . . ."

"You're not in Scranton, Pennsylvania?" the leading intellectual of Westchester County asked in astonishment.

"What the fuck would I be doing in Scranton, Pennsylvania?" From somewhere Jennifer brought into being a half of grapefruit and scooped out its innards with her buckteeth. "Where were you? I was gonna call the police," she said to me.

"Perry's right. Your husband's a sick man," Linda put in. "I've had the worst morning . . ."

"Go home, Linda. Linda, go home," I ordered, moving to her. I think my fists were clenched.

Linda backed into the foyer. "Come with me," she shouted at Jennifer. "You don't have to live in this house! You have choices; as a woman you have many, many choices!"

She may have said more, I'm not sure. I think I threw her into the street and slammed the door shut.

"I was in a little after three." Jennifer didn't look at me as she spoke. She didn't offer any excuse or apology. She turned and went upstairs to the bedroom. I soon followed her. She was lying in bed, facing the uncurtained window, her knees bent almost to her chin; the bony curve of her spine protruded sharply beneath the tawny sheath of her skin. The image of a skeleton came to mind.

I undressed and lay down next to her. I was too depressed to speak for a while. "Linda told me about the book. I know how disappointed you must feel," I began, softly, staring at the nape of her neck.

She moved closer to the window. "I'm not a writer," she mumbled. "Who said I was a writer? I'm glad it's over. You don't know how glad I am it's over."

"Where have you been going nights?"

"Friends."

"What friends?"

"My friends. People I enjoy being with."

I could feel her love for me cracking and splintering in a thousand pieces.

"Jen?"

No answer.

"Linda told me . . ." I tried to concentrate on the ache throbbing in my skull. "I'd like for us to have kids. I would. I didn't know . . . I mean, I didn't know it was that important to you."

No answer.

"Would you like me to meet Doctor Zamichow?"

No answer.

"I didn't tell you but I am planning to pick up the horn again. I didn't forget my promise. As soon as I . . ."

"Oh, God, don't talk! You're hurting me!"

Her voice didn't sound human.

It paralyzed me.

"Jen, listen . . ."

"Don't talk, please! please!"

I said nothing.

Eventually we both fell asleep.

But even after that there were times when Jennifer was very affectionate toward me, nights when she'd hold me for all she was worth and tell me how much she loved and needed me; there were times when we went out together and it was like it used to be. I smiled at fire hydrants. There were also times, however, when neither one of us pretended that things hadn't changed between us. We made wide circles to avoid meeting. We hoarded our words. I suppose I was imitating the behavior of my parents. I don't know who Jennifer was imitating. Perhaps me.

On another occasion I brought up the subject of our having a child.

"I'm thirty-seven!" she screamed at me, clawing at the curtain of bangs on her forehead. "You don't have children when you're thirty-seven!"

I could have told her she was wrong. I could have phoned Doctor Zamichow, set up a meeting, and somehow convinced her . . . I let it drop. I had my limits, too.

In any event, during the subsequent months or years, she quit Doctor Zamichow and returned to her job at Starlight, the window-display company where she had been employed when I first met her. She attended as well evening classes in drawing and sculpting at the Art Students League. She was doing wonderfully. Busy, busy, busy. You should have seen the wardrobe she bought for herself, the best of everything, sleek, silky dresses, bright, pleated skirts, sheer, boldly patterned blouses, glinting high-heeled shoes, stunning boots, a mink coat, a raccoon coat, jackets of leather and suede, hand-knitted bulky sweaters, scarves, gloves, hats, jewelry. You name it, the little lady had it. And she started using makeup, creams, cleansers, colognes, let her bangs grow, and brushed her jet black hair flatly away from her lovely forehead. She was always out, always had plenty to do.

259

Saturdays there was a body fitness session, and Sundays she swam and played tennis with some girlfriends. I didn't have to be home for dinner or do any household chores. She hired a West Indian woman to do all of that for us.

I had no complaints.

Still I had problems, don't worry. Businesswise, things weren't going too hot for me. The variety special with Jackie St. Claire had bombed, the comedy sit-com had been placed "on the back burner," and a new game show of ours, "The Honey Pot," was staggering through an abortive season. The network executives took to the hills. "May I speak to . . . ?" "He's in conference, Mr. Davis. He'll return your call shortly." You could die of arteriosclerosis before he returned your call. I knew that Perry was hanging out with Barney Zim, a hustling, mentally retarded independent producer. What I didn't know was that he was plotting to do me in.

I worked as if it were a matter of life or death. And the more I worked, the less I had to show for it. Everything was sliding away from me. I couldn't get anything going. I was unable to focus on a single project but was involved frantically in at least a dozen potential blockbusters. Nothing was happening. I wasn't moving, building, connecting, achieving. My income now equaled my expenditures. My bankbooks weren't multiplying. Inflation corroded interest and capital, and there were no new deposits to provide for the future. I was losing it all, letting it get away from me. A coldness spread like fire in my chest. The air seemed to be filled with vile, noxious fumes and I couldn't get enough oxygen into my lungs. I was slowly suffocating to death.

If Perry shared any of my anxieties, he naturally didn't let me in on it. The skunk was operating at full speed, skating gracefully on the brink of financial disaster, not a hint of panic in his baby blue eyes. He was into so many deals that I couldn't keep track of them. He claimed to be making a fortune in the stock market, in a real estate conglomerate, in a Philippine Toyota franchise. But I knew he was lying. He had borrowed forty-five hundred from me and owed money to everybody and his brother.

My first adulterous relationship was with Rosey Posey, the reader in our office. My first quickie was with an actor's wife in a Winnebago on location in San Diego. My first holiday weekend affair was with a Lufthansa reservation clerk at an oceanfront motel in . . .

The weirdest thing just happened. As I was writing I could have sworn I heard the young horn player in the purple beret playing under my hotel window. I snatched my coils of gold and rode the elevator to the street, not bothering to put on a coat. But when I reached the sidewalk I saw no one. I asked the doorman.

"Was there a horn player out here, Joe?"

"A horn player?"

"Skinny, wearing a purple beret."

"I didn't see him, Mr. Davis."

I looked up and down the street. I could still hear the horn, faintly, a resonant, rumbling sound that reverberated in the gray, leaden sky. But there was no sign of him.

Where was I?

Oh, yes.

Adultery.

Fornication.

A social gesture introduced in our day and age to replace the handshake.

I could give you a goodly number of reasons for getting into that scene, but I don't believe any of them would be particularly persuasive. Least of all my marriage.. In my gut I knew it would straighten itself out. Jennifer and I were bound together, inextricably inseparably. Of that I was absolutely certain.

Looking back I'd say that I wasn't (once again) morally strong enough to ward off contamination. My resistance was low. I was too weak to disassociate myself from the prejudices that prevailed. In the streets the populace cried, "Liberation! Cunnilingus!" I was merely swept along with the mob.

And why not, my friend? You only live once, right? Was I to march into the valley of dust without having had two women in bed with me? without having felt a seductive finger lodged in my rectum? without having provoked, ever, a series of spasms and a concatenation of multiples? No way. No way. You can ask so much of a human being and no more.

So it went. And so I went. Another day, another ejaculation. Squish-squish-squish. In and out. Over and under. Here, there, everywhere. A matter of routine, an "alternate life style." The booze helped. The Gucci shoes helped. Boobs and buttocks. Wooden tubs and Japanese lanterns. Half a lude. A sniff of the white stuff. Squish-squish-squish. In and out. Over and under.

Perry stood in awe of me.

"Don't go crazy now, Eddie. I'm warning you, you're going to get into serious trouble." He was, on the face of it, genuinely concerned. "I've seen it happen before, buddy. Hundreds of times. You're not covering yourself. If Jenny finds out . . ."

"Is that it, Per? I have to go. Matilda's waiting."

"Will you listen to me? What the hell is this? Did you give up? Did you resign? We have work to do here, damn it! You're not doing your share! You're not delivering! I'm running my ass off and you're out whoring! Eddie, I can't do everything myself. You have to . . ."

I didn't hear the rest of it. I walked away with my hands in my pockets, whistling "Raindrops Keep Falling on My Head."

It was during this period that I ran into Eleanor Goldsmith and I said to her, spontaneously, as a matter of routine, "I'd like to go to bed with you, Eleanor Goldsmith." It didn't as a rule take more than that (not in our day and age, my friend), and if it did, there were plenty of others around.

You give me my pleasure and I'll give you yours.

Which was frequently easier said than done, for as you know, the young ladies in our day and age insisted on their full ounce of reciprocal pleasure. There was no shortchanging those kids. They could become awfully nasty, vicious even, if you didn't come up with the goods. Yes, Sir. No question about it.

Oh, my sweet young lady, I wanted to cry out in the throes of my tenuous passion, let me, I beseech you, let me be your favorite vibrator! Take me in your firm, grasping hand and plunge me headlong between your quaking thighs. Drive me deeper and deeper into the gushing vortex of your groin, and use me, my sweet young lady, I beg you, I implore you, use me as you would your plastic, drugstore lover!

(You've experienced it all, haven't you, my friend?)

I remember I was seated in a bar on Second Avenue, at a table in one of those glass-encased extensions built on the sidewalk. I was drinking Stolichnaya, neat and cold, with my old steady, Rosey Posey, not a very pretty girl, admittedly, her body a bit slouched, pudgy, melon-breasted. In the office she was conscientious, reserved to the point of timidity, and never asked any favors of me. I liked her. She was honest. A former lover had taught her that divinity could be discovered in orgasm. She was, privately, something of a sex freak.

When I was in town we'd leave the office about six, booze a little, cuddle a little, and wind up in bed at about eight.

This evening I was really going at it, hot to trot, Stolichnayaed out of my mind. I had my paws all over her, tugging at her garter belt, muzzling her ripe, responsive titties, stabbing my tongue into the pink, wet cavity of her mouth.

"Not here, Eddie. Let's go."

"In a minute. You're beautiful, do you know that?"

"People are looking at us."

"Let them look. They're jealous. I love you, uhhh, Rosey."

(He would say to them, without perception or discrimination: You're beautiful; I love you. He didn't know where the words came from or why he was saying what he said.)

"Let's go to bed, Eddie. Come on."

"In a minute," I murmured, dipping my tongue between her raw lips.

And then some devil or demon made me turn to the window, and there, staring at me with her wide, coal-black eyes, her face painted garishly, hideously, like an Ensor mask, was Jennifer, watching.

Or was it Jennifer?

I couldn't trust my eyes.

The woman at the window was wearing a ridiculously short, skin-tight dress and incredibly high-heeled shoes; mascara stained her rouged cheeks, and her black hair was permed into a wild, frizzly wig.

I squinted, pressed closer to the window. "Jen?"

The mask disintegrated in front of me, broke into ragged shards of papier-mâché, and flew off in every direction.

"Jen?" Did I call her again?

I don't know.

Strange sounds tumbled out of me and moaned pitifully on the floor.

"Shhh, Eddie. Shhh." Rosey begged me, and she tried to take the glass from my hand, but I wouldn't let her.

I squeezed the glass with all my might.

The glass screamed.

Knocking over the chair, I got to my feet and rushed into the street, thinking: It wasn't her; it wasn't Jennifer; I'm drunk; I'm hallucinating.

I held my cut hand to my mouth and tasted my own blood.

On the sidewalk I saw her. It was no hallucination. She was standing at the opposite corner, watching me, her frizzly-haired head jerking back and forth, indecisively, as if she couldn't make up her mind whether to run away or come to me.

I yelled at the top of my lungs, yelled everything I felt for her. "Jen! Jen!"

Her face brightened, exploded in a smile, shed its pain and

anger and confusion. She waved at me, excitedly, stretching on her toes so that I could see her. Blindly she darted between the parked cars at the curb, stumbled, and tripped in her high-heeled shoes as she crossed Second Avenue to reach me.

"Stay there! Wait . . . !" Did I shout that? I don't know.

When the pickup truck hit her, she was lifted into the air and drifted lazily in a web of invisible strings for a few seconds or minutes or hours before she fell with a thud on top of the truck's fender and slid down to the gutter.

I didn't, I couldn't move from the sidewalk.

A crowd gathered around her and chanted in hushed cadences.

The driver of the truck cradled her lifeless body in his arms and cried his heart out.

sixteen

For my part I'm done with the skinny horn player. I wash my hands of him. As I said previously, I am not responsible for him. His life is not my life. I need only tell you that he split with Perry Reese, rather he was royally shafted by Perry Reese, who moved with his family to L.A., where he negotiated with a competing network to develop several new game shows in association with Barney Zim, the mentally retarded producer. They have been very successful as a team. The skinny horn player subsequently told his lawyer and accountant that he was going off to Greece, cutting himself loose for a while, pressures of business, personal matters, etcetera, etcetera.

In actuality, he double locked the vermilion door of the town house on East 73rd Street and took a suite of rooms at the Geneva Hotel.

You wouldn't believe how much progress I've made these past few months on the horn, my friend. I'm better at it now than I've ever been. Forty-five or no forty-five. I'm convinced that I'm ready to sit in with any musical group in the country and hold my own. Yesterday I wrote to five out-of-town symphony orchestras: Cincinnati, Houston, Oregon, Fresno and Utah. In my letters to them, besides requesting an audition at their convenience and at my expense, I added a postscript: "Whatever your decision in regard to the possibility of my joining your orchestra, I want you to know that I am prepared to donate a substantial sum of money in support of your cultural efforts." I also wrote to Columbia Artists and ICM, asking for a meeting to discuss the feasibility of giving a concert, on a very small scale, guaranteeing them a handsome profit for their labors. I am not naive, my friend. I don't expect miracles. But you'd be amazed at how receptive these people can be when you dangle a stack of bills in front of them. Believe me, I've learned a thing or two. I know where it's at.

Incidentally, I've been searching for the young horn player in the purple beret. I want to give him a check, say a thousand. Why not? Isn't that what money's for? I'd love to see the expression on his face. "It's all right. Use it in good health." And I'd walk away. But he's not to be found. I searched everywhere. Third, Lexington, Fifth, Columbus . . . everywhere. I did come across an incredible assortment of street musicians: a string trio, a couple of guitarists, a cornetist, a flutist, a jazz group, a woodwind ensemble, a steel-drum band, almost every conceivable combination. The city seems to be spawning them in abundance, pushing them up between the cracks in the sidewalk, thin, spindly weeds that sing sweetly and arrogantly under the clear benevolent sky.

Often I've asked for him, waiting for the musicians to take a break before intruding. "Excuse me, have you seen a young French horn player? He wears a purple beret." But no one has seen him. I guess it's too cold for him out there. I've gotten into the habit of carrying my horn and my checkbook whenever I leave the hotel, in case I run into him.

Jennifer is gone.
Yet in every note I play I feel her presence.
Perversely I've a great need to rid myself of everything I own: the money I have accumulated in banks throughout the

city, the town house, the eleven acres in Manchester, Vermont, and the pension and insurance policies.

I mean to get rid of it all as fast as I can.

Then, if necessary, I'll find work, just to meet expenses.

It has been frigid this winter. A few days more and we're into the New Year. I should move to another hotel or another city. I should live somewhere else, somewhere warmer, quieter, less of a hassle. But where? I can't get myself to move, anyway. I should do something, though. The odor in this room has become positively foul. I should have them remove the cruddy trays and dishes, the pillowcases stuffed with garbage and the piles of dirty laundry. I should buy myself some decent clothes. I should exercise, join a gym, jog in the morning, visit museums, bookshops, attend concerts, recitals, the theater, etcetera, etcetera.

I should and I will. As soon as I'm set with the horn. I've renewed my pledge to call no one, meet no one, initiate no relationship, seek no diversion, until I'm gainfully employed as a professional musician.

I gave Mr. Burton, the desk clerk, a twenty and he's promised to bring my mail to me, the minute it arrives.

I feel optimistic.

My sex goes into my music, by choice, and my dreams float around the room like a host of angels.

God! Almighty God! Why have You been so good to me? Why do You give me such joy? Why have I been chosen from all the multitudes to realize myself? to be able to create beauty? to be able to sing and dance?

The odd thing is that I think I know why. I have waited a long time to speak. And He has rewarded me for my patience.

I tell you, my friend, I feel terrific. Like a million bucks. Who wouldn't? Last night I went searching for the young horn player. With the coils of gold under my arm, I walked toward the Bowery bank, my head butting the icy wind, my legs sliding and spinning along the glazed sidewalks. Of course the young horn player wasn't there. It didn't matter. I moved up 57th Street. Snow fell from the livid sky. No one was about and yet it couldn't have been much after eleven. I hurried along, clutching my Burberry collar. Icicles dripped from the frozen buildings and the pavement crackled beneath me. I wasn't sure where I was going until I got there. I stood under the marquee of Carnegie Hall and raised the coils of gold. Friend, believe me, those first notes I blew broke the sound barrier. It was my Mozart, then my Beethoven, my Bach, Mendelssohn, Strauss, Weber, etcetera, etcetera, etcetera.

The snow-hooded taxis slowed to a crawl as they passed, noses and eyes pressed to the vaporous windows, but none of them pulled over. A pair of bent, shriveled bagwomen crept out of a doorway and with their arms loaded with bundles sat on the steps behind me. A Puerto Rican kid, in soggy sneakers and torn pea coat, was the next to stop. My audience was growing, no doubt about it. A young man with his leg in a cast, hobbling on a crutch, and two hard hookers in flimsy dresses and ratty fur coats stopped; and a middle-aged man and woman staggered across from a bar on Seventh Avenue, martinis still in hand; and others, street people, night people, slipped out of the subway and out of the dark crevices of the frozen buildings. I swear there must have been forty or fifty of them, huddled together under the marquee of Carnegie Hall, all listening to me play the horn.

And I played, beautifully. Beautifully. A big, round, full tone flowed gloriously from the bell of my horn and danced with the snowflakes. I never played better. Never. I wore gold tails and a gold cloak and a gold, diamond-studded crown. My audience just stood there, huddled together, mesmerized, open-mouthed, their eyes saying, You're special, Eddie; you're a unique human being. No one moved. No one left. Coins dropped at my feet like falling stars and the wind stopped to listen, too.

I tell you, my friend, I have never been happier in my life.